MW00777965

ALSO BY JARED REINERT

WEST OF WANTING

THE DEVIL IN THESE HILLS

THE
DEVIL
IN THESE
HILLS

A NOVEL

JARED REINERT

WALKING MAN BOOKS

THE DEVIL IN THESE HILLS is a fictional work. Names, places, and incidents are of the author's imagination or are used fictitiously. Resemblances to actual names, places, or events are coincidental.

First printed April 2022

Published in the United States by Walking Man Books

For information on author appearances, bulk orders
or press, contact:
jaredreinertbooks@gmail.com

Printed in the United States of America

FIRST EDITION

For Heather,
my favorite story

AUTHOR'S NOTE

This novel includes several difficult topics. While this story was conjured in my imagination, there is nothing fictitious about the struggles of migrants, abused women and children, or the wrongly convicted.

I will be donating a portion of my royalties from this novel to the following charities:

URBAN RESOURCE INSTITUTE

TEXAS CIVIL RIGHTS PROJECT

ANNUNCIATION HOUSE

AMERICAN CIVIL LIBERTIES UNION (ACLU)

These issues are not plot devices in our world. And much like in this novel, there is an upright and ethical side. I pray — in our society and this story — this side will win out soon enough.

THE DEVIL IN THESE HILLS

Jesus in a Box

Late Summer 1983

Whatever you did for the least of these brothers
and sisters of mine, you did for me.

Matthew 25:40

1

H E DIDN'T SEE THE PRONGHORN until it was butchered between his headlights.

John Garner Ellis angled his truck onto the popping gravel and knee-high brush alongside the interminable ribbon of Interstate 27. It was nearing midnight and he was a half-hour past Amarillo, almost exactly halfway to Lubbock, when the pronghorn jumped the cattle fence and shuddered against his truck. He'd seen the wreckage they could do. Warping windshields like cellophane and rolling over the roof until the slaughter kicked languidly in the road. Luckily, he'd hit a young doe that froze when the Chevrolet barreled toward, then through it. John climbed from the cab to survey the damage. He pulled his hat over his eyes and squinted into the headlights. There wasn't much to see. Some tatters of viscera hung from the truck's brush guard, and the passenger headlight was cracked and glazed crimson. He searched the roadside for whatever was left, hoping a .45 round in its suffering direction wouldn't be needed. But he found little evidence the animal had ever existed.

The truck was running so he didn't bother picking the gristle from the bumper. He'd been in high school when his friend left his truck running while parked in sagebrush. And, as the friend told it, he was unfastening a girl's belt when she grabbed his hand and said she smelled burning. By the time his jeans were back on, the flames cast long shadows. He and the girl walked nearly fifteen barefooted miles to town while the truck was reduced to a sagging, achromatic frame.

John pinched a small clump of dark red muscle from the front of the truck and took it back into the cab where he held it in front of his dog's nose. Merle devoured the viscera happily.

It was Memorial Day weekend — the last, oppressive days of summer — and John Ellis was driving home. He'd spent a couple weeks fifteen hundred miles from home in Wyoming where his brother, Shawn, was trying to scrape together a living as a rodeo cowboy. Shawn rode in Cody, in Cheyenne, and in a town they didn't bother to learn the name of. None of Shawn's rides qualified him for another, so they spent most of the next days drinking cases of Budweiser and frying thick slabs of ham on a hissing camp stove. They unfurled their bedrolls and slept in a truck bed under the clear, pin-poked skies of Wyoming.

As John drove south, he continued his habit of studying constellations. He tracked them through Colorado, a corner of New Mexico, then the familiar sky over Texas.

Home was the town of Uvalde. Fifty miles from the Mexican border and two hundred from the Gulf, it was a day's travel to just about anywhere save for San Antonio. And even that drive was hardly worth the tankfuls of gas. Uvalde was only more than a highway crossroads in the Texas Hill Country because the former Vice President had called the place home as well. His mother was a quiet supporter, so John Garner Ellis owed the man his name. John Nance Garner once had an office overlooking Uvalde's city square. The town was, at one time, famous for its *guajillo*, and although the sorghum had been replaced with the darker sludge of crude oil, John thought the winds of Uvalde still smelled honeyed. Especially in the darkest and quietest hours of the night.

It was in those hours that Interstate 27 split the town of Abernathy. Silos and oil derricks towered and flickered their halogen lights into the ink-black night, giving the vague appearance of a distant city skyline.

The change in landscape reminded him of the growing pressure in his bladder. John clicked on the cab light and checked his wristwatch. The dashboard clock hadn't worked for years, and the prosaic miles of the Texas twilight gave no hint of the time. It was just past one in the morning, according to his watch. He cleared his throat and spat out the open window, then pulled the truck into a paved lot just off the main road. A single-bulbed traffic light hung over the intersection and clicked a rhythm in time with the flashing yellow light. John parked behind a small brick building in the lot, cut the lights, and climbed from the truck. He unbuckled his clattering belt buckle and peed against the brick, his legs wide to keep the splatter from his leather boots. He was wringing out the last drops when the wall glowed red. The cop was out of his patrol car by the time John's pants were buckled.

"What brings you to Abernathy, son?" the cop asked.

John bit his bottom lip. The cop showed his hand early with the drawling *son*. "Passing through," he said. "Nearly home."

The cop nodded. "Didn't recognize the truck when it passed by. You from Lubbock?"

"Uvalde," John said. "You know every truck in this town?"

"Goddamn right," the cop emptied a mouthful of tobacco froth. "Suppose you don't know what you're pissing on, do you?"

John shrugged.

"Come 'round here," the cop said and rounded the brick building.

He clicked on his Maglite and pointed the beam into the front windows. What John thought at first was a corpse was only a sculpture. It was a roughly made, but towering, rendering of Jesus on the cross entombed in a window-fronted brick box.

"Good God," John gasped.

The cop pointed his light above the glass panes. *Jesus In A Box* was painted in red block letters. "You a Christian?" he asked.

"Yeah," John said. "Most days."

The pair stood in silence for a minute, with Jesus's roughhewn eyes glaring at them. The cop walked back to the truck, leaving John in the rhythm of the traffic light.

"This your dog?" the cop asked when John came around the building. Merle's head stuck from the truck window.

John nodded. "His name's Merle."

"Like Merle Haggard?"

"That's the one."

"You're a long way from home to be saying you're almost home, ain't you?" the cop asked.

"Closer to home than I was this morning."

"Where're you coming from?"

"Started in Cody, Wyoming a while ago. Woke up this morning north of Pueblo. I was hoping to make Lubbock tonight but my truck got tangled up with a pronghorn about an hour ago."

The cop walked to the front of John's truck. He bent and inspected the blood-splattered bumper. "We don't have any hotels here," he straightened. "And I'm afraid what you'll piss on next if you stay any longer."

"I didn't know it was Jesus in there," John offered.

"Yeah, well—" the cop scowled. "Got anything in the truck I

4

should know about?"

"A pistol under the seat, but it's legal."

The cop peered in the truck window. "Okay. I'd ticket you for pissing on church property but I suppose that judgment's not entirely mine."

"Fair enough."

"You're not making it to Uvalde tonight and I don't want you hanging around Abernathy."

"I was planning on sleeping in my truck outside Lubbock."

"Well, get on then," the cop said and walked back to his cruiser.

A half-hour later, the truck was pulled off the road north of Lubbock and John was in his truck bed, stripping down to his underwear. He realized the fly of his Wranglers had been down since Abernathy. Lying on top of his makeshift bed, he laughed. "Jesus in a fucking box," he said to himself and howled until it turned to coughs that reported over the plains like shotgun blasts.

2

By noon the next day, John was pulling into the long dirt driveway. It was the same pale ochre as the dried kindling of the lawn. August was not kind to most vegetation in Texas, even in the lush Hill Country. He pulled the truck close, nearly nudging the chrome rear bumper of a Cutlass, hoping the faded carport would provide some shade.

The Oldsmobile was his mother's. John had packed her belongings from his childhood home into the vinyl backseat, helped her into the passenger seat, and drove east until they arrived in Uvalde. He parked the car under the carport that evening, promising his mother the spot, and the shade it provided, was hers. The car had backed out of the carport once; to take his mother to Uvalde Memorial Hospital when she'd coughed up a gobbet of blood and lung, and his truck's serpentine belt snapped and whipped against the hood when he frantically turned the engine over. When he returned home by himself, he parked the Cutlass in the shade and went to work on his truck. It made him feel better, keeping his hands greasy and moving. He'd almost rebuilt the engine by the time he scrubbed the oil from under his fingernails and went to her funeral.

His mother often said the most excitement in John's life had happened the day he was born. John was born and brought up in the town of Valentine. Three hundred or so miles to the west, the place was such a distilled nothingness it felt vacuumous. But, amongst the nihility of the town and its surrounding desert, his parents built a placid life and had enough children to run their modest farming operation.

John was born on the fourteenth of February. The only notoriety the Ellis family could claim — to that point — was the birth of their baby boy, born on Valentine's Day in Valentine, Texas. His birth made the front page of the regional newspaper, the paunchy newborn's picture printed on the fold. A reporter from the San Antonio Express called John's father and asked a few hurried questions, then ran a release touting an exclusive interview with the parents of the "Cupid Baby." When the papers in Dallas seemed uninterested, John's mother penned an anonymous letter suggesting they write about the Cupid Baby, but the news had already moved on.

For almost two decades, John Ellis began every school year with that story. Each class's first lecture was some variation of the same at Uvalde Regional High School. Mr. Ellis would ask the students to share their names, favorite baseball team, and favorite book. Invariably, the answers would morph into a common thread, which the anxious and awkward were able to hide behind. After his students finished the exercise, he would reach into a desk drawer and take out a laminated, yellowed newspaper clipping. "And this," he'd hold it up, "is me. The Cupid Baby."

The desks would squeal and shudder as the students pushed forward, hoping to get a better view of the portly baby. Gasps and giggles would swell through the rows of students until Mr. Ellis had to put the clipping back in its locked drawer and hold his hands up in an act of suppression. The students knew it was coming. The newspaper clipping had become a local sensation of sorts, after a student during his first year teaching came into Mr. Ellis's class and asked if he was the Cupid Baby. His mother recognized the name on their report card, the student told him.

As a promise he made halfheartedly, he told the boy if he was accepted into a university, he would bring the newspaper article, complete with a photograph, to show him. Two years later, when the student barged into Mr. Ellis's classroom with an envelope from Texas Christian University, John kept his promise and found the article in a box of his mother's keepsakes. Soon, students he had only known in passing would come to him with their college acceptance letters and ask to see the picture. It was a badge of honor at Uvalde Regional High School. One which felt ridiculous just weeks after graduation, like most high school memories do.

The first day of the 1983 school year started the same as every year before, and John Ellis looked forward to another year free from complication.

3

Gabriel Jiménez was skirting through his first day at Uvalde Regional High School. He kept his head low. His eyes darted to every face that passed by in the hallway. He wore an immaculately white button-down shirt. The kind that boys wore once every few years when a relative passed or someone remarried and they needed formal attire with little time and less money. The shirt was stiff from starch and still had the deep wrinkles acquired from its packaging. Gabriel's arms were hidden inside the wide sleeves. Its measurements were for a man twice his size and triple his age. He knew the shirt looked ridiculous, but he'd begged his mother to buy him one. He'd seen a young man on television wearing one like it, and since they didn't have the money for the faded Levi's jacket he really wanted, the white dress shirt was what he got. Especially after it had been repackaged and its price marked down. When his mother finally agreed to buy it for him and he got home and tried it on, he knew kids would make fun of him. But he also knew he had to wear it. At least for one day or risk his mother asking about it for weeks.

But Gabriel was surprised how ignored he'd felt during the morning of his first day. Even the blazing whiteness of his bedsheet-fitting shirt wasn't enough to distract the students from catching up with their friends, realizing which girls had filled out over the summer, and discussing the summer's newest Star Wars movie.

The vibrating anxiety he'd felt all morning was beginning to dissipate and, in its place, exhaustion settled into his muscles. He hadn't slept well for a week in anticipation of his first day. By lunchtime, he felt like he was beginning to belong among the other students trudging through the halls.

He sat alone at lunch and was thankful for the solitude. He was grateful for a hot meal until he had his first bite. Even on the first day, the lunch ladies used some sort of mystery meat to make chili. How long the leftover meat had been stored, and whether it had been sitting in the cafeteria kitchen all summer, were the whispers students muttered to friends as they gnawed on beef fat and spit half-eaten mouthfuls into their napkins.

Gabriel was opening a carton of orange juice when he felt a hand grip the back of his head. It tightened, the fingers straining and tangling in his hair, until he could feel hot breath on his ear.

"Listen here, you fucking beaner," the voice hissed. "We don't need you 'round here."

Gabriel swallowed hard. He fought against the hand but felt it tighten in response.

"I said we don't want you here. So go back to wherever the fuck you came from."

Gabriel's eyes searched the cafeteria, desperate to find someone who might be watching. A girl a few tables away looked at him, then at the face behind Gabriel, but looked away. Just as she turned away, Gabriel felt the hand shove his head down. He was jerked toward the table. His face smashed into the bowl. Chili splashed and squelched onto his face, over his ears, in his hair. The hand kept his head held down, submerged in the scorching chili, until his lungs screamed for a breath. As violently as he was forced down, the hand ripped his head back up. His eyes burned. A bean dripped from his chin and plopped onto his pants. Streams of brown, pepper-flecked chili ran down the front of his shirt. Gabriel struggled to catch his breath.

"Fucking wetback," the voice boiled. "Better get the fuck outta this town while you got the chance."

The voice hissing in Gabriel's ear was Bobby Kershaw, the loudest, but far from the meanest, of the Kershaw clan. The Kershaw family was a part of Uvalde since white men had first borrowed the West Texas land with no intention of returning it. The Kershaw family tree grew in snarled branches and sudden offshoots from knobby trunks. It grew and sprouted without warning. The roots so entangled in the Hill Country dirt, there is no possibility of stymieing its growth, let alone uprooting it.

It seemed, at any given time, there were dozens of Kershaws milling around Uvalde and its neighboring towns. Locals' first thoughts after hearing police sirens, firecrackers, gunshots, or extended yelping and hollering was that a Kershaw was responsible. Kershaw children grew like desert plants: tall and hardened, sun-beaten and callused. Every Kershaw that had gone through the Uvalde public school system had quit by eleventh grade for a job at the mill. The lucky ones found work on an oil field. There, they would collect paychecks that seemed obscene for a sixteen year old. A few months after dropping out, they would drive into the school parking lot in whatever rumbling pickup or humming sports car they'd financed earlier in the week. They were proud, they were menaces, they were bad influences, and they were pervasive. And, above all, the Kershaws were hotblooded supremacists. Living in a town less than a hundred miles from the border, they still felt it was their duty to cleanse Uvalde of any persons darker than their sun-battered selves.

Gabriel didn't prove to be any less elusive with his face buried in a melamine bowl or with dregs of chili running down his white shirt. No one spoke up or moved to stop Bobby. Gabriel had to wipe his face clean with his hands and search for the bathroom with his eyes scalded from spice. If anyone saw anything out of the ordinary in Bobby's attack on a new Mexican student, no one offered their help. That was the unspoken expectation inside Uvalde Regional High School and the roads webbing from it. Speaking in defiance of a Kershaw was an attack against all of them. It only lengthened its beatings, heightened its violence, and turned its vitriol and fists toward those that had opened their mouths. Surrendering silence meant stepping in front of the rifle barrel and placing the crosshairs between your shoulders. Uvaldians knew the best way to handle a Kershaw was to walk away and let them tire themselves out like a petulant pup. Eventually, they would take their vile, frothy-mouthed incivility back to their dilapidated trailers.

If someone would have spoken up, not even against Robert Kershaw but with advice to Gabriel Jiménez, the tie that bound them would have unraveled itself. *Just keep your head down for a few days,* they could have offered. *Let him be an asshole. As long as you don't fight back, he'll be bored with you by the end of the week.* Gabriel would have taken the advice seriously, and told his brother he'd spilled the chili on himself. Instead, when he walked into their rented house piled with moving boxes, and his brother asked about his shirt, Gabriel told him the truth.

"An asshole," he said. "Some big guy at lunch."

4

Their mother worked often and late, leaving Gabriel and his older brother, Martín, to spend most of their evenings together. When Gabriel told him what the bully had done, Martín fumed. Gabriel shook his head and tried halfheartedly to assuage him. "It was an older kid," he explained. "You know how it goes."

Martín pursed his lips. "What'd he look like?"

"I didn't really get a good look at him."

"Then why do you think he was messing around?"

"I could just tell," he shrugged.

"Tell me what he looks like."

"You're looking for trouble," Gabriel said.

"If you don't teach the kids at school to leave you alone now, it'll just get worse."

"Mom's going to be mad if either of us get into a fight."

"But first she's going to be mad when she sees that shirt."

By the time their mother came through the sagging screen door, Gabriel's white shirt was bleached and hanging to dry above the bathtub. The brothers slept in front of the television which played the Rangers game, then the nightly news, through the colorless snowfall of static.

5

John Ellis was the youngest of three sons. His family lost the middle brother, Shawn, to the glinting buckles of the rodeo circuit. Colter, the oldest of the brothers, had died twenty years before. John was a teenager and Colter was in his twenties when he passed.

He had been baling their eastern field on one of the hottest days of that summer when he'd taken a break around lunchtime. He ate a slick-warm ham and cheese sandwich, and drank two or three cans of Coors in the shade of the tractor, his back leaning against its hulking rubber tire. It was almost three in the afternoon when he woke and realized the shade and the trundling engine lulled him to sleep. He drove back to the barn to refill the gas tank and grab another lukewarm beer. When their father heard the tractor approaching, he walked from the shade of the barn.

"If you're finished already, you might as well go back and do it right!" he yelled to Colter.

"Had some engine trouble," Colter lied. "Put me an hour or two behind but I can get it done. Long as I don't have to stand around bickering with you."

His father shooed him with his foam trucker hat and went back inside the barn.

Their land was not expansive by any measure. The crop barely covered its expenses, but their father was stubborn in his belief that if they owned the land it was their duty to plant and till it. The field could be baled or planted in a day, but Colter liked to make the job last longer in an attempt to avoid other chores.

Because of his siesta, Colter was still working the field when dusk fell over the farm. The sky was aflame in auburn and purple in the last minutes of daylight. The shadows cast by the tractor stretched and warped until they disappeared altogether. One of the tractor's headlights had burnt out seasons ago, so he drove through the inky black field with a single quivering beam. He was nearly finished when the tractor's engine shook vengefully and Colter smelled the mineral scent of motor oil. He climbed from the cab, cursing, and made it to the second step from the cab before his boots slipped on the dew-damped metal and he tumbled headlong into the prickling crop.

When he hadn't returned for an hour past sundown, their father wrestled into a flannel and went back to the barn. He primed and started their old tractor, then drove gingerly down the path and across the corner of the field. He held a spotlight in one hand and scanned the crops until light glinted off the other tractor. He shifted into a higher gear, feeling his anger beginning to boil over, and sped toward the scarlet Farmall.

He swore he hadn't felt his wheels roll over Colter. His wife believed him. Shawn believed him. And the town never publicly questioned it. But John thought it was only a way of coping. Some people in the town suggested Colter may have already been dead from his fall; that the whole thing was just bad luck heaped on itself. John, however, had seen his brother fall from haylofts, rooftops, barbed fences, and he knew the fall from the tractor wouldn't have killed Colter. His brother's last breath was mashed out of him by that massive, studded tire.

Before Colter died, Shawn was already growing restless with the town of Valentine. After losing Colter, Shawn thought the place had a stench. As if the fields had gone rotten and covered over with flies. His muscles rippled like a racehorse, the pads of his fingers rubbed on themselves like he was considering something deeply. He had no plan though. Only a hankering for shimmers of sunlight off gold buckles as big as pie plates, women who nursed cowboys' bruised loins, snow-drifted rails of cocaine tallied across bar tops, and benders on whatever else their winnings could buy.

Shawn left Valentine two days before his eighteenth birthday. He quietly packed his clean shirts and best pairs of jeans, shined his boots, and brushed his Stetson clean. He shushed his truck engine as it rolled over, and drove through the grass to avoid the popping gravel driveway. The ghosts of his tires in the grass were the first sign he had gone. Their mother found a note he left behind, with a halfhearted explanation scratched on a scrap of paper. She read the note every day until the pencil marks eventually faded from the page.

Four years later, their phone rang late in the morning. A neighbor that had moved out of town was calling, telling them she was reading the morning's paper and recognized a name. Shawn Ellis had won seventy-five dollars at a rodeo near Amarillo.

John was in Wichita Falls for the next weekend's rodeo. His brother turned out of the competition, but John found him in town among a thrall of wide-stanced cowboys.

"Hiya Shawny," John said to the back of his brother's tanned neck.

Shawn turned as quickly as his whiplashed neck would allow. John had a thick new mustache and a fancy pearl snap, but the same old and faded black Stetson hat. They embraced, jostling and spilling over murky glasses of cheap draft beer. The men, who were crowded around only seconds ago, turned away and gave them space.

"My brother!" Shawn explained to the barroom. They found a booth away from the bandstand and talked for the rest of the evening. Empty glasses and spent Coors bottles speckled the Formica table by the time the bartender wiped the tables around them. They pushed through the doors into the cool North Texas twilight.

John rode the prosaic miles of highway alongside his brother for the rest of that summer, taking part in all the rodeo had to offer, save for the riding. They took turns driving through the nights, the Silverado resting only when they reached the next town where banners were already hung, grandstands hosed off, and livestock trailers parked as tightly as a deck of cards.

One of the last weekends that summer, the rodeo rolled into Uvalde like a circus of sinners. Shawn had won a hundred bucks the week before, so John's smile was slightly broader that weekend. It was that smile that caught Abby's attention. She crossed the bar and sat next to John. It was early evening and he'd been set up since breakfast.

"Shouldn't you be at the fairgrounds riding?" she asked.

John turned and looked her over. "Ain't the bulls I came to ride," he slurred. Abby had rarely heard a worse line, but it worked.

Seven months later, he signed for the down payment on a ranch house with a brand new carport in Uvalde. Two moving trucks parked outside, one his and the other Abby's. They were married for just over a decade when she started going out more, coming home wafting that slick, oily scent of alcohol.

That year's last day of school, John came home with a bottle of middle-shelf champagne and a case of Budweiser. It was a tradition he'd started to celebrate their first married summer. His dog, Merle, was laying on his side in the front yard and picked his head up, ears high, when John's truck pulled into the driveway. When he shouldered open the door and put the bottles on the countertop, he saw the note. Abby was already gone. Halfway to Dallas or Tulsa or wherever she had it in her mind to go. He balled it up and threw the *Dear John* letter away without reading it. But when he tossed an empty Budweiser in the trash, he saw it was written on a stationary pad from the hotel where she'd been meeting the other guy.

6

John rarely missed details. Perhaps it was hindsight from his willing dismissal of the small changes detailing his wife's infidelity, or that his students' most common mischief dealt in the minutiae, but he felt he rarely missed a thing. So, when Gabriel came into his classroom on the second day of school, John scribbled a note in his grade book before beginning his lesson. When the bell rang at the end of the day, John Ellis stood in the doorway of his classroom and nodded to the students departing in huffs, their arms crimped on stacks of books and notebooks. He kept an eye out, using his years of teaching experience to pick a single face from the middle of a throng.

"Gabriel!" he shouted over the din of the students. Gabriel turned and John waved him over, making sure he plastered a warm smile across his face. "Just wanted to check in," he said when Gabriel was inside the classroom. "Make sure you're getting used to the new school. I know it's not the easiest thing to do."

Gabriel shrugged. "It's going alright."

"Good-alright or bad-alright?"

Gabriel chewed the inside of his lip. "Both, I guess," he said finally.

"Anyone giving you a hard time?"

Gabriel shook his head.

"Not even one of those Kershaws?"

"I don't really know anyone's name yet," Gabriel said.

John sighed. "I've got to ask about those bruises, Gabriel."

Gabriel's gaze dropped. He stood still.

"I could get in trouble if I didn't ask," John lied. He wished it were true, but teachers were mostly told to stay out of their students' lives. If he wasn't confident the bruises had come from a drunk father, he would have never brought it up. "Just need to make sure you're safe here. At home too."

Gabriel chewed his bottom lip before replying. "Got them from moving furniture, I think. Lots of moving."

"Sure," John said with a forced smile. "I know how that goes."

Gabriel stared at the remnants of scribbles on the chalkboard.

"Okay. Well, have a good night and I'll see you tomorrow."

Gabriel turned and joined the stream of students.

John graded a pile of homework until the hallways grew quiet and the evening glimmered through the long windows. He walked the empty corridor and descended the echoing stairwell. He knocked on the door, cracked it open, and peeked through without waiting for a response.

"John," the man inside said, "Come in. Sit."

"Dr. Hendrick," John nodded and sat in the drab fabric chair across from him.

"You're my first visitor in two days. Would you believe that? Not a single student in trouble yet. Must be a new record."

"Guess so," John shrugged. "I have a new student, Gabriel Jiménez.

Pretty shy. Quiet, at least for now. But you know how new kids are. Then today he showed up with bruises all over his face. Looked pretty beat up. I asked about it but he didn't have much to say."

Dr. Hendrick let out a breath like a leaking tire. "I wouldn't get involved," he said dismissively. "Probably a senior trying to act tough."

John turned his hands over and held them palm up. *Isn't that trouble?* he would have liked to say.

"What did you say his name was?"

"Gabriel Jiménez," John said.

Dr. Hendrick tsked. "I wouldn't lose sleep over it. Good chance it happened at home," he said. "You know how those Mexicans are."

John blinked slowly and stood. "Sure," he said. "Thanks for the help."

Dr. Hendrick continued talking, but John was already closing the office door behind him.

John went back to his classroom, checked his class roster, then packed his bag and left the school building. It was a few weeks from the earliest days of fall, and the air was as heavy and oppressive as it had been for months. John climbed into his truck and rolled his sleeves up to his elbow. He turned the truck over and headed into town, then through it. His favorite radio station was just beginning to fizzle out of range when he parked in front of the Jiménez house.

John walked as gingerly as he could through the sun-bleached grass. It snapped like toothpicks under his shoes. The screen door was stretched and split like abused pantyhose and the faded wood front door was open. He knocked on the aluminum frame of the screen door. It shuddered on its hinges and the screen rattled inside its brackets. John could hear the TV volume had been turned down so he knocked again. That time, he heard socked feet padding toward the door. He didn't recognize the boy who turned the corner into view but his features were similar enough to Gabriel's.

"Hi," the boy said suspiciously, keeping a safe distance from the flimsy door. "Can I help you?"

John removed his Stetson to offer the boy a better view of his face. "I'm a teacher over at the high school. Gabriel is one of my students."

The boy put his hands in his pockets. "What did he do?"

"Nothing," John smiled. "He's not in any trouble. Do you go to Uvalde High?"

The boy nodded and took a step closer to the door, close enough to open it and shake the man's hand, but he didn't. "I'm Martín," he said. "Gabriel's brother. I'm a senior."

"Nice to meet you, Martín. Any chance your mother's home?"

"She's at work and won't be home until late."

"Would she be around tomorrow around dinnertime?"

"Probably not," Martín said. "She works late most nights."

"Maybe I could call in the morning before she leaves?"

Martín shrugged. "She's usually at work before we're up."

"How about your father?"

Martín shook his head vaguely.

"What does your mother do?"

"Do?"

"For her job. Where does she work?"

"The hospital."

"She's a nurse?"

"Cleaning, I think." Martín's eyes studied the inside of the stamped metal on the bottom of the door.

"I see," John looked over both shoulders to take in the dilapidated neighborhood. "Well, next time you see her, please tell her I was here and she can call me at the school."

Martín nodded.

"I'm John Garner Ellis, but Gabriel knows me as Mr. Ellis."

"Like the vice president?" Martín asked.

"Just like that. Again, Gabriel isn't in any kind of trouble. Maybe tell her that first," John said with a smile. "Take care, Martín. And tell your brother I said hello too." John pulled his hat on and turned toward his truck. His boots crunched through the yard. He rounded the front of his truck and saw Martín still standing on the porch, shielding his eyes from the setting sun.

"Want me to drop off some dinner?" John called to him.

Martín dropped his hand. "No," he said. "We can manage." He went back inside and the screen door squealed shut.

7

They moved to Uvalde late in the summer. Soon after moving in, Martín had done yard work for a half-blind elderly man that lived on their new street. He gave some of the money to his mother, who smiled proudly but refused to accept it. Martín put three dollars on the table before going to bed. The cash disappeared by the next morning, and the fridge had a new carton of eggs and gallon of milk in the morning. Martín found a Milky Way on his nightstand after his mother kissed her sons' foreheads and left for work.

He invested the rest of the money on a used Huffy Thunder Road bicycle. The woman he bought it from explained her son had gotten it for Christmas a few years before, but for his most recent birthday an aunt had mail-ordered a new Schwinn, and the Huffy had been relegated to a corner of the garage. Before rolling the Huffy to its dusty corner grave, the boy was sure to remove the black placards, leaving only a simple black frame with a massive vinyl seat as large and scarcely padded as a saddle. Without the placards, it didn't look much like a Thunder Road, but Martín knew it was. He promised himself he would go back in a month and two to offer the boy a few dollars for them. In the meantime, he rode a bike that was a ghost of the one he'd seen a few summers ago in a magazine; a scrawny blonde-headed boy pushed a shining black bicycle. *As seen on TV!* it said, promising it was *The bike most wanted!*

To his brother's delight, the bike had pegs screwed into the back axle. Martín figured the boy had forgotten to remove them. Gabriel loved standing on them, his hands clamped on his brother's shoulders. Martín pedaled furiously and Gabriel stood on the pegs, leaning at an angle close behind his brother, eyes squinting against the wind.

Gabriel arrived home not long after Mr. Ellis left. He went inside, threw his notebooks on the countertop, and rummaged through the cupboards until he found a half-eaten box of cereal. He poured himself a bowl and was adding the last dredges from the milk carton when he caught its sickly sweet odor.

"Martín!" Gabriel shouted into the hallway.

"What?" Martín yelled back over the din of the television.

"The milk's sour!"

"Just drink it! I had some yesterday and it was fine!"

Gabriel huffed. "It's not fine! It smells like ass!"

"You wouldn't know an ass if you were inside one!"

By the time Martín was finished laughing, Gabriel was standing in front of his brother and pounded a television knob, quieting it to a faint crackle. "Let's go get some milk," Gabriel said.

"I'm not going to the store! And don't touch the TV!"

"Then I'll ride *your* bike there."

"Like to see you try. It's locked up and you don't know the combination."

"18-34-7," Gabriel said and turned from the room.

Martín shot from the chair. "How the hell do you know that?"

"Are you pedaling or am I?"

Martín huffed and shook his head but he was already tying his shoes. "Hope you have money for milk," he said.

"You can pay with the dollar in your pocket."

"What're you talking about?"

"Mom left money on the table."

"I didn't see it if she did."

"You sure?" Gabriel asked and unfolded a note in their mother's handwriting. *Money for milk.*

"Figured the milk was fine," Martín shrugged.

8

Gabriel and Martín retraced their path while they each cradled a carton of milk. Martín pedaled as quickly as he could without dropping the milk, or Gabriel off the back. A rainstorm was swelling in tumorous clouds from the rocky western hill country. A growl grew and echoed over the streets and low buildings. They thought it was the low rumbling of thunder. But when they turned to face the grassy square of the town center, bordered by downtown streets, they saw a different storm. A couple of Kershaws were holding court with a group of school-aged boys. Their volume was otherworldly in the quiet, empty streets of Uvalde, and the air emanating from the group was charged, as if by lightning, with the electricity of disorder.

Gabriel recognized the boy by his thick fingers and grubby nails. His grip tightened around his brother's shoulder and the carton of milk.

"That's him," he said to the back of his brother's head.

"What?"

"That's the guy," Gabriel repeated.

"What guy?"

"The guy from lunch. The one that bullied me."

The brakes on Martín's Thunder Road squealed until they stopped and he put his leg out like a kickstand. "Which one?" he asked.

"The big one," Gabriel said. "In the flannel."

Martín stared at the group, looking at the tallest of them. His round head and home-cut curly hair rose above the other boys. His face lit into a half-smile, his eyes thin, a plan of mischief on his lips. The boys around him listened as if he was delivering a sermon.

Without saying another word, Martín stomped on the pedals toward the congregation. Gabriel nearly fell backward into the street. Martín steered the bike toward the group, then leaned to the left and tilted the handlebars to start a sweeping turn that would bring them within spitting distance of the boys. The group saw the brothers coming and spread into a straight line as if they were infantry holding their ground. Bobby Kershaw tilted his chin up in a sign of defiance. His minions glanced to him for direction. But as the brothers continued by, Martín threw the carton of milk toward him. It hung in the air for a long moment before hitting the asphalt just in front of Bobby's thick-soled boots. The carton exploded as if detonated and sent thick white splatters up to Bobby's shoulders. Martín pedaled with even more fury before turning back and calling to Bobby. *"Gordo hijo de puta!"* he yelled. Bobby took a heavy stride in their direction but the bike had already carried the brothers out of view.

"What the fuck does that mean?" Bobby asked the group. All but one, Jack MacAnally, shrugged. Jack had taken a semester of Spanish and, although he failed, he possessed a working knowledge of only vulgar vocabulary. He almost said it. If his bottom lip wasn't pinched around a pouch of Skoal tobacco, it might have slipped out. *He called you a fat motherfucker, Bobby.*

9

"You shouldn't have said that," Gabriel said when they reached their street. It had been a feverish ride from town. His eyes were dry and his hair was blown stiffly behind his ears.

"Said what?" Martín scoffed.

"Called him a—" he stopped himself. "Called him that."

"Well," Martín shrugged, "isn't that what he is?"

Gabriel felt the back of his neck grow hot. He tasted bile in the back of his throat. Or maybe it was cafeteria chili forced down his nose so far the flavor was lodged in his throat.

"That kid's trouble," he said. "Don't start anything. I can handle it."

"Were you handling it when you got half a bowl of soup thrown on your shirt?" Gabriel almost corrected him, but instead allowed Martín to believe the chili was thrown at him, rather than feeling like he'd been drowned in it.

Massive raindrops began to fall. They splattered on the road like the milk against Bobby Kershaw's Wranglers. The street went from dotted to patchwork to uniformly covered in seconds. Martín hung his head and leaned into the pedals with whatever energy he had left. Gabriel hopped from the back of the bike and sprinted onto the porch, carefully holding their only remaining milk carton. Martín followed behind and leaned the bike against the house.

Gabriel grabbed a tea towel from a kitchen drawer and wiped his face dry. His hair dripped rhythmically onto the shoulders of his oversized t-shirt.

"Your teacher was here," Martín said, watching his brother.

Gabriel lowered the towel. "What are you talking about?"

"Your teacher. Guy with a cowboy hat and mustache. Mr. Ellen or something."

"Mr. Ellis? Why would he come here?"

A drop of rainwater fell from Martín's chin onto the floor. "Wanted to talk to Mom."

"Why?"

Martín shrugged. "That's as much as I know. He asked if Mom was here, and when she'd be home."

Gabriel worked the threads of the towel between his fingers. "I'm not in trouble, am I?" he asked.

"Probably," Martín said and turned down the hallway before his brother saw him smile.

10

Rivulets ran in pointed currents from the Jiménez house, past the cluster of boys with their ball caps and shirts washed of milk splatters, and continued past the house with the faded carport. By the time the rainwater reached his street, it was so thick and polluted with litter and dust it resembled oil field runoff. John Ellis slept under the awning in front of his house. The porch was large enough for him and his dog, a faded blue webbed lawn chair and a side table with a small potted cactus that sagged dismally, and an ashtray wisping smoke from a spent cigarette. Underneath the chair was a TV dinner tray with sludgy remains of gravy, and a half-crinkled can of Coors Banquet. John was reclined on the chair with his feet balanced on the railing in front of him. Fat raindrops collected from the edges of the clogged gutter and dripped onto the toes of his boots. Neither the rain nor the whipping winds that preceded it woke him. But finally, a chorus of thunder from the west shook John and his dog awake.

His boots hit the cracked concrete porch with a wet slap. He collected the remnants of his dinner before they were taken up by the storm and went inside. He threw the tray on the floor and scooped some ALPO kibble on top of the congealed gravy. Merle lapped it up eagerly. His wristwatch showed half-past seven. He removed it, along with his boots and jeans, stretched on the sofa, and fell asleep in his pearl snap shirt and underwear.

11

Her lunch break came around eight, and in the form of a room-temperature egg sandwich, a dixie cup of tap water, and ten minutes to down it. When she was finished, but still chewing the last corner of crust, she walked the fluorescent-lit hallway where the stench of urine was underlaid by stinging bleach. Being able to track the scent of piss-soaked bedsheets was a skill that made her job easier so she'd learned fast. On her first day, when her nose felt burnt from the Clorox, nurses turned her in every direction, demanding she redress the beds, change the diapers, mop the floors in this room or that hallway. It was dizzying. It was humiliating. So she learned to stalk the corridors, tracking scents like a hound through undergrowth. Alma Jiménez was tasked with picking up the sopping wet diapers of the elderly, bagging tepid piles of feces into baggies, and mopping acrid sick from the tile floors, but she did it well. It was the penance asked of her to support her sons.

Through the degrading hours, she thought of her boys — the brightest lights in her life. She hadn't seen them in a couple days. Double shifts turned into triples, and sleep came violently when she arrived home.

She had double-checked her wallet after she punched in that morning, making sure she'd left money on the table. She vaguely remembered doing so, but waking at random, groggy hours of the day covered her memory in an opaque film, like fingerprints on a lens.

While she ate her egg sandwich, she watched the deluge outside. Visitors and outpatients ran through the parking lot, heads ducked under umbrellas and newspapers. Alma hoped her boys had been to the store and back home before the rain. She hoped they were getting along. She hoped they were making friends, doing well in their first days at school, eating enough for dinner. She hoped a lot and worried more. In the glaring whiteness of the hospital, worrying was most of what she could do.

12

Bobby lifted a bag of potato chips toward his face and funneled the crumbs into his open mouth. He took the bag and crumpled it into a ball, then tossed it into the wind. It tumbled through the yard until a wrinkle met the floodwaters and it was swept away. He reached down and rubbed his barbeque dusted fingertips clean on the wet grass. He wore a slicker that used to belong to his father until Bobby claimed it. It was tight around his wide shoulders and would probably fit his younger brother better. But he figured if he wanted it bad enough he could fight him for it. Bobby was a foot and a half taller than his brother, Donald, and only one of his dozen cousins stood over him. He was hardened from the day he was born, and he never wanted to be anything but mean.

He reached into one of the slicker's pockets and brought out a small copper bullet, fingering it into the chamber. He brought the .22 to his shoulder and aimed at a water-filled soup can balanced on a rock across the yard. His father had told him not to take the gun out in the rain. And his mother, years ago, had told him not to shoot it toward the rock, warning him it would glance off and hit him. Only a week later, a bullet had deflected off the rock and broke a neighbor's window. It left a neat hole with a latticework of cracks. He walked toward it, grabbing a rock as he went, and threw it through the windowpane. He figured it was already broken and his neighbor deserved it.

Sitting in the pelting rain, he squinted down the sight. As he was clicking off the safety, a rabbit jolted behind the rock, desperate for shelter. Finding none, it took a few tentative steps toward the garden next door. Bobby swept the barrel to the right and pulled the trigger. The rabbit hurtled in a frantic turn before falling on its side and kicking its hind legs against the soggy ground. It was still twitching, eyes wide and searching, when Bobby picked it up by the ears and tossed it like a beanbag into the neighbor's yard.

He wiped the blood from his fingers and turned toward the house. Watching him from the back door was his younger brother, Donald. "You're lucky Mom didn't see that," he said.

"Lucky?" Bobby scoffed.

"She would've been mad."

"Caught it in the stomach or I would've brought it in for supper. Wouldn't be too mad about meat for supper, would she?"

"That rabbit didn't do nothing."

"Didn't do nothing?" Bobby laughed. "Didn't have to do a goddamn thing but walk in front of me."

Donald turned back into the house.

Bobby followed him, dripping a trail of water through the kitchen. "Not like that fucking beaner I saw today," he said, mostly to himself. "Next time I see that motherfucker, he'll be sorry."

13

Before dawn the next morning, John Ellis sat up in bed and squinted around the room. His head felt like it was in a tightening vice. His back was damp and his shirt stuck to his skin. He leaned on one arm and ran the other hand through his hair, which was soaked through. He swept the covers off his legs, but when a shiver traveled through his body he pulled them tighter around himself. John reached across the mattress to the nightstand. He grabbed the phone and dialed the school, leaving a message for the front office.

"This is John Ellis," he said. "I'm not feeling great, so I won't be in today. Call me at home if you need me."

John put the receiver on the nightstand, off the hook. He went back to sleep and only put the phone back in its cradle when he woke to use the bathroom sometime after noon.

He called out again the next day.

And the following day. After calling the school the third day, he dialed the hospital and scheduled an appointment for Friday afternoon.

14

By Friday morning, the ground in their corner of West Texas had dried. A football game was scheduled that night, and the players were gracious the field wouldn't be a mud pit by halftime. The weather stayed dry and moderate, a meeting of two rare occurrences that caused people to leave their houses in groups and head into town. It was opening night of the football season, and a massive, eager crowd was expected. In Uvalde, like most Texas towns, the week was a gradual crescendo toward Friday when the aluminum bleachers became packed with townspeople. They came to Honey Bowl Stadium wearing their maroon shirts and howled in support of their Coyotes.

The stadium was edged by a high fence on three sides and the fourth was demarcated by thorned brambles. Football boosters sat by the gates with a coffee tin in their hands, and admission was only granted after plunking two quarters into it. For students, only one.

Martín and Gabriel came late and stood outside the fence furthest from the bleachers. They were surrounded by noticeably younger kids, so Martín was glad his classmates were on the bleachers and were too far to recognize him. The brothers tried to position their eyes in the spaces of the chainlink fence, but they realized by halftime they were too far from the field to see anything more than vague movement.

At halftime, as the marching band shouldered their glinting instruments, Martín elbowed his brother. "Ready to go?" he asked.

"Don't really feel like going home."

Martín reached a hand into his front pocket. "I've got a couple bucks saved up if you want to check out that arcade."

"Someone at school said they have the new Star Wars game," Gabriel beamed.

The brothers walked along the fence until they reached the street. With the sun beginning to set, they headed into town with their shadows stretched in front of them.

15

Bobby Kershaw trudged into Honey Bowl Stadium during the second quarter with his younger brother, Donald, in tow. Donald had begged to come along, and Bobby agreed to bring him on the condition he pay both of their admissions. Bobby lied, saying it cost a dollar each to get in, then rushed his brother through the gates as he tossed the quarters in the bucket. He told his brother to scram when they reached the steps to the bleachers, but Donald only put a step or two between them. Bobby climbed to the top corner of the grandstands where his friends were standing against the railing. Although Bobby had the build of a Uvalde Coyote linebacker, he had no interest in being told what to do. He'd told the coach to fuck off during his freshman and sophomore years until he stopped asking Bobby to consider joining the team. He preferred showing up during the game, his breath sour from his father's cheap bourbon, hoping to start — or at the least join — some trouble. He and his friends crowded together with their backs to the game, smoking cigarettes, and hatching plans of small town mayhem.

Donald found a spot in the fringe of the group that kept him within earshot but out of his brother's sight. He could hear them whooping in laughter.

"You all think it's so goddamn funny, huh?" Bobby snarled.

"Now hold on, Bobby," one of the boys said. "You gotta admit it was a pretty good throw."

"Yeah!" another chimed in. "Maybe he should be our new quarterback! He threw that fuckin' thing ten yards!"

Donald wasn't sure what they were hollering about, but from what he could piece together, someone threw a gallon of milk with sniper-like accuracy from his bike. He looked away from the group to hide the smile curling his lips. Donald thought that if he could shake the person's hand and thank him for his service, he would.

"You should've heard what that spick said too!" the first boy laughed. "Jack, tell them what he said!"

Jack squirmed a bit before saying, "He called him— he said 'you fat motherfucker.'"

The group of boys erupted into convulsions. They tipped their heads back and smacked their knees and the backs of the boys next to them. They repeated *you fat motherfucker* like an incantation until Bobby lifted a boot and slammed it against the aluminum bleacher. It clanged like a car crash and sent vibrations down the row. "I'm leaving," he said.

"Aw, come on Bobby! You ain't gotta leave!" the boys apologized halfheartedly.

"Ain't a goddamn thing going on here. I'll find something worth my time somewhere else."

Some of the boys stayed, but most of them shrugged and followed Bobby down the bleachers. As they passed through the gate, Bobby saw two boys walking toward town. They looked like the ones from the other day. The Mexican ones. They might not be the same brothers, but they were close enough.

"Let's go," he said to the group. "I just got a hell of an idea."

16

With most of the school-aged kids in Uvalde at the football game, they only had to wait a few minutes before the Star Wars machine was open. Martín fed a quarter into the game and balanced the remaining stack on the edge. They would have to take turns, but Gabriel was more than happy to watch his brother play first. Martín jiggled the joystick in anticipation before the screen went black then displayed a galactic battlefield where a war was to be waged. Martín and Gabriel alternated as pilots of TIE fighters until the galaxy was obliterated. They had a few quarters left, so they went across the arcade to play Donkey Kong.

The place was about to swell with the excitement of a Friday night. The football game was nearly over and the bleachers were emptying. The Coyotes were less than a mile away and losing by forty-nine points at that point.

Gabriel was playing and Martín was jingling their last quarter when the door opened and the band of boys walked in. Gabriel was too distracted with avoiding the falling barrels on the screen, but Martín heard the voice. If he'd known it was directed toward him, he would have turned. And the night might have happened differently.

"Finally," the voice growled. "Thought I'd never find that motherfucker."

17

The wretched hands shoved Martín from behind. He was looking at the quarter in his hand, running his thumbnail over the grooves along the edge, when his head met the solid wood of the arcade machine. Another hard push from behind split his forehead open in a gash on the corner of the game. By the time the same hands turned him around, blood was dripping steadily into his eyebrow, filling it and diverting like a clogged gutter. When the hand tightened around his throat, he recognized the boy. Even though his vision was swimming, he knew it was the kid he'd thrown the milk at. *Gabriel had warned him*, he thought as the first punch collapsed his stomach.

Gabriel had trouble understanding what he was watching until Martín was bloodied. His eyes refused to tell his brain what he was seeing. His first movement was away from the game. He staggered a few steps back and watched with wide, miasmal eyes. He watched as Bobby punched Martín in the stomach. The blow would have doubled him over if Bobby didn't have a hand around his throat. Another punch, then a knee to the crotch. Bobby let go and, when Martín hung his head, hit him with a vicious uppercut that threw a splatter of blood from Martín's forehead onto the wall. He crumpled onto the dingy carpet, his bloody face in the brightly patterned pile, and stretched his arms in front of him in a vague attempt to crawl away. Bobby calmly put a boot on Martín's back to stop him from getting away. He pinched at one of his knuckles, where Martín's teeth had put a small cut. "Anybody got any milk?" he yelled into the scattering group of teenagers.

Bobby put the toe of his boot under Martín's chest and kicked him over as if he was roadkill. Martín's vision was narrowing and whatever fight he might have had in fairer circumstances was gone. Bobby reached into the shaft of his right boot and knelt beside Martín, his knee on Martín's chest.

"See this?" he said. He held a gleaming clip point knife just above Martín's eyes. "Pretty nice, ain't it? Stole it off the last Mexican that looked at me wrong." Bobby looked at the blade with reverence, then ran his thumb over the carved bone handle. "Except he didn't call me no motherfucker, so I figure you deserve more than getting your pockets emptied. Don't you think, fellas?" he turned to his friends. They studied the carpet in front of them. Jack MacAnally chewed the inside of his lip. Bobby's brother was the only one to speak up. "Bobby," Donald said, "maybe we should just get going."

Bobby laughed. "The hell are you doing here, Donnie? Thought I told you to get lost an hour ago."

Donald faded back into the group.

Martín, in the last bit of consciousness he could muster, shoved Bobby's arm. The knife was airborne for a long moment before clattering on the floor and bouncing out of reach. Bobby watched it skitter away. "Well," he sighed, "that was gonna be a whole lot quicker, but—" he shrugged and raised his fist. His knuckles crushed Martín's face, pulping his cheek, his teeth, his nose.

"Hey!" a voice screamed from the stunned crowd. "Get off him!"

Bobby let his fist fall once more before he looked toward the voice.

"That's enough," the same voice said and raised an arm. He was gripping Bobby's knife.

"I'll be damned," Bobby laughed. "Looks like this whole goddamn family wants to die tonight. Almost didn't recognize you without that fuckin' dog food all down your face."

"Get off him," Gabriel said, pointing the knife at Bobby.

Bobby stood and Martín gasped a sick, gurgling breath. Bobby took a step toward Gabriel. "Give me the knife," he hissed. "Give me the knife or I'll do you worse than that," and tipped his head toward Martín.

"Leave us alone," Gabriel said.

Bobby shook his head. "Ain't going no damn place," he said and cocked his arm. He stepped toward Gabriel like a pitcher winding up. When he threw his arm forward, Gabriel met him in the void between them. The blade slid through Bobby's shirt silently. It made no sound when it gouged the skin or pierced his intestines. Bobby felt heat in his stomach as his punch missed. He felt his shirt grow heavy with dark, sticky blood. Then he fell to a knee and felt nothing else.

18

The flashing screens and bulbs on the arcade games and pinball machines continued their rhythms. As the blue and red lights from outside swept across the walls, only a few people remained in the arcade. Their faces were cast in purple, blue, red light. The police separated the teenagers and asked questions. The teenagers answered as best they could. The arcade owner gave an impassioned speech on the current generation. Gabriel and Martín were on opposite sides of the room. Gabriel searched for his brother, but Martín was being loaded onto a gurney and was wheeled away.

Gabriel fidgeted in the darkest corner, a deputy keeping silent watch over him. Gabriel's eyes were on the floor, tracing the patterns in the carpet. The other kids were telling the cops something, then pointing at him. He wasn't sure what to do. Wasn't sure how he should feel. Was it a time for pride? He'd surely saved his brother's life. Or maybe solemnity? A boy had just died. Shame? It was his hand that plunged the knife into him, after all. But at that point, it hadn't crossed his mind to put on a face for the police. He was simply embarrassed that kids from his new school were pointing at him. He was no longer invisible.

Gabriel raised his eyes when he heard another gurney being rolled in. He briefly felt muddled hope that Bobby would survive. The medic kneeling by Bobby stood. Another crouched and placed a finger on his neck then shook his head. A long tarpaulin pouch was unfurled and Bobby was placed inside. The bag was zipped shut, making the same whizzing sound as a long winter coat. Four men grabbed the corners of the body bag and hoisted Bobby onto the gurney and rolled him outside.

Gabriel's vision warped as his eyes began to water. His mouth flooded with thin, acrid-tasting saliva. As Bobby was being loaded into the coroner's van, Gabriel vomited onto the carpet. It splattered onto the deputy's silver-tipped cowboy boots. Over the sound of his retching, Gabriel heard sobbing. Only when his stomach was empty did he realize it was him.

19

Donald told the police officer what he'd seen while fighting away the searing sensation in his eyes and refusing to let the cop see him cry. He wanted to be a cop when he was older so he figured the man would never hire him if he remembered him as a blubbering kid. As he answered the cop's questions and shared what he knew, he saw them put his brother in a tall black bag. They zipped the bag and started loading Bobby onto the gurney when the Mexican kid puked on his own legs. The sight of the Mexican kid — the only person in the place that was his age — comforted him, even though he had just pointed to him as the person that plunged the knife into his brother. Seeing him puke, smelling the sick, distracted him from what had happened. The perverseness of it lifted him from the place so he could pretend he hadn't been standing next to his brother's body and the puddle of blood that grew underneath him.

The cop wrote in his small notepad and knelt in front of him. "Donald," he said, breaking the trance and bringing him back to the place that smelled metallic from the blood and vomit and sweat. "Do you need a ride home?"

"Home?" Donald asked, dazed. He hadn't thought of home.

"I can give you a ride if you need one."

"I'm okay," Donald said. Then after thinking a moment, "What happens now?"

The cop let out a long breath that hissed through his nose. "I think it's best if you go on home. We're going to finish up here, then I'll come by your house to talk to your parents."

Donald nodded and left. He walked out of the arcade into the cooling evening. The sun was set but the horizon was still painted a hazy orange. He was halfway home before he realized he would be the one to tell his mother. Donald considered walking the town in circles until he was sure the cop had broken the news but thought better of it. He was afraid the Mexican kid would come to find him too. Maybe do him the same way he did Bobby.

The front door was propped open with a cinderblock and he could see from the street that the light over the kitchen sink was on. Donald heard the TV murmuring. Standing on the wood-slat porch, he closed his eyes and turned an ear toward the living room. It was the new episode of *Dallas*, which meant his mother was home. And she never fell asleep during her shows. He walked in loudly, banging the screen door against the cinderblock and trudging through the hallway. Donald hoped the noise would bring her to the doorway, but she remained transfixed by the screen.

"Hi boys," his mother said. "Wash up before bed. Not gonna fight with anyone about it."

Donald's chest constricted and squeezed out the breath he'd been holding. His mother was the sole example of kindness his life had given him. He'd heard other boys say their fathers were nice, that they were good men, or decent husbands and dads when they got home sober. But Donald's was none of those. The closest his father had ever edged on kindness was a few years before when he mentioned over dinner that he'd gotten a B on a geography quiz. "King Shit," his father scoffed, pieces of chewed peas flying from his lips. "Your mother sure does think you're something. But I seen you when I needed help with that clutch. Wouldn't know a goddamn flywheel if it sucked you

41

off."

He wasn't lying. Donald still didn't know what a flywheel or any other part of a clutch was, and his mother did think he was something. She would joke that the baby she delivered and Donald were switched at the hospital. "No way you're filled with Kershaw blood," she teased. When Donald got high marks on his school exams, he would quietly tell his mother so his brother and father wouldn't tease him. Sometimes, she would sneak into his bedroom and slip a dollar bill under the front cover of a textbook.

"Hi Mom," he said quietly.

"Where's your brother? Did he send you home?"

Donald shook his head and looked at her. Seeing her face finally brought tears.

"What happened?" She muted the TV. "Did Bobby do something?"

Tears streamed over his cheeks and collected on his chin.

"Donald," she whispered, her voice reaching across the room to him.

He went to her and sat beside her on the sofa. She reached over and wiped his cheeks.

"You can tell me anything."

Donald swallowed, took a deep breath. "Bobby's dead," he said.

20

One of the medics gave Gabriel a handful of crackers and a cup of water. He downed the water and its refill and nibbled the corners of the crackers. He was sitting cross-legged on the floor, still able to

THE DEVIL IN THESE HILLS

smell the bile from his vomit. The deputy had taken up spitting into a handkerchief and cleaning his boots while scowling at Gabriel.

"Son," another uniformed cop stood in front of Gabriel. "Your stomach alright?"

Gabriel shrugged.

"I'd like you to tell me what happened."

Gabriel fiddled with the rough edges of the crackers. "I don't really know what to tell," he said quietly.

"Well," the cop sighed, "where were you before this?"

"The football game."

"With your brother?"

Gabriel nodded.

"Then what happened when you came here?"

"We were playing the Star Wars game. Then it started getting crowded but we had a few more quarters so we played Donkey Kong."

"Then?"

"Then I was playing Donkey Kong, and all of a sudden Martín was bleeding."

"What had happened?"

Gabriel shrugged. "He got pushed, I think. Then that kid choked him and pushed him around and started punching him." His eyes were beginning to sting again. His lids were irritated and puffy, and his eyes felt gritty and dry. Whatever tears would have come then had already been wiped away. "I was scared," Gabriel said shakily. "Martín couldn't breathe."

"How do you know he couldn't breathe?"

Gabriel stared at his glimmering badge. He hadn't known any more clearly than you know a rainstorm is coming without checking the skies; you can sense the smallest changes in the things you've always known. "I could just tell."

"Was your brother being choked while he was on the ground?"

"Yes. Well—" he thought. "I think so."

"So you were concerned he couldn't breathe but can't remember if he was being choked?"

"I— I guess so, yeah."

The cop wrote something in his notepad and underlined it with two quick gashes. "And how did you become involved?" he asked.

Gabriel fought to collect his thoughts, beginning to understand the gravity of each answer. "Martín was on his back and he was getting punched by the other guy. Punched in his face. And Martín couldn't fight back."

"Was he conscious at that point?"

"I don't know," Gabriel shrugged. "But he wasn't fighting back."

"Was that your knife?"

Gabriel shook his head. "It was his— the other guy's. He pulled it from his boot and was putting it in Martín's face."

"Was he moving it in a threatening way?"

Gabriel looked into the cop's eyes for the first time. The cop was younger than he'd thought, but indigo bags ringed his eyelids. "Is there another way to hold a knife to someone's face?" Gabriel said. He studied the cop's face, his eyebrows raised in surprise, before staring at the cop's badge.

"No, I wouldn't say so." The cop checked his notes, then asked, "How did you get the knife?"

"I just picked it up. Martín knocked it out of his hand and it landed right by my foot."

"I thought he wasn't fighting back?"

"That was the only fighting he did."

"Okay. Then what?"

"I told him to get off of Martín. He got off of him and came toward me."

"Did you step toward him?"

"I— I don't know. Maybe."

"Did he hit you?"

Gabriel shook his head. "But he was going to."

"Did he threaten you?"

Gabriel nodded.

"What did he say?"

He tried to put the words back into the boy's sneer. "I can't remember."

"Tell me what else happened after that."

"I was afraid Martín was dead. And I was afraid he was going to kill me next. So I tried to hold the knife out in front of me to keep him away. But he tried to hit me. I guess— Then the knife went— it went into him."

The cop scribbled some more notes and pursed his lips. "Well, son," he sighed. "Some of those other boys said you two were looking for a fight, and when your brother bit off more than he could chew, you stole that boy's knife and killed him with it."

Gabriel's eyes began to prickle again. His chest shuddered as he tried to breathe. "That— that isn't wh— what happened," he stammered.

"Yeah." The cop watched him, standing over him. "I know how you all are," he said.

Gabriel retched again, vomiting over his crossed legs, covering his jeans with sick.

"Stand up."

With his stomach heaving, Gabriel stood. He was expecting anoth-er Dixie cup of tepid water or another stack of crackers. He thought the cop placed a hand on his elbow to steer him toward a drinking fountain or a ride home. But when he stood, his limp arms were pulled behind him and Gabriel felt the cold binding grip of metal clicking into place around his wrists.

Utopia

I ain't crying,
that's West Texas in my eye.

The Panhandlers

1

SHIRLEY KERSHAW SWORE she was cursed. She knew it before she became a Kershaw. Even before she'd met the man that would bring her into that fold. She reasoned she must have come from a damned bloodline. Perhaps an ancestor had made a sordid deal at her expense. For generations, men from her lineage have dropped like whitetails in rifle season. Her father reached through time and butchered his children's futures, ripping holes in the fabric that would be patched together to create his unborn grandchildren.

Shirley's father was a drunk and often came home from his shifts at the sawmill to beat her mother. One night, he called the kids — Shirley and her two brothers — to the kitchen table and had their mother make them all dinner plates. Then he took a bite of boiled potatoes and spit the mash into his wife's face. He balled up the rest of the food on his plate and threw it against the wall where it stuck fast for almost a minute before dropping to the floor. He smacked their mother a half dozen times before Shirley's oldest brother pushed his chair from the table and stood. He caught his father's arm and turned him. "I'll kill you," the brother said. "You do that again — you *ever* do that again — and I'll kill you." Their father stared at him until he spit in his son's face and stormed from the house. It took half an hour for Shirley to clean the potato mash from the seams in the linoleum floor.

Not even a week later, their father staggered into the house reeking of Everclear and pulled his wife's head by her hair. Shirley's brother grabbed him and took him through the back door. He took their father through the dewy yard and kicked the backs of his knees so he collapsed in front of him. Shirley's brother pulled a pistol from the back of his belt and pulled the trigger without hesitation. A price tag still hung from the gun. He'd gotten it from a pawn shop the day after he made his promise.

Shirley's brother was taken to jail that night and died in a cell some years later. The only tragedy, as far as anyone could see, was that her brother's squandered life was a byproduct of their father getting exactly what he deserved.

For a few years, the three of them made do. But when her brother turned eighteen, he joined the Army and was shipped to Vietnam. They buried him in a closed casket the next year. They were promised his dog tag if it was ever found, but Shirley suspected it — like her brother — had been blasted back to dust.

Her mother still had Shirley, but she'd lost every man she'd known. Her father had died in an accident at the sawmill when she was nine, and her own family was ravaged — save for her daughter — by the time she turned forty-five. She became quiet and spent days and nights without sleep, barely blinking, in front of a television. Shirley set dinners on a tray next to her only to scrape the hardened food into the trash before she left for work the next morning.

It was at work that she met Dwayne Kershaw. He was loud, abrasive, and rude. But he was handsome and paid her all the attention she could want. He talked a blue streak and, coming from a house that had grown silent, it felt like a luxury to have his words in excess. He rarely drank too much, though he ran with a group that did. Under different circumstances, Shirley's mother may have looked from the television screen when her daughter came home, dropped off late by the rumbling Dodge pickup truck. *Best be careful,* she might have said. *Never can be too careful around a Kershaw.* But she never said a word about it.

Most nights, Shirley would leave the grocery store, still wearing her kelly green apron, lock the door behind her, and climb into Dwayne's truck. He drove her around Uvalde, taking her down the county roads that split the Hill Country and seemed to go on forever. She liked when he'd take her to a town called Utopia, less than an hour northeast of Uvalde. Shirley figured he had no idea what utopia meant, but she felt a thousand miles from her cursed life in Uvalde. *Welcome to Utopia,* the sign said, *A Paradise.* Dwayne never drove her through the town, but would park with the truck headlights shining onto that city limit sign. Just reading the sign outside Utopia was enough of an escape from the tragedies her life had collected. If not for her silent mother, she would have left for some other utopia years ago and sowed her crop in her own Elysian field.

A few miles outside of Utopia, on a backroad with the headlights off, she made love to him. That was the night they'd made Bobby. She swore she could feel it by the time Dwayne had his Levi's pulled back up. That was when she knew that paltry town of Utopia would be the closest she'd get to getting away. The nearest she'd ever be to utopia.

So, Shirley was not entirely shocked to hear of Bobby's death. It was enough of a curse to raise a son as mean as him. The most surprising part of it all was that it had taken so long for him to meet his match.

2

It had been months but she still wasn't used to the bleach. The caustic fumes made her lungs feel shriveled, and there hadn't been a day it didn't make her eyes tear. Alma had found the effects of the bleach were worse in the nebulous and alien hours of a Saturday, pre-dawn, near the end of a double shift. She was sloshing some of it into a toilet when her co-worker came into the restroom. Alma didn't know the woman well, but she was the type that was maternal to everyone. She was older than Alma, a slight figure that moved through the hospital quietly and effortlessly, which made her indispensable as a housekeeper.

"Alma, it's Melissa," the woman said.

"Hi, sorry. I'm almost finished. Just need to scrub this stall."

"I'm not your boss, honey," the woman put her hands on her hips. "Listen, what are your boys' names again?"

"Gabriel and Martín," she said. "Gabe's the youngest."

The woman bit her bottom lip, studying the toilet seat. She reached into the front pocket of her work uniform and began fidgeting with something inside.

"What is it?" Alma cut in. The unexpected mention of her boys on another woman's lips sent waves of panic through her limbs and put a cold, copper-lined pit in her chest. She was still standing in the restroom stall, the bleach vapor surrounding her, choking her. "What is it?" she panicked.

"One of the girls was working in a room, and she said there was a patient— a boy— named Martín."

Alma shook her head. Her eyes flooding from the bleach, from what the woman was saying. "I'm sure it was a different boy," she said.

The woman shook her head.

"What are you saying? You really think that's my boy? If it was my Martín someone would have told me!"

The woman was silent, her eyes pained. Her hand worked furiously in her pocket. "I guess I'm telling you now, Alma. I'm so sorry."

Alma fell backward, seating herself on the gleaming toilet.

"To thee we cry, poor banished children of Eve," the woman whispered with her head bowed.

"I— he— what happened?"

The woman pulled a kerchief from her pocket and handed it to Alma. "I don't know, honey. But he's alive."

"*Alive?*" Alma sobbed. If that was the indication of his condition — alive versus dead — she couldn't fathom what might have happened. She could barely make sense that something *had* happened to her son.

"He's in room 214. I can go with you if you want."

Alma wiped her face with the kerchief and shook her head.

"Here," she reached into her pocket and took out a rosary. Handing it to Alma, she said, "You need this more than I do."

Alma sat on the toilet, swimming in the cloud of noxious bleach, clutching the beads and the kerchief. She stayed until her legs went numb and tingled until her body was devoid of tears. She sat and prayed. Her legs refused to move. She thought she might sit until the whole thing revealed itself as fiction. If it weren't for the totems clasped in her hands, she wouldn't have believed something could happen to her son.

Alma found room 214 at some point, though her mind was a muddled haze. From the doorway, a rush of relief went through her. It stilled her trembling hands and settled her chest. She looked at the hospital bed and the bandaged person lying in it. Heavy gauze bandages wrapped the face in thick stripes around the forehead, nose, and chin. IV lines hung from their limp arm, a catheter from under its gown to the foot of the bed. "Thank the Lord," she sighed, clutching the holy beads. She stepped quietly toward the patient, careful not to wake them, although they were far from the grasp of consciousness. As relieved as she was this patient was not her son, they were another mother's son. Alma said a prayer for them all the same.

She was standing by the bedside, ready to lay the rosary on the bedside table. Alma looked at the patient, wondering what kind of grim injuries would require such bandaging around their face. Her heart broke for the nameless man. She could tell he was handsome before the injuries and the layers of gauze. His thick and wavy black hair was unruly but attractive. She wished Martín would wear his hats less so people could see his similarly handsome hair.

Alma reached for the patient's hand. She began a prayer and interlaced the rosary between his fingers. On the man's right hand, along the wrinkles of the first knuckle, was a scar. It looked like a scar that might have come from a fistfight, from a sharp blade. Or from running with a glass bottle of cola and tripping, landing on a shard and cutting the knuckle so deep she could see the white bone underneath. As it did with Martín.

Alma shuddered. "My boy!" she cried. She bent at the waist and put her head on the chest of the man, the boy — her boy — in the hospital bed. The sight of the seeping bandages was too much to bear.

There was no disconnect between her pain and that of her son's. The scaffolding holding her insides together collapsed. Yet, she would use each broken piece of herself to cast her son together again.

3

Alma was still in that position — on her knees, back and head bent as if worshiping the bandaged body before her — when the police officer came into the room. "I'm sorry to interrupt," he said. He held his silverbelly hat in front of him and bowed his head. "Are you Martín's mother?"

Alma turned her eyes to glance at him. "Yes," she croaked. "This is my son." Then she rose, bearing the weight of Martín's pain while he slept. "What happened?"

"I'm Officer Simmons. I'm leading the investigation into what exactly happened last night."

"Last night?"

The cop nodded.

"Why didn't someone tell me?"

"We tried. We went to your home and tried calling but we couldn't reach you."

"I was here," she said. "I was working. I was a floor away this whole time." New tears came then, conjured up from some reserve. "What happened to him? Will he be okay?" she cried.

"I'm sorry, ma'am. I'm not his doctor. But I can gladly get him for you if you'd like."

"Just please tell me what happened."

Officer Simmons sighed. "There was a— an altercation last night. At the Pocket Change arcade."

"I don't understand."

"A fight, ma'am."

"My boys wouldn't fight. Somebody did this to him."

"Maybe so," Simmons shrugged. "But a boy died because of it."

"*Died?*" Alma's mouth hung open.

"Yes, ma'am. Your son was certainly in the middle of something. I was hoping to speak to him, but I guess he's been out since he got here."

"Why would you need to speak to him?"

"About Gabriel."

"What does Gabe have to do with this? Was he there?"

"Yes," Simmons took a deep breath. "He was there."

"Is he okay?"

"Yes, ma'am. But—"

"But *what?*"

"—he's under arrest. Charged—"

"*Arrest?*"

"—with first degree murder."

Although Alma thought she was already at the bottom of whatever well she'd tumbled down — whatever tortuous maternal gauntlet she was in — she felt herself descend further with a jolt.

4

John Ellis was back in school on Monday. He'd gone to a doctor Friday afternoon for his first visit in several years and was given a brown bottle of thick sludge that he was ordered to take a swallow of twice a day. It tasted of metal shavings and felt similar when it hit his empty stomach, so he'd begun taking it with a whiskey chaser and an apple. "It's just a head cold. Maybe the flu," the doctor said vaguely before handing him the bottle and shooing him back to the front desk. Over the weekend, he began feeling more like himself and was resolute that he would be in school on Monday.

John stopped by the office on the way to his classroom, and his mail cubby was stuffed with rolled envelopes and papers. He tucked them under his arm and was a step into the hallway when the principal called from behind him.

"Morning Dr. Hendrick," John turned.

"How are you feeling?"

"Better. Thanks."

"Listen, I got a call about some goings-on Friday night. I don't have much to tell, but if you hear anything, let me know."

"Sure," John nodded. "I saw something about it in the paper but it didn't say much." All the teachers at Uvalde Regional knew Dr. Hendrick's reputation as a gossiper. Nothing got him to work harder than whispers of a sordid rumor.

"I've been hearing it was some of our students."

"What happened?"

"Hell of a fight, from what I hear." He put a hand on John's shoulder and leaned close. "I probably shouldn't be saying this," he whispered, "but I heard the coroner was there."

John felt the principal's breath on his ear. "That's not true," he shook his head. "Is it?"

Dr. Hendrick pulled John even closer. "Heard it might've been a Kershaw."

"A Kershaw?" John pulled away. He picked at a corner of an envelope. "Guess they were bound to go too far sooner or later."

"No, John. I heard a Kershaw died."

"Hard to imagine a Kershaw on the receiving end."

"My thoughts exactly," Dr. Hendrick said. "That's why I'm asking the staff to keep an ear out for talk of it. I have a feeling there's more to this story."

Later in the morning, there was a knock on Dr. Hendrick's door and an older police officer poked his head into his office. "Come in," Dr. Hendrick said. "Please sit."

The cop sat facing Dr. Hendrick's desk. "I came to discuss an incident involving some students over the weekend."

Dr. Hendrick nodded gravely, feigning surprise.

The officer explained the events from that Friday night at the arcade. How there was some investigative work still to be done, but it seemed obvious enough that at least one party arrived hoping for trouble. "Either way," he explained, "Robert Kershaw is deceased, and Gabriel Jiménez was arrested."

Dr. Hendrick reached for a pen. "Can you say that name one more time?"

"Gabriel Jiménez," he said. "I believe he's a student here."

"Sure, sure! But I'm sure you know how it is. More of them every year. Hard and getting harder to keep them all straight."

The cop watched Dr. Hendrick scribble the name on the edge of his desktop calendar. "The other boy — the one that got beat up pretty good — he's a student here too. Gabriel's brother. Martín Jiménez."

Dr. Hendrick wrote the other name.

"Have you heard anything from last week that might've started this?"

Dr. Hendrick leaned back in his chair. "Haven't heard a thing. But, in your opinion," he said, lowering his voice, "what do you think happened on Friday?"

The cop reached into a breast pocket and removed a carton of cigarettes. He took a cigarette and rolled it, unlit, between his fingers. "That I can't say. But kids talk. So if you hear anything that might be of use to our investigation, please give me a call." He pulled a business card from his pocket and put it on the desk, then lit the cigarette and left.

5

"You said you wanted to see me?" John called into the office later that afternoon.

"Come in, John. Have a seat," Dr. Hendrick said. It had been a long day for him. The phone was ringing constantly, and his secretary had to leave at noon so his calls were being fielded by a senior student that helped around the office. She was lightning quick with a typewriter, but she'd accidentally hung up on three calls before she learned how to place them on hold.

"What was the name of that Mexican kid you were bent out of shape about the other day?"

"Gabriel," John said. "He wasn't in today. I talked to his brother a few days ago about those bruises but he didn't seem to know anything about it."

"What have you heard about Friday night?"

"Not a thing."

"Well, I had a visit," Dr. Hendrick said. "From an Officer Sim-mons."

"Okay."

"Turns out that kid you were so worried about *was* having some issues. But nothing like you thought."

"Did he get caught up in something on Friday?"

"You could say that!" Dr. Hendrick scoffed. "Officer Simmons — along with a bunch of witnesses, apparently — seems to think that boy killed Bobby Kershaw."

"I— what— that's not possible," he stammered.

Dr. Hendrick sat back in his desk chair. "I'm not the judge and jury, but that cop seemed pretty sure of it."

John shook his head slowly. "Gabriel is probably the shyest student I've met this year. Haven't heard him string more than a few words together. I honestly don't think could do something like that."

"Well, you know how Mexicans get when they get angry."

"Stop," John said. "Don't start with that. I'm sure it's just a misun-derstanding. Are you sure it wasn't his brother?"

Dr. Hendrick referenced his desk calendar. "Martín? He's at Uval-de Memorial for whatever injuries he got that night."

"And what about Gabriel?" John asked. "Where is he?"

"He's in jail, John. Where else would they put a murderer?"

6

The truck cab was stifling but John drove through town with the windows up. With each intersection he crossed through, it seemed the neighborhoods became more ramshackle. The houses soon began looking like they would, or had been, losing small bits of hardware — a shingle, a mailbox door, a ribbon of siding — any time a Hill Country storm rolled through. He pulled in front of the Jiménez house and finally cranked the window open. He took a deep breath and rubbed his face, then crossed the small yard and rapped on the door. After a minute he knocked again, but there was no movement inside.

John went back to the furnace of his truck cab and rifled through his bag. He'd brought along a few mini-bottles of Jim Beam to aid his medicine taking. There were three left, so he twisted the cap on one and downed it. He opened another and sipped it slower.

A humid wind blew through the window and felt cool on the droplets of sweat stippling his face. He wasn't sure what to do next. What he should do was go home, but he knew it would be a long night wondering about the Jiménez boys if he did. Why did he feel so kindred to these brothers he hardly knew? To a shy new student and his wary brother? Maybe, he thought, he felt he needed to reconcile the Gabriel he'd met with the Gabriel that went toe-to-toe with a Kershaw. The biggest and meanest of them, no less. More than that, he felt a stream of responsibility which connected to the larger story. At least in his mind. If he had been in school, rather than sweating out a fever in his bed, he may have been able to do something for that young brother who was now sitting in the Uvalde County jail. He knew it would be easier to feel a detached incredulity about the news, as most people would, but if he was willing to dismiss the emotions and needs of the young men then, most likely, he never would have considered teaching.

Each student came to their teachers with peace offerings. Small pieces of themselves that were handed over in essays, discussions, poster boards. In return, they were gifted slivers of their teachers. Assignments, private conversations, lectures. By the time these students vanished from the hallways and classrooms, they were a patchwork of themselves and all the mentors that had given themselves over. It would seem each student benefits greatly from this, but what about the teachers? At what point do they give away the last shard of themselves? They were pails of water left in the rain. Eventually, with each drop that falls into the pail, a drop trickles to the ground. There must be a time when the bucket is filled with only rainwater, and its original contents had all soaked into the earth to begin a new life as rain once more. Perhaps that was the watershed moment in their careers when they either feel enlightened or indentured.

It was his incurable solicitude that was the reason John enrolled in the educational program at Southwest Texas State in San Marcos. One of his high school teachers was an alumnus, and once pointed to a framed picture on his desk. "One of my classmates," the teacher said with a coy smile. The photo showed him with an arm around Lyndon B. Johnson. John wrote the teacher a letter soon after graduation telling him it was the best decision he'd ever made, especially considering the alternative was being sent to Vietnam.

He drained the last swig of whiskey and put the truck in drive. He drove back across town, seeing the dilapidation in reverse. Like the houses had been nailed back into repair. The macadam parking lot was soft from the heat and made a sticking sound on his boot heels as he walked toward the hospital. He hadn't been to Uvalde Memorial Hospital in many years, and now he was walking through the heavy doors for the second time in a week. The crisp air conditioning sent a shiver through his limbs when he went inside.

"Here for an appointment?" the woman at the front desk asked.

"No, ma'am. I'm here to see someone."

"What's the name of the person you're visiting?"

"Jiménez," John said. "First name is Martín."

The woman flipped through some papers. "Let me make sure he's taking visitors right now," she said with a practiced smile. She pinched the phone with her shoulder and shuffled more papers, then asked a few hushed questions. "M-hm," she nodded. "I see. Yes, of course. Thank you kindly." Turning her attention back to John, she said, "I'm sorry, sir. Mr. Jiménez is just out of surgery, and won't be taking visitors today."

John studied the corner of the countertop. "Thanks for your help." He turned and went back into the steaming air outside, pulling his hat low to shade the late summer sun glinting off the blinding windshields.

7

By Tuesday, there wasn't much left of the inside of John Ellis's cheeks. He hadn't chewed his cheeks until they bled or his nails down to the quick since he was a teenager. His thumbnails on both hands were gnawed down to puffed and irritated skin. The act of lighting a cigarette and flicking the grey ash usually scratched whatever had been itching at him. But since hearing about Gabriel and his brother, his trusted Marlboro reds tasted bitter and left a lingering film on his tongue that made his stomach roil.

He knew enough of the boys and what had happened to have it seize the machinery of his mind. Still, he knew so little that his thoughts spiraled quickly out of control when he was reminded. It seemed, for the past day, every time he tried to turn away from the anxiousness that seeped into his muscles, he would bump into a new way to think about it, a new place to drill a pit in his stomach.

John had a psychology professor in college that loved to lecture about *papancha*. "Avoid papancha," he would preach. "Propagating thoughts will drive the soundest minds to madness. Always avoid papancha." With only a few semesters to go, John had enough coursework to keep his mind busy then, and he thought the professor was pretentious. But after spending a day wading through his proliferating anxieties, he wasn't as sure. All he knew was avoiding papancha that day was as simple as keeping his fingernails from a prickling rash.

John stumbled through a morning of lessons, explaining to his students he was still feeling under the weather, then sat at his desk over his lunch hour. He had forgotten his medicine on the nightstand but he still had a nip of whiskey in his bag. When he rifled through it, he could hear the bottle clinking against some binder clips. He didn't trust the notion that whiskey calmed nerves — and he'd put it to the test — so he sat with a warm can of Coke and a cold turkey and cheese sandwich in front of him. He tore off a chunk of clammy turkey lunchmeat and chewed on it until it became a tasteless pulp. When the bell chimed somewhere down the hallway, he tossed the sandwich into the garbage. It made a shuffling sound when it settled in the mess of paper.

John had one class left after lunch period, then an afternoon of desk work. He was usually grateful for the time and used it to grade assignments and exams, but he'd stayed up late the night before, mindlessly marking papers with a red pencil.

After his afternoon lesson, John grabbed his bag, which was already packed, and locked his classroom door behind him. He went down the side stairwell and out a fire exit that hadn't been connected since he started working there. Out of habit, he lit a cigarette after starting his truck. He cranked the window down and took a drag. Wishing he hadn't scrapped the turkey sandwich after all, he held the Marlboro out of the truck window and pulled away from the school. By the time he parked at the hospital, it was burnt to the filter. John sat for a minute, mindlessly flicking it with his thumb. He thought about coming up with something to say, some way to explain why he was visiting in the middle of the day, why he was visiting at all. But there was hardly a reason that made sense to him, so he didn't bother.

8

Martín was still on a gurney in room 214 when John entered. He knocked on the metal door jamb. "Come in, doctor," a voice called from the bedside. John stepped hesitantly into the room and went around the curtain partition hanging from the ceiling, covering Martín's upper half. From his waist down he appeared uninjured. But the thin hospital sheets tented over his feet gave him the same anonymous appearance as the hospital's other hundred patients. When he rounded the curtain, he saw Martín. His face was swollen, a patchwork of bandages. He heard the slow beat of the beeping heart monitor, and he saw his eyes, closed from sleep or swollen shut he couldn't tell. A woman was sitting at Martín's bedside with her back to the door. She was leaning forward with her head bowed near Martín's shoulder. One of her hands held a rosary, the other grasped Martín's.

"I'm sorry," John looked to the mint green tile floor. "I should go," he muttered.

But the woman turned to him. "Are you with the police?" she asked. She seemed to sing the words, even through her grieving. Her skin was tanned and perfectly smooth. It reflected the harsh after-noon sunlight streaming through the window as softly as moonlight. She was nearing 40, but her skin belied the years. Even the difficult times in her life, which were burdensome on her heart, were absent from her face.

"You're Martín's mother?"

The woman nodded. "Are you from the police station?"

John scratched his chin. "I'm just a teacher at the high school."

"You're Martín's teacher?"

John shook his head. "I have Gabriel."

The woman looked him over again. His shy, wide smile under his thick but neat mustache. He wrung a straw cowboy hat in his hands, and his hair was shoddily slicked with product in an attempt to tame his cowlicks.

John knew he owed the woman a better explanation, but he had none to offer.

"But you know Martín?" she asked.

"We met," he said. "Briefly."

"Oh?"

John could feel embarrassment growing from his neck and blos-soming into his cheeks. Abashment was not a common feeling for him, whether from avoidance or confidence, but he recognized the air growing thin between the two strangers as unease, or something like it, settled in. He considered leaving. His foot even stuttered on the floor in the direction of the door. But he knew if he left then, with the image of Martín's gauze-mottled face and his distraught mother in his memory, he would struggle even more to turn away from thoughts of the family. Instead of rationale, he offered what he had: honesty and compassion.

"I've been a teacher for a long time," he said. "And I try to pay some extra attention to my new students. They don't usually need it, but just in case. Gabriel seemed pretty shy, even for a new student, so I took some extra notice to him. So when he showed up at school with bruises on his face, I was fairly concerned. I talked to the principal but he hadn't heard anything, so I drove out to your place."

"You came to our house?" Alma cut in.

"I was hoping to talk to a parent."

"About what?"

"About the bruises."

"I didn't notice any bruises," Alma said. Then, understanding the implication, added, "I promise. Gabe is a good boy."

"I know," John nodded. "But I've seen kids go through things they never should. I just wanted to talk to someone. To make sure it wasn't something at home. I figured someone was giving him a hard time at school."

"Was someone?"

"I don't know. Gabriel wouldn't say. But I talked to Martín when I came to your house. He seems like a good kid too. Told me you worked here and that you weren't home. I was going to call or stop by again, but I got pretty sick for a few days and then—" he trailed off.

Alma was quiet, running rosary beads over the pad of her thumb. "I just don't understand it."

John studied the way the tiles came together, how some of them were laid crooked so a crevice would grow along its edge to collect dust and debris. "I don't either," he said. "I did hear there was a Kershaw there. Heard he might've been right in the middle of whatever happened."

"No, I know *what* happened. I just don't understand."

"What happened?" John asked before he could stop himself.

Alma placed the rosary in her pocket and turned the chair to face him. She told John what she knew. She shared everything Gabriel had told her when she was finally allowed to visit him at the jail. Alma had called the police station and the county jail every waking hour since she'd picked herself up from Martín's bedside. They gave her routine and perfunctory answers. *He's still in the intake process,* they'd said for close to forty-eight hours. *He'll have access to a telephone to call you before he's able to take visitors,* they began saying after that. Who was she to question the process? Surely her son would be taken care of until everything could be sorted out, and he would be sent home.

When she was finished recounting the past three days to the stranger in her son's hospital room, she felt a faint trace of peace.

John's face was slack but his eyes were darting like he was furiously working to piece together shattered fragments of glass. "I appreciate you sharing that."

"You're the first person that's asked."

"Not even the police?"

She shook her head. "An officer came and told me what happened. But I haven't heard from them since I visited Gabriel."

John wanted to ask about the boys' father, about their family, any of Alma's coworkers. "Nobody asked?" is all he said instead.

Alma held her hands open as if to say *this is who we have.*

John reached into his pocket and pulled out the Marlboro pack, then grabbed a pen from his breast pocket. He ripped off the lid of the carton and flattened it. "My name is John Ellis," he said as he scribbled on the paper. "And if there's anything you or your sons need, please call me or come to the school or even to my home. Here's my phone number and address." He handed her the ragged scrap. "I mean it," he said. "Anything."

Alma looked at the thick paper, *JOHN ELLIS* written in block letters, and realized she hadn't told him her name. She looked up to introduce herself, but he'd already disappeared into the hallway.

9

On the day Gabriel Jiménez first walked into the Uvalde County Courthouse, the flotsam in the cool spring water of the Frio River were offerings from tourists — spent beer cans, crumpled cigarette butts, popped and deflated inner tubes. Summer elsewhere was dissolving, but the southern Hill Country had a way of grasping it like a flour sack towel and wringing every sweltering day from its fibers.

The courthouse was altogether more impressive than Uvalde's Tuscan-inspired City Hall. The county courthouse appeared collegial and welcoming, and many had mistaken it for the city's library while driving through the town on State Highway 117. But whatever friendliness the architecture emanated was unintended. Its exterior was sparse for a courthouse, with its ionic Roman columns extending only partway to the ground. It's said there are five pillars of justice, but the Uvalde County Courthouse was supported by four. The building looked as if the dirt surrounding its foundation had washed away in a flood. The top two levels were beige brick with wide-set columns planted firmly in a wide, open balcony. If the ground were piled twelve feet higher, it would have made a proper entrance. Instead, the first floor was mismatched white stone, the front door was shadowed — and mostly hidden — by the arches supporting the balcony.

Gabriel did not enter the courthouse through the shaded front doors. He was driven to the courthouse in a police car, and led inside with the cop's hand grasping his elbow. Gabriel's hands were shackled behind his back. The cop steered him through the humid, cavernous halls of the courthouse until he was shoved into a small, windowless room with a low metal bench in the middle of the floor. He stood behind it for a time that was meaningless in the sterile room until his attorney arrived. He stayed just inside the doorway as if the walls might close around him if he entered a step too far.

Gabriel had met the attorney a few days ago. He was sitting in a cell, on another cold metal bench, and coloring patterns on a legal pad when he was called to the door, shackled, and led to the tables he and his mother sat at during visits.

"I'm Ron Diedrick. I'm your attorney," the man said tersely.

"Attorney?"

"Court-appointed," the man said. "Although I'd say you're going to need a bigger gun than me for this hunt."

"Okay," Gabriel said vaguely.

"You've got a hearing in a couple days. Your arraignment. Do you know what that means?"

Gabriel shook his head.

The attorney sighed. "It means you're going to be charged and your bail is going to be set."

Gabriel didn't know what that meant either, but he thought better than to say so. The attorney continued to rattle through jargon and flip pages of his notepad until the words became static in Gabriel's mind. When the attorney finally stopped, he spoke up. "What's going to happen?"

"Well, you got yourself into this mess. Now it's up to everybody else and there's not much you can do."

"Will I go to jail?"

"You're already in jail."

"But—" Gabriel tried to grasp the words, but the dread of it made them elusive. "Will I be in jail for a long time?"

The attorney dropped his pen onto the notepad. He pushed his glasses up and pinched the bridge of his nose between his fingers. "You're going to be charged with first degree murder."

"Okay."

"If you're found guilty, you'll be sentenced to a hundred years."

10

John was scooping steaming soup into his mouth when the phone rang. He swallowed the searing broth and let the spoon clatter into the Tupperware bowl. "This is John."

"Mr. Ellis, it's Alma Jiménez. Gabe and Martín's mother."

"Alma," John straightened his back and wiped his mouth. "How are things?"

"Gabriel had his arraignment today."

"Okay."

"They charged him with murder. They're trying him as an adult."

John leaned hard onto the chipped kitchen countertop. "How?" he asked eventually.

"They said the crime was too violent for juvenile court."

"Violent? It was self-defense!"

"Not according to the police report."

"What about bail? Can he get out on bail?"

"No," Alma said. "The judge said he was a flight risk. That we might take off across the border if he's let out."

The muscles in John's shoulders had cinched so tightly they were almost touching his ears. "I can't believe this," he said, mostly to himself.

"I know."

"What can I do? Tell me how I can help."

"I don't know. But thank you."

"How's Martín?"

"He's coming home next week, hopefully. His doctor said he probably won't be back in school until after Christmas. Said he hopes the speech problems will go away in a few months."

"Speech problems?"

"He can understand when I talk to him, but he talks like it's in slow motion. Martín's frustrated by it. Says he knows what he wants to say but his mouth won't say it."

"I'm sorry. But like I said, I'll help any way I can. And I appreciate you calling. Please tell the boys I asked about them."

"Of course. Thank you," Alma said and left the pay phone for Room 214.

11

Gabriel and his attorney entered the courtroom side-by-side and sat behind a small oak table. Two men sat at the tables to their left, and they all stood as the judge lumbered to the bench. He was a broad, older man with white hair growing in a ring around the glimmering top of his head. He reached under his black robe and pulled a pair of wire-rimmed glasses from his breast pocket. He balanced them near the end of his wide nose and looked down at Gabriel, then to the paperwork piled in front of him, then back to the wiry young man in a faded prison jumpsuit.

"You're Gabriel Jiménez?" the judge asked.

Gabriel nodded.

"I need you to speak, son. She can't type head shakes," he pointed an arthritic finger toward a woman sitting behind a stenotype.

"Yes sir," Gabriel spoke as loud as he could muster, but his voice did little more than sputter through the courtroom like an engine on its last drops of fuel.

"Mr. Jiménez, you have been charged with the crime of murder, which is a first-degree felony. Do you understand the crime you are being charged with?"

"Yes, sir."

"Are you prepared to enter a plea today?"

"Yes, Your Honor," his attorney said for him.

"How will you be pleading?"

"Not guilty."

The judge took a pen and flipped through the rest of the paperwork. "As discussed previously with both the prosecution and defense, I will be declining bail today, as you are believed to be a flight risk." He referenced the pages again. "We'll reconvene on November 2nd."

As soon as the judge collected the papers and hammered the gavel, Gabriel was led back through the tangle of hallways, into the back of the stifling car, and closed into his lonesome cell.

SADNESS LIKE JIMSONWEED
FALL 1983

Main Street isn't Main Street anymore.
The lights don't shine as brighly as they did before.

James Taylor

1

Dusk approached earlier each night. Soon, the foliage would mark its own change. The trees patching the Hill Country wilted under the weight of cool fall rains before leisurely turning — one spot at a time — to a marigold overstory. The leaves flaked off like scabs and dropped into the cola bottle green water of the Frio River. They floated south along the wide, rippling stream into the valley of the Rio Grande, which hung like a dribble of sweat from the stubbled chin of South Texas. The waters clogged with them as they turned to a brown mash behind deadfall branches and lazy eddies. Some haggard clumps were jarred loose. Others sat cast aside on the banks when the waters shrank and ran cold, left to shrivel and flake like cured tobacco detritus.

In those desolate and solitary months, as he waited for his trial, Gabriel had been remolded as well. He'd grown taller but had withered. Like dough left to rise too long, in too much heat, he collapsed to a sunken toughness, to disheartening blandness, while left unattended in a sealed oven. Gabriel had given up on anger. His indignation required upkeep. It needed watering and pruning to keep it flowering. After lonesome weeks of gardening his ire, it no longer seemed worth the effort. Sadness was easier. Despair crept like a vine in the untended soils of his thoughts. The sorrow seemed to grow more naturally, with much less effort. Anger is an exacting, thorned rose bush. And sadness is like jimsonweed; invasive and fetid, flowering and hearty, but barbed all the same.

Alma had visited Gabriel at least once a week during those months. She saw the change in her son no more than she saw their home's painted siding fading through the summer. But John Ellis gasped when he saw Gabriel. He hadn't seen him since the first week of the school year. A hundred-some hours past Labor Day, almost three months before.

John spoke to Alma once a week as well. She usually called when she got home from visiting Gabriel and had cooked and cleaned whatever soft foods she'd made for dinner. Martín was home from the hospital, but he didn't talk much. Alma would beg him to speak to her, but his words still came after effort, and his jaw had mended in a way that made speaking uncomfortable. Chewing anything tougher than gelatin was so painful, bolts of light would shoot through his narrowing vision. He ate boiled dinners most nights. Alma sat across from him and ate exactly as he did, slowly forking pallid half-mouthfuls. Martín's eyesight in his left eye was like looking through a milky cup of tea. The retina in that eye, at some point during his beating, had given up and released itself from the back of his eye. He began watching dramas on the television most of the day. Sports moved too quickly and he struggled to keep up with only one eye. When he sat with the volume turned up and his good eye turned toward the screen, Alma snuck back to the kitchen and made herself a plate of more palatable dinner. On the nights she visited Gabriel, she sat at the table eating her pork chop or salami and mayonnaise sandwich with the phone pinched in her shoulder.

A few weeks before the trial, John asked if he could visit Gabriel.

"Oh god," Alma choked on a bite of Salisbury steak. "I never even thought—" she wiped her mouth. "I didn't even think to ask."

"You've got a lot on your mind," John said. "I didn't want to ask. I thought Gabriel might think it's strange. His teacher visiting him, you know? I'm basically a stranger."

"No, not at all. He's happy to have you on his side."

"Of course. How could I not be?" John asked like there was no other side to be on. Like the loudest voices in Uvalde weren't screaming for their idea of justice. Like he hadn't heard the gossip in the school hallways, in the stores, in the men's rooms. *An illegal, no doubt* once voice said. *Send 'em all back. Use a goddamn dump truck if you got to,* John had heard. An older Mexican woman said, *makes us all look bad.*

Uvalde had a large but discreet Mexican population. Being an hour's drive through dusty, sagebrush-covered nihility made the town seem oasitic, so many travelers spent the night in the shade of the place, then slowly unpacked their belongings one garment at a time until it had been a decade and they were still sidling the streets of the town like they didn't belong. Like they were still, after all those years, just passing through. Many had congregated at the border towns, then bumped along the windswept highways between Ciudad Acuña or Piedras Negras into Uvalde, where the roads converged. The highways continued in dark taupe ribbons, but many of them never saw the other side of Routes 90 or 83.

The town's namesake was a Mexican governor, but the men in control of the place had taken it for themselves several generations ago. There was no longer tension at the borderland. The lawlessness that seeped from every establishment and street had become only a romanticized notion. A John Wayne film or a dime store book. Like every town of every place they'd gone, white men grappled power and respect from the natives and implemented their own providence. They preached their predestinations with crooked smiles and turned back to the denizens with peace offerings of sneers and spit in their faces.

So there was only one spoken opinion on Gabriel Jiménez in the streets and businesses of Uvalde. The common stance had been chosen by those that saw their kind killed by an *other* — by their lessers — as unrest. It was a vague attack on their own lives. They would agree it had been a tragedy but argue who had been the victim. After centuries of spilling blood for the sake of their ideas, they pointed to small cuts in their flimsy skin and called it slaughter.

John stood out like a wraith from that lineup. He heard the gossip and the hearsay, but it hardly registered. He told Alma a dozen times in the past months that Gabriel would be home soon. The town would hear the facts and understand they'd been mistaken. *Everything will work out.* Alma nodded along. "I hope so," she would say. But she'd seen enough from the other side of the curtain. John had a cushioned seat in the auditorium, while Alma grunted and blistered her hands pulling ropes to raise the curtains. She knew the actors that sang scripts of peace could snarl at those below just as easily. She knew John was naive to the backstages of being a minority. That he'd never watched a show from the stage wings. She knew even if Gabriel shed his orange jumpsuit and walked the streets of Uvalde toward home in penance, their lives would never be the same.

2

Gabriel's attorney was almost twenty minutes late to their nine o'clock meeting. If Gabriel was allowed a watch or clock in his cell, he might have been bothered. But he was led through the rows of cells into the visitation room with only a low-grade excitement for being any place but his cell.

"Hi Gabriel," his lawyer said without looking up. He continued writing on his legal pad. Still scribbling, he said, "I got a plea offer from the prosecutor. They don't think this has to go to trial. And I don't either, honestly. We've talked about that already, but they sent an offer over that I'd like you to think about." He finally looked away from the notepad and slid a small stack of papers toward Gabriel. Gabriel looked at the first page, read a few half-lines of the minuscule font. "I don't really know what that means," he said.

His attorney sighed. "It means if you decide to take this deal and say you're guilty, you'll go to prison for less than a hundred years."

"How much less?"

Mr. Diedrick spun the papers to face himself and flipped to a page. "Sixty years," he read flatly. "In the Uvalde County Correctional Facility."

"Sixty years?"

"Better than a hundred. Almost half."

"I'd be almost eighty."

"Yeah. And I'm almost sixty."

Gabriel tried to calculate the time. He could barely remember what five years feels like. Sixty years seemed illusory to him. The years of his life piled up, then multiplied. Still, he thought for a long moment, it was shorter than a hundred years.

"You should think about it. You've got all day to think. Whenever you decide, just ask to call me and let me know. But this isn't the worst deal I've ever seen."

"What is?"

"A hundred years for stubborn pride." He collected the papers and filed them into his briefcase. He left Gabriel sitting at the table, counting the dimples in the cinderblock wall. He was trying to count sixty of them. He got to forty-seven before the guard told him to stand and led him back to his cell.

Gabriel spent the rest of the morning counting sixty of anything he could find. His notepad had fifty pages. He counted sixty hairs on his forearm, then counted forty more. It hardly made a difference. He stared at the patch of thin black lines as they coagulated into a confusing smudge. He struggled for hours to make sense of it. He counted the flickering fluorescent light outside his cell, imagining each ripple in the light was a year of his life spent in a cell. He counted sixty with a growing lump in his stomach, and was going to count to a hundred but staring at the light gave him a splitting headache, so he buried his head in his pillow and slept. The sun was high when a guard banged on the metal bars of his cell door. "Up and at 'em," he said. "Got another visitor."

3

"Mr. Ellis," Gabriel smiled.

"Hey, Gabriel. How have you been?"

Gabriel looked around the white cinderblock room. He raised his hands and the shackle chains chimed against the cold metal table.

"Don't know why I asked. Sorry."

"Mom says you've been keeping up with—" he paused, "all of this."

"Of course. You're a good kid. You don't deserve this."

Gabriel studied the swirled scratches on the tabletop. "How do you know I'm a good kid?" he asked quietly.

"Well, I've been a teacher for a while and we figure out how to pick the good apples from the rotten ones."

"What about Bobby Kershaw?"

John sighed. "I never had Bobby Kershaw in class, but I've had some of the other Kershaws. And I can tell you every Kershaw I've ever met — and probably most of them I haven't — are bad apples."

"Do bad apples deserve to die?"

John reached out his hand but stopped himself before the guard could stop him. "I don't know," he scratched his cheek. "I don't think anyone *deserves* to die, but some people probably have it coming."

"Wouldn't killing someone turn a good apple rotten?"

John shook his head. "You didn't mean to kill anyone."

Gabriel rubbed the palm of his right hand. "I was holding the knife," he said.

"It was self-defense though."

"Not according to Mr. Diedrick," he shrugged.

"Your attorney?"

Gabriel shrugged again. "He said I'm guilty any way he looks at it. Said any judge in Uvalde County would love to lock up a Mexican for a hundred years. Told me my only hope is to have Mexicans on the jury and have them pity me."

John stared at Gabriel. He stammered for a minute. "Your attorney said that?" he asked. "He shouldn't have. It isn't that simple."

"Well," Gabriel sighed, "he's my lawyer." After a quiet moment, he said, "He wanted me to take a deal today. Mr. Diedrick told me if I plead guilty I would get sixty years instead of a hundred."

"What? Sixty years? You've got to be kidding. Sixty years for self-defense? What the hell is he thinking?" John's chest was so tight he struggled to breathe. A guard edged closer to their table and John's raised voice. "Gabriel, listen. I know your attorney said it's a lost cause but it's not. *You* are not a lost cause."

Gabriel looked up and swept his eyes over John's. John could see they were welled with tears. Two drops fell and ran over his cheeks and disappeared into the corners of his mouth. "I told Mom I didn't want to move again," he whispered. "I should've never gone back to that school after he messed with me."

"Who? Bobby? He messed with you?"

"Shoved my face in a bowl of chili," Gabriel cried.

"Is that where the bruises on your face came from?"

"The bruises don't matter much now."

John's thoughts webbed like a crack in a pane of glass. If Dr. Hendrick had taken him more seriously about the bruises. If he'd been more stern with Gabriel, forced him to admit where the bruises came from. If Alma had been home when he went to the house. If he hadn't gotten sick and missed a week of school. If Martín had known more. If he knew to say *Kershaw*. If the football game hadn't been a blowout. If someone would have said anything, two families might not have known what tragedy felt like. *If,* John thought, would be an echo that continued to reverberate through the remaining days of his life.

If only he'd tried harder. If only he'd done more.

John pulled to the curb near a diner to use the pay phone outside. He fed his quarter and dialed. "Alma," he said. "I was just out to see Gabriel. He's okay, but I wanted to talk about something."

"What is it?"

"I think we should get him a new attorney. He told me what this one is saying. Things like he's guilty and has no shot at getting out. The guy's court-appointed and I don't think he's even trying. We need someone that wants to keep Gabriel out of jail."

"John," Alma said quietly.

"This guy doesn't give a shit about Gabriel. Just wants to get it over with. He tried talking Gabriel into taking a plea deal! Did you know that? Sixty years! He'd be an old man when he got out! Sixty fucking years, Alma! Did you know that?"

"Yes."

"That's bullshit, Alma. We can find someone better. We *have* to."

"John."

"What?"

"I can't afford another attorney," Alma said calmly. "He's still around because he's free."

"What? Gabriel could go to jail for a hundred years!"

"I know. But knowing that doesn't put money in my purse."

"Jesus," John sighed. "Let me— let me just think about this. Let me see what I can do."

"You've done enough, John."

"No," he said. "No, I haven't. Not until Gabriel is home."

4

John came through his front door crumpling a pack of cigarettes he'd smoked in succession on the drive from the jail. His dog, Merle, ran toward the door to meet him, his paws struggling for purchase on the linoleum. John rubbed his head and kept walking to the kitchen. He grabbed the heavy ALPO bag from atop the fridge and filled Merle's bowl. He grabbed the Yellow Pages near the phone and sat at the table while the dog crunched happily. Flipping through to the A's, he wrote a list of names and phone numbers on a scrap of paper. Checking his watch, he grabbed Merle's leash as quietly as he could. But the dog heard and abandoned his food bowl for the door. With his tail sweeping the floor, he sat in feigned patience as John latched him to the leash and took him into the breezy, late afternoon.

It had been almost nine years since John was driving home from a summer spent with his brother on the rodeo circuit and returned with his new dog. He couldn't remember the town, but driving south, somewhere in Oklahoma, he was passing the lonesome hours through the unchanging miles by singing with the radio. Windows down, his straw cowboy hat on the passenger seat, he sang along to the country and western stations as loud as he could. When his truck rumbled too far from the towers and the stations turned to static, he tuned into another. It was hard to spin a radio dial in Oklahoma and land on anything besides a country station.

South of that forgotten town, the station's signal fizzled out just as Merle Haggard was getting to the chorus. John kept singing, letting the static play along like an out of tune fiddle, hoping he could crest a hill or glide around a turn and the song would abruptly fill the speakers again. *Turn me loose, set me free,* John sang. *Big city turn me loose and set me free.* He finished the song himself, singing with just static, then began fiddling with the dial. He was near the highest end of the frequencies so he twisted it all the way back to 85.0 FM. He looked up for only a moment and saw something crossing the road.

It was the first living thing he'd seen since he had stopped for gas forty-some miles before. With a few hundred feet between them, John thought it was a fox. But as he pumped the brake pedal and prayed his wheels wouldn't lock and throw the truck into the gulley, he saw it was a dog. His truck squealed and whined but eventually stopped in front of where the dog had crossed. From the opposite gulley, it watched the truck curiously, its ears perked from the screeching brake pads. "Hey!" John yelled across the road from his open window. "Almost killed both of us!" As John let out a short string of obscenities, the dog's tail began wagging. John stared at it for a minute, the radio continuing to crackle in the background, the dog's tail keeping time to some song on a different frequency. "Pretty damn cute though, you know that?" he said. He would swear for years the dog nodded in response.

By the time John opened his door and his boots hit the macadam, the dog was at his feet. John put a hand up to shade his eyes and studied their surroundings. Nothing. And the sweltering heat wasn't going to let up for weeks. "Let's go," John said and lowered the tailgate. The dog hopped into the truck bed and sat, smiling at him.

They drove twenty miles before finding another town. There, John pulled into the gas station and went inside to ask the attendant for a hose. With it, he showered the dog and dried him with one of his dirty undershirts. The dog yipped at the cold water, but that was the last time John would see him without a wagging tail.

He was afraid the mutt might blow out of the truck bed like a beer can, so he spread the damp t-shirt and let the dog sit in the passenger seat. As they drove toward the Texas border, 85.0 FM came to life. "No shit," John smiled. "More Merle." He joined in with the choir as loud as before. *Silver wings shining in the sunlight.* The dog turned and licked his ear until John had to push him off, then he stuck his head out of the window and howled along to the steel guitar. "Good boy," John laughed. "Everyone should sing along to Merle." Then after a minute, he scratched the scruffy fur on the back of the dog's neck and said, "You look like a Merle to me. What do you say? The Okie from Muskogee, or wherever the hell you're from."

Merle walked by John's feet, only veering from his shadow to track an interesting smell or lick at a dirty puddle. Neither were fans of the heat, so the milder temperatures of fall were their favorite days to walk. John lived on a quiet street, but the town seemed quieter than usual. Everybody was resting up for something, he supposed. Preparing to go to their favorite bars, or to stay home and drink. Maybe some would even take their other halves to dinner. John was wondering whether they could make it to the grocery store and back home before sundown when Merle barked. He let out a screaming sort of bark, then hunched down and growled. He acted aggressively but was careful to stay behind the protection of John's legs. John followed Merle's stare to the row of low bushes lining a yard. He didn't see anything and figured the squirrel that had caught Merle's attention snuck away. Merle, emboldened then, took a few timid steps toward the bushes and began sniffing the ground in front of them.

Out of one of them came a fat black rat snake. It slithered out, eyeing Merle, and continued by them and across the road. John watched it slink away while Merle barked and pulled on the end of the leash. When the snake reached the other side of the road, it coiled itself and stared at them. It could have hidden in the sagebrush, but it decided to raise its head and keep its glassy eyes on John.

"Is this what I get for pissing on that Jesus in a box?" John said to it. It didn't move. They walked a few blocks before turning back toward home. When they passed by the row of bushes again, the snake was gone. When the house was within sight, John unclipped Merle from the leash and let him run ahead. John watched him trot toward the porch and wondered if, maybe, both he and the snake were cursed. He thought about how each decision a dozen people made over months had led to so many lives changing and intertwining forever. Choices that were overlapping and somehow connected, like the oil black scales of a snake.

5

John continued to fight a cough but silently refused to see another doctor. The medicine he'd been given made anything but sleep difficult and didn't seem to help his cough much at all. In the months since, he had passed through several storms of fevers, head colds, and chills. He hadn't been sick in several years prior, and prided himself on his record of near-perfect attendance since beginning his career at Uvalde Regional High School. He wrote the recent sicknesses off as effects of stress. He'd woken one morning in early October with a cramping pain below his sternum, and although it had been indigestion and passed within an hour, he was momentarily convinced it was a heart attack brought on by another day worrying about the Jiménez family.

A week and one day after seeing the snake, John called Alma for the second day in a row. "Can I come over?" he asked. "I have some news." He hung up and fell into a fit of coughing. His chest rattled with the deepest hacks. He checked his palm for blood, but it was dry. The coughing hadn't brought anything up in weeks.

John drove through Uvalde toward the Jiménez house and sipped a mason jar of tap water to quell his tickling, ragged throat. He parked and jogged up the porch steps and into the house without knocking. He was always struck by how the ramshackle house could feel so comfortable with its family photos, a murmuring television, the smell of cooking wafting from the kitchen, a mother's doting voice.

"H— Hello," Martín said slowly, turning his good eye away from the TV to look at John.

"Hey Martín, how are you doing?"

Martín shrugged and returned his attention to the playoff baseball game. Shrugging had become his default answer to most questions — *what would you like for dinner? Would you like to go for a walk? How was your day? Will you be okay if I run to the store quick?* Speaking was still an onerous task for him, so he stayed quiet most days. The last time he'd strung sentences together was the only time he'd felt up to visiting Gabriel at the jail.

"In here, John!" Alma called from the kitchen.

John went through the living room and when he turned the corner into the kitchen, he could smell simmering stock and the unmistakable hint of cumin.

"Almost done if you want stay for dinner," Alma offered.

John nodded noncommittally. He didn't want to leave the temptation of Alma's cooking behind for a microwave dinner, but he was anxious she might rebuff the invitation after he told her what he'd come to say.

"I'll just have some water for now," he said and filled his mason jar from the sink faucet.

"We have cups, you know."

John shrugged and gulped from the jar.

Alma lowered the blue flames on the stovetop and wiped her hands. "What's this news you're so excited about?"

John took another long drink. "Before you say anything, it's already done and can't be undone."

Alma pursed her lips and sat across the table from him. "What is it?"

"My mother died a few years ago. I moved her out of my parents' place in Valentine, and she moved in with me for the last few months she was alive."

"I'm sorry about your mother."

John shook his head. "It was years ago. I'm only bringing it up because she left my brother most of the land and I got the house. It's a decent plot in Valentine, a few hours from here. Anyway, I made some calls and — well — I sold it."

Alma nodded.

"Just the house, but it was pretty nice the last I've seen it. I'd been renting it on and off since Ma moved out. It sold pretty quick, which is good."

"That is good news."

"But—" John paused for a coughing fit. "I'm gonna use that money to pay for an attorney."

"Why do you need an attorney?"

"For Gabriel. A better one."

Alma shook her head and pushed her chair from the table. "No," she said. "Thank you, but no. We don't need you to pay for anything. We're doing just fine."

John picked at the Formica tabletop. "None of this is just fine, Alma."

"Maybe not. But we can manage."

"I don't want you and the boys to manage. I want this to work out. I want Gabriel to have a good attorney so he can come home."

"Then what?" Alma wrung a towel in her fists. "What happens when he comes home?"

"What happens is he doesn't spend a hundred goddamn years in prison, Alma!"

Alma turned and opened a kitchen drawer. She rifled through it and pulled out an envelope and handed it to John. "Read it," she said.

John took out the letter and read the slanted, halted handwriting.

You fucking spicks are getting what you had coming and this whole town is glad for it. Wish we could lock all you Mexicans up. Keep showing your face and we'll finish the job on the cripple like they shoulda done the first time.

"When did you get this?" John studied the envelope.

"A couple times a week."

"What?" John howled. He stood quickly, almost knocking over the table. "How many of these have you gotten?"

Alma tapped the same drawer with a finger. "I stopped opening them after the first few. I imagine they mostly say the same sorts of things."

John held the letter up. "We have to tell the police! People can't do this!"

"What are the police going to do, John? They all think Gabriel is guilty. You think they'd help us over a stack of mean letters?"

"They're threatening you and the boys! You can't just ignore it!"

"I can ignore it, John, and you should too. It's the only way it's going to end. These people aren't going to just wake up and decide they don't hate us anymore."

John stammered for a minute before he sat and stared at the letter. It was addressed to the *Himenez Trash*. "Well," he said, "I sold a house to pay for Gabriel's attorney." He reached into the breast pocket of his denim shirt. "I'm driving out to Valentine tomorrow to sign the paperwork, but I brought a check tonight to pay for a better attorney. If you don't cash it tomorrow, I'll bring a money order. If you don't take that, I'll bring cash and leave it right here on the table."

They both stared at the check, flittering on the tabletop between them.

"Why?" Alma asked. "Why do you care so much?"

"Because Gabriel is a good kid, and—"

"No," she cut in. "What's the truth?"

John sighed, and struggled against a cough. "Because I think I could have stopped it," he said. "I think I could have said or done something else when I saw Gabriel's bruises. If I made him tell me,

I don't think it would've shaken out like it did. I could've told him to steer clear, to tell the principal. He couldn't have ignored a new kid with bruises like that. I should have done more and none of this would have happened like it did. This is—"

Alma put a hand up. "If you say this is your fault, I'll smack you."

John stared at her. "Well, what if it is?"

Alma stared, then took the check from the table and placed it in her pocket. She reached across the table and patted John's stubbled cheek. "Everything can't always be your fault, cowboy."

6

Shirley Kershaw scanned the grocery store parking lot and, when she was sure no one was watching, she slipped around the corner to the back of the building. The arch of her left foot pulled with every step and her legs were exhausted from her shift, but she walked into tufted, shin-high grass behind the store and continued steadily toward home.

Months before, in the weeks after Bobby's death, her boss had given her time off. She didn't ask for it and, as the days dragged by, she wished to tie the green apron around her waist and walk into the air conditioned store. She had done just that the Monday after Bobby died. She was aligning labels on Campbell's soup cans when her boss walked by the aisle and stopped short, his shoes squealing. "What are you doing here, Shirley?" he asked. Shirley continued twisting the cans into order and shrugged. "You should be home," he said. "Please go home. I'll call you when I need you to come back."

"Are you firing me?"

"No, Shirley. Of course not. But you should be home with your family."

She half nodded. "Let me just finish these cans," she said calmly.

Her boss gave her a sympathetic look and left her. He watched from a distance as she organized and primped the entire aisle before wiping her brow and walking slowly to the door.

She went home to an empty house. Not even Donald was home. The momentary relief that filled her turned quickly to shame for feeling it. She had been sent home, banished from the safety of the canned goods aisle, to spend time with her family. To be a mother. Still, when she stepped into the sweltering house, she was glad there would be no maternity required of her just then. No listening to her husband, Dwayne, bellowing about the Mexican who killed his boy. No placating Donald as he seesawed through waves of distress and culpability.

Shirley pulled a chair from the table and sat. The tie around her apron strained across her stomach. She ran her fingernails over the woodgrain on the tabletop, digging out small splinters from the widest vein. The quiet scratching was the only noise in the house, but the stillness wouldn't last.

As word of Bobby's death spread across town, throughout the dilapidated tin-roofed houses and rowdy barrooms where Kershaws and their friends were found, their home swelled with her husband's cousins, nephews, uncles, and old buddies until the walls seemed ready to burst. They filed through like a seething, choleric receiving line. Instead of condolences, the men left vitriol. It fanned the flames of their deepest hostilities but placated them. Pointing their bitterness in a direction opposite themselves, they were able to avoid the questioning eyes that searched within them, and their ancestors before that. It made no difference to them whether it was a stairway they climbed or a pile of those they'd been convinced were lesser than themselves.

Donald kept to himself while those distant branches of his family tree swooped and crashed into the house like they were downed by a gale. He was quietly receptive to the enmity he could not avoid, but it added weight to his scrawny back the same way it breathed levity into the other men. He listened attentively to the chorus of blustering voices, but when the men grew bored of him and his silence, they would close the circle tighter with Donald marooned to retreat to his bedroom. There, he mulled over what he'd heard, and carefully studied how it compared to his own experiences.

Shirley was sure to make a plate for him every night. She'd begun cooking dinners that could feed half of Uvalde, though she wasn't sure how they were to continue affording the trunkfuls of groceries it required. Sweat dripped from her chin and was stirred into tomato sauces, mashed potatoes, salad dressings. The men were too loud, too preoccupied, to hear her announcements that their dinner was ready. But she'd learned the easiest way to quiet the crowd was to take the steaming pans and clatter them onto trivets in front of them. Before doing that, she would make a plate for Donald, scooping from whatever casseroles she'd made and filling in the missing corners. While the men shoveled the food straight from the pots to their mouths, she carried a foil-covered plate to her son.

"Thanks," Donald said one of the first nights the men sat around the table. "Can I stay in here until bed?"

"Sure," Shirley grabbed his ankle. "Maybe I'll join you."

Donald pushed peas over a hill of mashed potatoes and into a pool of gravy. "I don't want to go tomorrow."

"Go where?"

"The funeral."

"Right. Of course." In her fervor to finish dinner, she'd slipped into the cool waters of placidity, of forgetting. She forgot the next day was the day she would slip into her only black dress, lower her eyes, and attend her son's funeral. She had forgotten her son had died for a moment.

"Do I have to go?"

Shirley watched the peas swimming in gravy. "Yes," she said. "I think you do."

"I don't want to though. Bobby wouldn't care if I went."

"Maybe you're right. But when you're older and think of your brother, won't you be sad to remember you didn't go?"

Donald was silent for a moment. "I won't think of him at all," he muttered.

Shirley took the plate from him and placed it on his nightstand. She grabbed his elbow and pulled him into a hug. She held him silently, tightly, for long minutes before his breathing splintered.

"I didn't mean that," he cried.

She kissed his head, where his hair swirled into a whirlpool of porcelain white skin. "I know," she said. "I know."

The following morning, Donald was the first one dressed. He sat at the table, behind the mess of leftovers and tableware the men had left behind. His slacks were too short and he had only white socks. His tie's knot was as crooked and gnarled as an ancient oak. His father crashed down the stairs and out of the house in his customary Dickies coveralls without saying a word. Dwayne's truck turned over and chattered from the driveway. A minute later, Shirley came downstairs, fixed Donald's necktie, and led him to the front door. They walked hand-in-hand for a half-hour until they were under the early morning shade of the church. Shirley powdered her forehead. Across the street, Donald could see his father sitting behind the wheel of his pickup truck. He watched him take long drags from Newports while droplets of sweat seeped into the back of his cheap polyester shirt.

Most of the town would remember how Bobby still looked mean, even under all the mortuary makeup and peacefulness of passing on. Perhaps the mortician had spent frustrating and fruitless hours attempting to massage the scowl from Bobby's face, to force his sneer to relax from the corners of his mouth. As the congregants stood by the cemetery plot in their threadbare blue jeans, dirt was poured over Bobby's casket and his eternally malicious face.

But it was fall then, when Shirley limped across the abandoned lot behind the store after her shift. She knew she'd return to a house that was quieter, but just as volatile as before. Dwayne filled the silence with his hot-breathed animus. Their silent apathy went unnoticed under his steady current of hatred.

Shirley came into the house, a drop of sweat rolling in front of her ear, and saw Dwayne and his pal at the table. "You're not working today?" she said. Ordinarily, she would have stopped herself, but the pain in her foot had grown to a piercing throb, and her patience had worn through like pantyhose.

Dwayne didn't look at her. Instead, he looked across the table to his friend, and they laughed before returning to their work. Dwayne had a yellow legal pad in front of him. His friend had a small stack of pages torn from the pad. They wrote laboriously, as if their compositions would bring Bobby from his grave.

The friend read his scribbled note, nodding proudly. "Hey," he called to Dwayne. "I called her a no-good whore in this one. Pretty good, huh?"

7

The night warped as John tossed and slept fitfully. He climbed from the bed sometime in the silent hours of twilight, walked out onto the porch, and lit a cigarette. He stood in his boxers in the cool, dewy air and thought about Gabriel in his cell, Martín sitting silently in front of the television, Alma's hand on his cheek.

He'd woken from a dream where he was walking through the pastures of his childhood home, taking long strides through the high grass. Every step, his bare feet landed on a pulsing nest of black snakes. He felt their cold skin against his toes, their searching tongue flicking his ankle. No matter how he tried, he couldn't run. His legs continued their steady march through the field. When the grass finally opened to the house's mowed front lawn, a snake followed him, close behind his heels. Turning to look, John realized the snake's body stretched in coiled black knots throughout the brush. The snake was miles long. It stalked him through the yard in a straight line, like yarn being pulled from a skein. Through the prickling grass, onto the porch, and through the back door. Up the stairs and into his childhood bedroom. The snake followed and stretched its body down the stairs, through the house, past the yard, and into the pasture. John laid on his tiny, creaking bed and closed his eyes. He felt its cold breath over his face.

He laid still for minutes, for hours, and when he opened his eyes, he saw a garden hose pinched under the door, its nozzle at his bedside.

When he woke in Uvalde, he searched the floor before stepping out of bed. On the porch, the air breezed lazily and sent a wave of goosebumps down his arms. He took a drag and threw the cigarette into a potted plant where it glowed gently and sent wisps of smoke into the inky night.

John went to the bathroom to shower, scrubbing the itchy slickness from between his toes and over his ankles from the black scaled snake. His body felt like it was bubbling each time he thought of the thing, but the scalding water eventually boiled the uneasy feeling from his limbs. His skin was red and rubbed raw when he cinched a towel around his waist and went to the kitchen, leaving a trail of droplets on the linoleum like a wounded animal. There, he fried eggs and started a pot of coffee. He sat and read the previous day's newspaper. By the time he was finished, the streaks of egg yolk on his plate had congealed into orange gelatin, and the sky was beginning to glow faintly.

He dressed and went outside, climbing into his truck. Merle followed curiously, his eyes swollen with sleep. Lighting a cigarette, he backed out of the driveway and pointed the truck westward. He would be in Valentine by noon.

8

Just past Del Rio, the water of Walk Lake shimmered in the hot morning sun. John studied it as he crossed over the bridge. The first sight of water in many miles made his tongue swollen and sticky with thirst. Then, the urge to urinate struck him suddenly and with ferocity. Traffic had been light since the sun rose over Highway 90, but there were a dozen trucks parked at the bridge abutment. Their drivers were somewhere on the banks of the lake, spending the Saturday morning lazily holding fishing rods. Merle stretched his head out of the window into the whipping wind to track the faintly sulfurous smell of the water.

When the highway straightened, John pulled over and strode into the high grass to pee. The Pecos River was a few hundred feet in front of him. When he was climbing back into his truck, another glint of water caught his eye. He stood on the truck's floorboard and searched the western horizon. It was the Rio Grande. The Mexico border. Just then, a gust of wind swirled and blew in that direction. John leaned his head back and spat with as much force as he could. The glob flew over two lanes of macadam before he lost sight of it. He started the truck with a rumble and pulled back onto the road, and he was sure the spit had flown clear into Mexico.

With the sun high, John drove past the sign welcoming him back to Valentine. When he left the town for the honey-tinged air of Uvalde, and any time he drove from the handful of streets clustered into the cheerless place as a teenager, he would raise a middle finger to the sign. In the years since he stopped calling Valentine home, they'd updated the sign and its promised population. 328. It no longer accounted for John Ellis, his brother, his mother, his father, or any person he could recall at that moment. The scant number had decreased steadily since the earthquake that shook half the state fifty years before.

With the results of each census, one of the city councilmen — who was more accurately a millworker, a roughneck, a carpenter — would march to the outskirts of town with the new sign under their arm, unscrew the faded and wind-worn sign from the post, and ratchet the new one in place. Its glaring, lush greenness would be the talk around town for a month.

John pulled into the long driveway and walked to the house. There were still tenants renting it, but he'd been unable to reach them for the past week. He knocked on the door; the same door he and his brothers had kicked and shouldered open when they flew into the driveway, their feet only touching the porch once or twice. A woman opened the door. She wore a linen skirt and a dingy white camisole. A chubby, drooling, red-faced baby hung on her hip. Her thin arms strained to hold it. John knew she was in her twenties, but those years must have been onerous.

"Can I help you?" she asked. A cigarette with a long pillar of gray ash bobbed in her lips.

"Yeah, sorry. I'm John Ellis."

The woman stared at him.

"I own— I'm your landlord."

She sighed. "Look. I know we're behind, but he's out looking for work right now. We don't have nowhere else to go. We'll pay whatever we owe by next month."

John nodded. He'd been too busy to remember the rent checks. The little rent the family paid was hardly worth the trip to the bank to cash the checks. He wondered for a moment how far behind they were, but then the baby began gurgling up chalky white vomit. The woman wiped its mouth with her thumb and brushed her thumb clean on her floral skirt.

"Don't worry about that," John said. "I've been trying to call but couldn't get through." The phone bills were surely piled in a stack of other unpaid bills on the table. "I just wanted to tell you that I sold the house."

The woman's face went slack. "What are we gonna do?"

"You can stay. Your lease isn't up for another couple months and the new owner can't kick you out until then. I just wanted you to know. If he tried to make you leave before that, call me or— something."

The woman nodded slowly. "What about what we owe? Should we send that to you or him?"

"Let's call it square. But just know the new owner might not let rent slide."

"Thank you, sir. Thank you, thank you."

John nodded. "I hope your man finds some work. Might not be a bad time to move east if there's no work here."

"Is that where you're from?"

"I'm from here. Grew up in this house. But I'm in Uvalde now."

"What's it like there?"

"Bigger than Valentine, thank the Lord." The baby started crying then, a dry and hungry wail. "I'm meeting the new owner today, so I'll be around for a bit. But don't mind us." John turned away from the house.

"Mister," the woman said. "Since you grew up in this house, did you wanna come in and see it before you go?"

"No, thank you though. I've already seen it for the last time."

The transaction took less than five minutes. A deed, a check, a few signatures, and a handshake. Compared to the mess of paperwork and realtors and bankers involved in buying his home in Uvalde, it was little more than a gentleman's agreement. The house was sold to a man that owned neighboring land. He had a decent sized cattle operation and was hoping if he owned the house, John's brother would be more willing to sell him the land as well. John wrote his brother's phone number on a scrap of paper and wished the man luck. At that moment, he couldn't conjure any concern about what might happen to the homestead. He thought that afternoon, the land smelled like the blood of his family and that oil-slick snake.

John wolf-whistled into the pasture and could see the high grass give way to the running dog. Merle galloped from the field with the remains of a cottontail hanging between his teeth. He laid at John's feet and continued his work of pulling the pelt from the cloudy pink meat. John kicked the rabbit away, and they both hopped into the truck. At the end of the driveway, he pulled next to the mailbox. He opened it and slid in two twenty-dollar bills before heading east on the highway. His stomach was grinding. He'd be lucky to be home before sundown and there wasn't a damn place to eat between Valentine and home.

9

On Monday evening, John left school as soon as the last bell rang. He drove to the hospital and parked under the shadow of the building where he could watch the front doors. He leaned his head against the headrest and wiped beads of sweat from his forehead. After a few minutes, he rifled around the glove compartment for a pack of Marlboros. He found an old carton and was sitting up to light it when the passenger door opened and Alma climbed inside.

"Christ!" John huffed. "Scared the shit out of me. I was trying to keep an eye on the door for you."

Alma pointed to a beige door fifty feet from John's front bumper. "I use that door," she said.

"Right. Well, let's hit the road." John pulled through the parking spot and weaved toward the road. "Mind if I smoke?"

"I do," Alma said simply. "Makes me car sick."

John turned the cigarette over and sniffed the frayed tobacco inside. It was so stale it smelled like paper, so he tossed it out the window. "I'm glad we're doing this," he said as he made the turn onto the highway. Another drive on Highway 90.

Alma was quiet. John tried calling a handful of times over the weekend until she picked up. He told her the house was sold and the check was ready to be cashed. He offered her a ride to the bank. He even said he'd bring the cash in a shoebox. She was quiet then too.

Alma still wasn't happy with the idea of John paying for Gabriel's attorney. She felt responsible for the loss of John's childhood home, no matter how much he promised he was glad to be rid of it. But when he called the night before, she agreed to meet with an attorney he'd found. His unrelenting persuasion did less to change her mind than when he vaguely mentioned leaving her alone, and she realized how much she hoped for the opposite.

But she was still uncomfortable, so she didn't say much. They drove in the long evening shadows toward Hondo. The town was less than an hour west of Uvalde; near halfway to San Antonio. John talked erratically about nothing the entire drive.

Ray Frazier's law office shared a building with a dentist. John parked his truck in front of the dentist's sign. "Want me to go in with you?" he asked.

"No. Thank you. I'll be right out."

"Take your time," John called to her through the window. He leaned back and closed his eyes. He thought of his dog, hungry at home, and let the dull traffic noise lull him to sleep.

The sound of the passenger door startled him awake an hour later. He wiped drool from the corner of his mouth with his sleeve.

"Maybe you should lock your doors," Alma said. "Or just stay awake."

"Yeah," he said groggily. "Haven't been sleeping well, I guess. How'd it go?"

"Mr. Frazier is very nice. He was very helpful." *Way more helpful than the last guy,* she thought but didn't want to say.

"Will he take Gabriel's case?"

Alma nodded. "He said he looked at the file and it should be a simple self-defense case. He's happy Uvalde's mostly Mexicans. Said it's going to help if they're on the jury."

John gripped the steering wheel. "I told you!" he blurted.

Alma turned and looked at him. Even the traffic through the town seemed to hush. "This isn't yours to win," she said. "I hope you know that."

"I'm sorry, Alma. I'm just happy to hear Gabriel's got a lawyer that hasn't given up on him before it started." Alma was quiet, so he pulled the truck from the lot and searched for Highway 90. A few blocks later, they passed an Old West hotel that had been remodeled into a bar. The Deep Elem Bar. "Want to stop for some dinner?" John asked. "That place looks neat."

"No, thanks. I need to get home to Martín."

A mile or two past the restaurant, a flash of green caught John's eye in the rearview mirror. He turned on the bench seat to look behind him. "I'll be goddamned," he gaped and pulled to the side of the road. "Look at that sign!" he hung out the window and pointed at it.

WELCOME TO HONDO, TEXAS
THIS IS GOD'S COUNTRY
PLEASE DON'T DRIVE THROUGH IT LIKE HELL

10

Dark came quickly. The truck's headlights vibrated a yellow beam onto the road and cut into the lonesome caliche of the Hill Country when John cleared his throat and decided to say something. His hands were jittering against the steering wheel. It was probably because he hadn't had a cigarette in almost twelve hours. Or, maybe, it was from the pressure that built between them in their silence, like a swollen storm cloud.

"I've been thinking about those letters," John said finally. He didn't know what to say next. He hadn't planned anything, even in the long miles of silence.

"John," Alma sighed.

"It's not right."

"Right, fair, kind. It's not any of those. It's not anything."

"I mean, it's *something*."

"I'm sorry it bothers you, but I haven't been thinking about them."

"How can you not think about it?"

"Because that's what they want. They want me and Martín and

Gabe and his attorney to be so upset by those letters that we pack our things and move to some other town."

"You guys didn't do anything wrong!"

"John," she frowned. "It's not about being right or wrong. I wish you understood that. It's not even about anything that happened. The only thing this is about is that we're Mexican."

"Jesus, Alma!" John snapped. "Half of Uvalde is Mexican! Half of Texas is Mexican!"

Alma looked out the window, watching the rocky bluffs beginning to catch the first glow of moonlight. "Mexicans that know their place," she said quietly. "That's what they want. We just had the bad luck of making a wave."

"I don't even know what that means."

"I know, John. I know you don't. That's what I'm saying."

John reached across the truck with a huff. Alma's breath hitched in her throat, thinking he was putting a hand on her leg. But he opened the glove compartment and let it fall open, the vinyl door knocking against her kneecap. John plucked the Marlboro carton from the mess of papers and slammed it shut. He pinched a cigarette between his lips and lit it, sucking in a lungful of tarry, papery smoke. The window was halfway open but he blew the blue smoke straight ahead, where it pillowed and fogged against the windshield.

When the cigarette was down to the filter, John said, "I'll be goddamned if I know how I turned into a bad guy in all this. I've tried damn hard to do right in my life. Never thought I'd get caught up in something like this but I think I'm doing well enough."

"I didn't say you weren't. You're not a bad man. You're a better man than most." Alma sighed. "I appreciate all you're doing. All the help you're giving. It just sits heavy on me sometimes. Me and the boys have gotten used to making do. It's not that I don't appreciate it. It's just hard to accept sometimes. Like when you sell your house to help us."

"That house didn't mean—"

Alma shook her head. "That's not the point. I'm only trying to say I'm not upset with you."

Passing through Sabinal, John lit another cigarette and offered the last one to Alma. "They're stale," he warned.

"That's what I'm used to," Alma said, surprising herself by accepting it. "Stale was all we had back when I would sneak around to smoke. I must've been sixteen." *Gabriel's age*, she thought.

John held the lighter in front of her. She inhaled cautiously, keeping the heat from her lungs. Still, she coughed until her head hurt. John laughed until she caught her breath and joined him. When he had smoked his and tossed it into the night, Alma passed hers to John.

"I appreciate you saying that," John said then. "That I'm a good man. I bet my mother would be happy to hear you say it too."

Then, the smoldering orange lights of Uvalde were in front of them. John pulled into the hospital lot and stopped next to Alma's car. It was Alma, that time, that reached across the bench seat. She put her hand on John's thigh and could feel his muscles ripple under his slacks. "Thank you," she said. They both stared at her hand. "I'm working a double tomorrow, but I'll call on Wednesday."

11

Her foot was still aching with each step, especially on the hard, bleach white tiles at the grocery store. She'd been spending more time helping at the registers than usual, diligently typing prices into the machine and placing groceries into the crinkling paper bags. She traded the discomfort in her feet for a different kind. Shirley normally liked to avoid the front of the store and its required palaver with women she knew only tangentially. The niceties of the interactions had never been of interest to her, and her discomfort had doubled with Bobby's death. Women — mothers themselves — would watch with commiserating eyes as Shirley balanced egg cartons and bread atop canned goods and waxy bunches of produce. They rarely spoke to her. Instead, they would talk to other women in the parking lot as the young cart boys loaded the bags into their trunks. *Such a terrible thing*, they'd shake their heads. *To bury your own child,* they would trail off. The sympathies were, for the most part, sincere. But they were only whispered, as if sharing them too nonchalantly, or looking the poor mother in the eye, would curse them to the same fate.

The fall afternoons were sweltering as she walked home, and the dry pasture grass tickled her legs. The pain in her foot had spread to a dull pain past her knee. Donald would be at school for an hour or two by the time she got home, and the cold glass of water and quiet she would enjoy was the oasis she plodded toward.

But when the trailer came into view, she saw Dwayne's yellow Dodge parked out front. Suddenly, she forgot about her foot. Her strides lengthened. Her purse pounded against her side furiously with each step. She ripped the screen door open so hard it slammed against the siding at the opposite end of its reach. Dwayne sat at the table by himself, his head down and surrounded by his arms. Three empty bottles of Schlitz surrounded him and his notepads.

Shirley kicked a table leg, sending a flash of pain through her foot. Dwayne sat up as if he'd been electrocuted. "The fuck—" he started.

"If you lost your job then you best go look for another one," Shirley cut him off. "If not, and you just decided to sit here and write your letters all day instead of going to the mill, then I'm taking the truck to work from now on."

Dwayne pinched his face at her. "What the hell are you talking about?"

"I'm talking about this!" Shirley picked up a finished letter from the table. "This isn't paying the bills! So if that's all you're gonna do all day then leave the truck key on the counter cause my foot smarts something awful and I'm done walking through that goddamn field every day!"

Dwayne started laughing, a deep rattling. "Heat must've gotten to you."

"Only thing getting to me is you."

He shook his head and laughed to himself.

"And leave that poor woman alone," Shirley said.

"*Poor woman?*" Dwayne howled. "That poor woman's a fucking spick and her kid that killed Bobby is too!"

"You really believe that?"

"Goddamn right, I do."

"Bobby got *himself* killed and we both know it."

Dwayne turned and tossed the chair across the floor until it rattled to a stop against the plywood cabinets. "You've got a lotta goddamn nerve!"

Shirley nodded. The room was starting to swirl in her vision. The fight, her stubbornness, was making her drunk. How many years had she wished to rile this man up with the words she held behind pursed lips?

He went to the fridge and grabbed the last three Schlitz bottles and blustered toward the door.

"Leave the keys," Shirley said.

Dwayne turned and his blazing eyes ran over her slowly. He reached into his pocket and threw the keys at her. She willed herself to stay still but felt her eyes flinch. She prayed Dwayne didn't see. The keys whipped over her head and shattered the glass in a family photograph hanging in the living room. The only picture of Bobby in the entire house.

Shirley waited a minute, but no longer, then went to the truck. She needed a shower. She wanted to change from her grocer uniform. She was afraid Donald might step on the broken glass glinting on the carpet. But she was worried she might lose her nerve if she took her eyes off the door too long. After a scalding shower, she may realize she was out of line, that her foot didn't hurt that much after all, that she should be starting dinner soon. All the thoughts she'd had since Dwayne moved her and her growing belly into the trailer. But that day, she was going to take the putrid yellow truck and drive it away from her torrid, sweltering house, her callous husband, her son's grave. Where she was going, she didn't know. But she was going. Anywhere but where she was standing was some kind of paradise.

12

The dusk outside of Uvalde partitioned the heavens in a gash. Most of the sky was a palette covered in shades of darkening blue. But above the horizon, in a perfect line, the sky turned blazing honey. The wheat-colored sunset stretched ahead, lighting her path to a fleeting deliverance, to Elysian fields.

The truck seemed to steer itself north on Route 83 toward Garner State Park. Maybe she would pull off the highway when she got there, stand along the banks of the Frio River, watch the yellow foliage rustle like a feather headdress. Drive through the parking lot fence, mark a path through the hiking trails to the top of a limestone cliff, and push the Dodge over the edge. Watch it plunge into the clear, shallow water below. Or maybe go over with it. Everything was another deep breath of freedom. Each possibility was itself liberation.

Shirley rifled through the pile of debris on the passenger floorboard until she found her Dolly Parton cassette tape. It had gone missing from the house months ago and she'd suspected Dwayne swiped it. She clicked it into the tape deck and *Jolene* crackled through the speakers. Near Garner State Park, Dolly begged her not to take her man. "You can have mine too," Shirley said and roared with laughter. She crossed over the Frio River when Dolly sang about a river of happiness. Shirley took it as a sign and took the first turn east. She still knew the way.

A *PARADISE*, the sign promised. WELCOME TO UTOPIA. Shirley parked in front of the sign, the truck's headlights trembling on the rusted sheet metal. It had been close to twenty years since she'd last seen it. The last time she and Dwayne drove to the sign, she'd been pregnant with Bobby for only a few months. She'd asked him to drive into the town that night. "Just tonight," she begged. "In case we don't come back before next summer." She hadn't told him she'd missed her period twice by then. She knew they wouldn't be back the next summer or any summer after.

"It's a shit stain of a town," Dwayne said. "Must call it paradise to be funny."

"I love it here," she smiled and stared at the sign. She longed for the paradise beyond it, but Dwayne put the truck in reverse, backed into the sagebrush, and turned back toward Uvalde.

But that fall night, sitting behind the wheel, she put the truck in drive and pulled past the sign, crossing over the city limits of Utopia. Shirley drove on Pecan Street, then turned onto East Lee, then Sycamore. She'd gone less than four miles and was back at the sign, having seen all there was to see of the place. The meager houses were locked and dark, the two businesses closed, the four-table café closer to opening than closing. Shirley pulled onto the gravel shoulder. Dolly Parton crooned, *I wondered where the love had gone that we'd found. And again, I felt the lonely coming down.*

Shirley put her forehead against the steering wheel. Her skin stuck to the cool, worn vinyl. Tears streaked down her cheeks, fell from her chin, and soaked into the filthy truck carpet. She cried in the stillness of that illusory promised land, in the hush of her splintered yearning. When the tears stopped coming, she sat back, pushed the crown of her head into the headrest and screamed. Until her throat was tattered, she bellowed into the night.

Then, with her silence being the only thing left, she drove toward home. South, away from Utopia, from the candle flame of hope that had flickered within her through her life's blackest hours.

There is hardly a change when a candlelit room is snuffed one flame at a time. But when that last, sole light is extinguished, the space is filled abruptly, grievously into utter darkness.

GOD'S COUNTRY

You might've seen me out in the country
but you lost me at the crossroad sign.
That was the old me, now you can't hold me,
all 'cause of this made up mind.

Tedeschi Trucks Band

1

O N THOSE COOL and soulless mornings of fall, the courthouse looked even more bleak than it had the first time Gabriel was led through the doors. Shirley Kershaw dressed in blue jeans and a thick knit sweater to fight the early, dewy cold. Her green work apron was stuffed in her purse. She slipped into the truck and drove quietly from the trailer. Dwayne was sleeping — or acting like it — when she left. Questions about his job at the mill went unanswered. If the neighbors or passersby recognized her or the truck, they would assume she was heading to the courthouse.

Jury selection was scheduled to begin, and her boss gave her the day off so she could be there. She thanked him but had no desire to be near Uvalde. She drove the long way through town, avoiding Nopal Street and the intersections where the two-lane highways cut through Uvalde.

That morning, Shirley went south. She'd already explored as much as she could imagine northward, nearly up to El Paso. Something about El Paso turned her away though. The planes whirring overhead or the sharply dressed Mexicans all heading into the city. So she drove south, where maybe she'd find some warmth. South toward Crystal City to get a hot breakfast and a few cups of coffee. Or all the way to Eagle Pass where she might park by the bridge, stare across the Rio

Grande into Mexico, and watch the faces coming through the check-points with expressions locked into overripe innocence.

John, Alma, and Martín were pressed into John's bench seat. The pressure on their hips, from the doors and each other, kept them firmly in place. John had offered to drive Alma to the courthouse, saying it wouldn't be a bad idea to have someone at least accompany them inside. Alma accepted the chivalry and surprised herself by being happy for it.

John slowed to turn left onto Leona Road. He waited for traffic to clear coming toward them. A yellow truck passed by, heading south. They parked down the street from the courthouse and walked in the brisk, blowing morning. The town was mostly empty, workers between shift changes and businesses just beginning to turn their placards over to OPEN. Martín hooked his arm through his mother's, keeping his good eye turned forward. Alma kept her eyes down. One arm pinched her purse against her side, the other arm kept Martín's hand tight against her. Feeling his knuckles on her ribs grounded her, the dull twinge plucking her mind away from the image of her son in shackles.

They entered the unadorned building and found the courtroom. Alma and Martín sat in the first row of the gallery. Alma clenched his hand. John stood against the back wall, arms crossed and eyes scanning.

Gabriel's attorney had suggested John keep space between Alma and himself. A few days before, Alma met with the attorney so he could explain the process and expectations of jury selection. He leaned forward in his leather chair and said, "I've got one last question. It would obviously be in confidence between us, but it would be helpful in the future if I was privy to anything going on."

"Going on with what?"

"With Mr. Ellis. Is there anything that might play a certain way with a jury?"

"I'm not sure what you're asking."

"I'm asking if there is any sort of romantic or sexual relationship between Mr. Ellis and yourself."

Alma scoffed. "No. Of course not. We— he's just helping in ways he can."

"I see," the attorney nodded. "If your relationship with Mr. Ellis happens to— blossom into something more, it may affect the way the jury sees you and, therefore, Gabriel. Juries are fickle beasts. They'll be happy to find any reason to doubt us."

"I understand."

"Either way, discretion is likely for the best."

Alma echoed the gist of that conversation to John, carefully walking the razor's edge of pushing, but not too far, and pulling, but not too hard. "The jury won't be able to ask about the man sitting next to me," she said. "So Mr. Frazier said it would be best to not put any questions in their head to begin with."

"Right," John said. "Makes sense." He half-listened to the rest of what she said, wondering what it all meant; the hand on his cheek, on his knee, the calls and smiles and laughs. He'd pushed those thoughts from his head easily a few months ago when they first gathered, but those ideas were no longer lanky calves. They'd grown into horned, unruly steer that refused to be herded or penned.

In the courtroom, John watched Alma and Martín talking nervously when Mr. Frazier and the prosecutor came in. They sat at their respective tables and unpacked folders, binders, and notepads of papers, then shuffled them around the table like blackjack dealers.

When their notes were disheveled in just the right configuration, a side door opened and a uniformed bailiff led Gabriel into the courtroom. Both Alma and John had visited him within the past weeks, and they'd silently forgiven his pallor, blaming it on the jail's sickly fluorescent lighting. But stepping into the courtroom, with its warm yellow bulbs, his gaunt and waxen complexion was haunting. Alma had gotten him a new button-down shirt and slacks, both a size smaller than the last ones she'd bought him. Still, the clothing seemed draped over him. His new skeletal shoulders were so angular it made the shirt look like he'd left the hanger inside. Gabriel had never been much wider than a fencepost, but he looked that morning as if he'd been rescued from some inhumane atrocity.

The judge entered soon after, proceeded by a bellowing bailiff, neither of which were small men. Then came the tedious and protracted task of sifting through dozens of random Uvalde County citizens until a group of men and women were agreed upon. They were interrogated on things related directly to the trial, and they were catechized about menial details of their lives. *Have you heard or read any details about this case? Do you have children? Do you feel capital punishment is appropriate for hate crimes? Do you or your spouse speak Spanish? Do you have any personal relationship with the defendant, or the victim, or their families?*

As the crowd was whittled down in batches, a couple of individuals took their seats in the jury box. "Get comfortable," the judge told them. "That seat is your new home."

All was going well, as far as John or Alma could tell, until the prosecution struck a potential juror. Gabriel's attorney, Mr. Frazier, was on his feet as if a spring had uncoiled under his seat. "Objection!" he hollered.

"On what grounds?"

"Your Honor, that is the third consecutive Hispanic juror that Mr. Wolfe has challenged."

"Mr. Wolfe?" the judge looked to the prosecutor's table.

"Yes, Your Honor," the prosecutor said. "Juror 37 was struck by peremptory challenge."

"Was Juror 37 struck on the basis of their race, religion, or gender?"

"No, Your Honor."

"Then, Mr. Frazier, your objection is overruled."

Ray Frazier fell back into his chair and glared at the prosecutor, who was busy shuffling papers into a new arrangement. The next seats were filled without issue. But after Mr. Frazier struck a white man who lived two streets from the Kershaw trailer, the prosecution challenged another Hispanic woman.

Once again, the attorney was on his feet. "Objection, Your Honor. At this point, it's obvious the prosecution is attempting to keep as many Hispanics from the jury as possible. I would like to request the prosecution's reason for dismissing Juror 51."

"Sir," the prosecutor started. "Forgive me for saying that, as Uvalde County's populace is something like eighty percent Hispanic, simple math leaves me with no choice but to challenge a fair number of jurors that happen to be Hispanic. As Mr. Frazier is aware, peremptory challenges may be used for any reason except those that are Constitutionally protected. I'm sure he is also aware that I am not obligated to give any reason for challenging a juror."

"Overruled, Mr. Frazier. If you'd like to file a Batson challenge, that is within your rights."

"No, Your Honor."

The next juror was seated and, with that, the faces that would decide Gabriel Jiménez's future looked at him in unison for the first of
many times. Gabriel's eyes remained on the edge of the table. But his
attorney looked from one face to the next until he'd stared at each
of them. He leaned over and whispered into Gabriel's ear, "That's a
good, honest jury over there."

2

If his students or the principal, Dr. Hendrick, paid enough attention, they would have noticed a change in John Ellis. His lessons,
once interactive and rousing, were now lectures read from textbooks
and lifeless examples scribbled on the blackboard. Assignments and
exam papers took longer to be returned, and the red marks scattering the page were no longer optimistic or understanding. *So close*,
and *Easy mistake to make* had turned into red gashes and X's. Where
in years past, his syllabus was memorized and practiced beforehand,
John now showed up minutes before his first class and checked his
calendar to remind himself what he'd be teaching.

There was a note left on his desk when he arrived that morning. If
he hadn't recognized the handwriting as the secretary's, he probably
would have crumpled and tossed it, and assumed it was a student asking for extra assignments to boost their grade. Instead, the note asked
John to meet with the principal before he left for the day.

After rushing to grade a pile of quizzes, John went down the stairs
and through the hall to the front office like a petulant student in line
for a scolding.

"Hi John," Dr. Hendrick said. "How's everything?"

"You know," John shrugged. "Always a struggle getting them to pay attention when they can smell the holidays coming."

Dr. Hendrick hummed. "Seems like they come sooner every year. And they just put pumpkins out, didn't they?"

"I think most of the kids would be happy putting Christmas trees up already."

"I don't doubt that," Dr. Hendrick laughed. "But while I have you here, John, why don't you take a seat. I want to talk to you about something."

John sat.

"I heard you and that boy's mother went to the courthouse together the other day. The one that got caught up with the Kershaw kid."

"Oh, yeah, well—"

Dr. Hendrick put a hand up. "It's not just that," he said. "I've been hearing you and the mother have been seeing a lot of each other."

"You got someone tailing me? Is that what this is?"

"Of course not, John. But this town is smaller than it seems. People see things. People talk."

"There's nothing to talk about."

"John," Dr. Hendrick pursed his lips. "I know how much your students mean to you. But — you've got to consider how it looks."

"Why would I be concerned about that? I'm helping a family that needs it."

"A young, pretty mother, you mean?"

"A mother whose son is in prison because he stood up to a Kershaw."

"Right," he sighed. "As your boss, I'm going to ask you to consider how driving around and going to court with his mother looks. We have a lot of other parents and families to consider."

"I should consider the optics," John repeated what Alma had repeated from the attorney.

"Exactly. Why don't you take a day to think about it? But if I were you, I wouldn't get involved. No matter how it turns out, you'll just find yourself in a mess."

"I'm happy to be involved. But I'll be sure to wear dark sunglasses and pull my hat low when I'm helping them."

Dr. Hendrick let out a long sigh.

"Thanks for your concern," John said. "Have a good night." Then he stood and turned his back to Dr. Hendrick. He was turning the doorknob when he heard the principal stand from his plush seat.

"Take the day off tomorrow. It'll be better for everyone."

"I don't need a day off."

"If you come here tomorrow, I'll send you home."

John left the office and slammed the door behind him. He was in his truck, its tires chirping on the macadam, lighting his second cigarette by the time the red faded from his face.

3

Half an hour later, John was racing past Hondo's welcome sign. Though it asked kindly that he didn't, he drove like hell until he found the place. He pulled into the parking lot of the Deep Elem Bar, his truck sandwiched in a row of a dozen others.

Inside, the bar was entirely what he'd hoped it would be. Small, high-backed booths against one wall, half of the floor stippled with leaning tables and chairs, and a bar that stretched the length of the building. At the furthest end of the floor was a stage. A band was milling around, taking guitars from cases, and plugging cables into a tangle of others. One of them sat on an amplifier with a guitar, singing. If the men lined on the barstools noticed John coming in, they gave no indication. He sat on a stool near the stage, his experience telling him the band would soon push everyone away from the speakers and he would have the area to himself.

"How we doing?" the bartender asked.

"Here at five o'clock," John chuckled.

"We all are," the man smiled. "Name's Lester, Jr. But everyone calls me Les. Family calls me Junior."

"Nice to meet you. I'm John. Can't say I've met a Lester before."

"Yeah, me neither. I was named after my dad's brother. Died in the war before I was born."

John nodded soberly. "A lot of uncles did."

"Then Nam took our brothers. Did they send you over there?"

"I was at college so they let me stay. Were you?"

Les shook his head and patted his leg. "This limp kept me out."

"Guess that's better than getting your limp over there."

"Now *that* is the goddamn truth! What do you want to drink, John?"

"Got George Dickel?"

"Yessir, we do."

"Dickel on ice then. And a Lone Star."

The man nodded and disappeared down the bar. He walked with a hard limp but was back in a minute with the beer and whiskey. John reached for the glass and took a few deep sips, the ice tumbling against his mustache.

"I don't recognize you," the bartender said after he poured another glass of whiskey. "You from around here?"

"Down the road a ways."

"How far of a ways?"

"About an hour that way," he pointed east.

"I ain't a local either. I'm from that way," the man pointed into the air. "From one of those shit hole towns between here and somewhere else."

"I'll drink to that," John raised his glass. "I was born in Valentine. Talk about a shit hole town. Born there on Valentine's Day too, in case I ever wanted to forget about it."

"That's some kinda lottery you won there."

John shrugged. "How far north was home for you?"

"Well," the bartender sighed. "Far enough I haven't got much reason to go back. Middle of nowhere Nebraska. Hayes County. My folks have a big piece of land up there. My brothers and my sister stayed, but I left on my eighteenth birthday to join the rodeo. Didn't stop driving til I got to Texas."

"You did the rodeo circuit? My brother's been cutting his teeth with that since he turned eighteen too."

"Seems like a better idea when you're that age, I guess."

"What'd you ride?"

"Bulls, mostly."

"Guess that explains the limp," John said.

Les nodded. "I wasn't any good at it, but I was too stubborn to quit. I was laid up in that hospital bed thanking God I had an excuse not to get on one of those things again."

John laughed and drained the rest of his beer. "Is this band any good?" he asked.

"Not unless you want to hear Conway Twitty for three hours."

"That guy was playing Willie when I came in."

"That guy?" Les pointed. "That's Mickey. He's the cook here."

John and Les laughed in tandem until they caught the attention of some other men sitting motionless at the bar.

"What do I owe you?" John stood.

The bartender took the empty glassware from the bartop. "Nothing," he said. "We're square."

John reached across the bar to shake his hand. "Appreciate it, Les. You here most nights?"

"Yessir. Either working or drinking. Sometimes both."

"I'll see you then," John said and pulled his hat on. As he drove back toward Uvalde, the wind streaming through the window felt less oppressive, the cigarettes tasted sweeter. It was probably the whiskey, but it was the first time in months he hadn't had to shove Gabriel and Alma from his mind.

John was careful to drive respectfully past the city limit sign. He'd almost forgotten to remember what he wanted to forget.

4

John spent his involuntary day working around the house; vacuuming, mowing the lawn, washing his truck, any menial task he could think of to pass the time. He was having a cigarette on the porch and scratching behind Merle's ear when the phone rang inside. It was the first unexpected thing to happen all day, and he sprang to his feet. Merle did also, growling offhandedly into the yard in case a snake —

or worse, a rabbit — was the cause of John's start. John grabbed the phone and heard Alma's voice on the other end. Again, his chest was awash in muddled emotions; equal parts excitement, reservation, and something between contrition and lust.

Alma said she had just gotten home from her shift at the hospital and invited John to dinner. "Of course," John said. "When should I come by? Want me to bring anything?" He remembered Dr. Hendrick's warning only when he parked outside the Jiménez house. But he didn't care enough to even muster a shrug, so he grabbed the six pack from the passenger seat and went inside.

Martín was in front of the television watching a boxing match. He watched it blankly, as if he either couldn't see or didn't understand what was happening.

"I heard this is supposed to be a big fight," John said. "Durán versus someone."

Martín shrugged.

"Not a boxing fan?" John asked him.

Martín shook his head. "Only thing to watch now that baseball's over."

"Yeah. Maybe the Astros will win it next year."

"I'm a Rangers fan."

"Well, I think they've got a better shot than Houston anyway. What do you think?"

Martín shrugged again.

"Not too much of a fan," John joked.

"I just like watching it. But my dad liked the Rangers, and their games are always on TV here."

John stood next to Martín's chair, both of them watching the fight. It was the first time anyone from the family had mentioned a father.

"That's how he hit me," Martín said then.

"What?"

"That guy Gabe killed. That's how he was hitting me."

John watched as Marvin Hagler pummeled the Hispanic boxer with a succession of punches that sent spit and sweat and blood into the air. Over the crowd and the commentators, he heard the gloved fists cracking against the man's face. John reached for the TV and flipped the channel. A young Tom Brokaw's face filled the screen. "Let's go see if your mom needs help," John said, pulling the sleeve of Martín's shirt.

In the kitchen, Alma gave each of them a job. She didn't need help finishing dinner, but she tasked Martín with mixing a pat of butter into the potatoes. John was busy finding the best matching silverware in the drawers and arranging it, then staring at it and rearranging it again. Alma leaned against the counter and smiled watching them. "I could've used you two an hour ago," she said.

After dinner, John stood at the sink with the sleeves of his Wrangler pearl snap folded to his elbows. He scrubbed the dishes like he was afraid of them, massaging them with the soapy rag, then passed the dripping plates and tableware to Alma. She was quiet, enjoying the nonchalance of the dinner and of having John over. The television murmured from the living room and John hummed a George Strait song.

"What're you singing?" Alma asked.

"I'm not singing," he looked at her, suds up his forearms.

"You were humming."

"Was I?" his face flushed. "Sorry to put you through that. I'm not much of a singer."

"It sounded nice. George Strait?"

John thought for a moment. "Guess it was. Been hearing it on the radio every day."

It was his new single. *You Look So Good In Love.* If John knew the title, he would have agreed that she did.

"Can I ask you something?" John stared at the dishes.

"I'm not going to sing a duet with you."

"Not about that," he forced a laugh. "Martín mentioned his dad was a Rangers fan."

"And you're not?"

"Oh, I am. It just made me realize I don't know anything about their dad."

Alma worked at the damp cloth in her hands, spreading it across the countertop, then folding it neatly.

"I shouldn't have asked. I'm sorry," John said. In the past months, he'd been having more trouble keeping his mouth shut. But it was out in the air now, that heavy question.

"It's fine, John. I don't talk about him much. Martín never did too much either. Gabriel was always asking about him though. He never met him."

"Really? Did he pass?"

Alma laughed thinly, her scratchy laugh that filled a room like music from a record. "Not as far as I know. I prayed for it for a while, but I guess prayers like that don't come true."

"Oh," John frowned. "That bad?"

"How much time do you have?"

"I'm yours for the night."

"Let's get some coffee on and I can tell you about it."

Sitting at the table with strong coffees in front of them, Alma leaned back in her chair and told John where she had been for the past twenty years.

5

Her parents had immigrated to the United States when she was a toddler. They originally lived in El Paso, but when her father lost his job, they moved east to Fort Worth. Alma fell in love with the city and its buildings adorned with neon cowboys. She would beg her parents to take her to see the cattle drives at the Stockyards, and when she was old enough, she hitched rides there herself and watched the proud cowboys riding in from the dust clouds.

One afternoon, in the amid of the throng of longhorns, a vaquero caught her eye. He offered to drive her home if she'd have dinner with him. They were married a year later. Neither her mother nor her father liked him. Their oldest son, Martín, was born less than a year after that. At first, the cowboy was a good father. Attentive and adoring. But after a while, the Stockyards began calling for him again like sirens. Not the steers or the horses, but the admiring young women. Alma was suspicious; of her husband's whereabouts, of her late period. A few nights later, when her husband returned at twilight smelling like manure and a perfume that wasn't hers, she told him.

"I'm pregnant," she said simply. She willed it to be the reveille that would bring him back to his family.

"No. You're not," he smiled wryly.

"Why would I joke about that?"

"What I mean is, you won't be pregnant by next week."

"What's that supposed to mean?"

He reached into his pocket with gold-ringed fingers and tossed a fifty-dollar bill at her. "I don't care how you do it, but that should cover it."

Alma stared at the money. "I— I'm not— doing— that," she stuttered. The back of her neck grew red and angry.

"I'm leaving," he said. "I'm gone."

"What are you talking about?"

"I'm not going anywhere. You are."

"What? What does that mean?"

"It's over. You can stay the rest of the week but then I want you and the boy gone."

Alma gaped at him. After a minute, she cried, "Where are we supposed to go?"

He shrugged.

"Please," she begged. "What did I do wrong?"

"Ain't done a goddamn thing wrong. But you're not Cindy, and she's my new wife."

"Cindy?" Alma spat, like the name was bitter across her tongue.

"She's moving in here in a few weeks." He pointed at the money. "That's for you. I don't give a good goddamn what you do about it, but it's none of my concern anymore."

Alma and Martín moved into her parents' house, cramming their belongings into corners and sleeping together on the sofa. After a month, Alma found a job as a housekeeper at a hospital in Austin and an apartment she could afford. They moved, and she did the best she could to keep her son safe and the bills paid. Gabriel was born at the same hospital she'd worked at, and came home to an apartment still stacked with unpacked boxes. They lived in the noise and bustle of Austin for almost fifteen years when Alma decided they would move. Her rent was becoming most of her paychecks, and as the boys grew the apartment seemed smaller every day.

She read about Uvalde in a Texas tourism magazine. It promised cool blue spring water and beautiful limestone bluffs. A quiet and kind town. It also had a good school and a hospital that was hiring. So they packed a U-Haul and drove toward the town like it was a mirage. They parked the square truck near the Frio River and dipped their feet in it. It was a baptism in the river of hope. In that water, she felt the seas she'd been drowning in had finally calmed.

6

When Alma finished her story, free the burden of it, she bowed her head and smiled. Like a priest pinching corners of bread, Alma broke off fragments of herself and her traumas at the faded altar of John's dashboard, of her chipped kitchen table, sharing the Eucharist of her tears as a sacrifice to the demons they shared.

She had never told the whole story before. Gabriel asked, but he always got the basic euphemisms of divorce. As he grew up, she could see he was bothered by the shallowness of the answers. She sensed his longing to meet his father, to find answers, to decide for himself. But she let him wonder about him. It allowed the flame of optimism to burn in him. The weight of his father might be his to bear someday, but Alma would shoulder it as long as she could.

"Stay here," John said and left the kitchen. Alma heard him go out of the front door and worried he'd left, but he returned in a minute with a six pack. He popped the cap from one and handed it to her. It was lukewarm but she drank deeply.

"Let's go for a drive," she said.

"I'll ask Martín if he wants to come."

Alma shook her head. She turned toward the living room and called, "Martín, can you hear me? Me and John need to run some errands. Will you be okay here for a little? We'll lock the doors when we leave." Then she stood and motioned to the beer. "Don't forget that."

John drove north, skirting Uvalde. Alma asked if they were taking the scenic route. *God forbid anyone else in this town sees us,* he wanted to say.

Instead, he told her about Abby. About how they'd met at a rodeo, about moving to Uvalde, about the day he came home and found her note, found her gone. After, in the silence of the flattening Hill Country, John lit a cigarette and watched the tobacco glow in a ring down to the filter; an effigy to his own demons.

He stubbed it out and Alma passed him another beer. "Guess we're members of the same club," she laughed. "If you see any place, I'll buy us another six pack."

Up the road, before crossing into a dry county, they stopped and bought two more six packs. Alma put them on the floorboard by the door and slid to the middle of the bench seat. John could feel her hip against his. "Where do you want to go?" he asked.

"Where do you want to take me?"

John bit the inside of his lip. "The state park's up this way. We could walk along the river or something."

"Okay," Alma said. "Let's park by the river."

Daylight was gone, and only the last embers of orange sunset glowed over the West. Parked amid the limestone bluffs, the night was as dark and still as the earth could muster. Frogs and grasshoppers surrounded the them and sang in their rhythms.

John reached behind his seat and pulled out a serape blanket. He went to the back of the truck, lowered the tailgate, and folded the blanket over the cold metal.

"Not bad for a cowboy," Alma smiled.

"Thank you kindly, ma'am," John tipped his hat.

Their laughs echoed off the limestone and filled the valley around them. They sipped at their beers and listened to the trickling Frio, the orchestra of animals, the shallow breathing of each other.

"Do you ever miss her?" Alma said after a while.

"Miss Abby?"

Alma nodded.

"Not anymore. My mom died a while back, so I miss her instead." He wasn't sure what to say then. He rubbed the palms of his hands down the legs of his jeans. "What about you?" he asked.

"I used to. Thought for a long time if he ever called, I would move back to Fort Worth. But I don't think that anymore."

"You like Uvalde enough to stay?"

Alma scoffed. "Uvalde's been nothing but bad news for me and my boys."

"What changed your mind then?"

Alma looked at him. Pinpricks of starlight reflected in her eyes. "You did." She put her hand on John's thigh again. The same place he'd felt her fingers for weeks after she took them away.

"Should we be doing this?"

"No," Alma said. "I don't think we should." Then she kissed him. On the cheek, but John put a hand to her face, turned her, and kissed her lips. They grappled with each other, clawing away the walls they'd built around themselves.

"Stop," Alma put a hand on his chest.

"Did I—"

She kissed him again, pulled at a button on his shirt. "Lay the blanket out."

They lay in silence for a while afterward, breathing heavily with the ebb and flow of the river. John put his arm around her. "This would be a better time to say 'Not bad for a cowboy.'"

Alma laughed. "You know what always bothered me about rodeo cowboys?" She rolled onto of him. "They only ride once a night."

When John pulled up to her house later, their skin still felt electric. Every touch capable of arcing a blue vein of spark. Alma kissed his cheek and left him to watch her walk across the yard barefoot. Martín had been in bed for a few hours. The dishes were put away and the lights were turned off. She went to his room to kiss him goodnight but stopped at the door. She turned away, afraid he would smell John's cologne on her.

7

The sky was gemstone blue the next morning. John drove to school casually and smoked the best tasting cigarette he'd ever smoked. He pulled into the parking lot and left his truck windows open. Crystal skies didn't make rain.

Dr. Hendrick was milling around by the stairwell. "How are you doing, John?" he asked.

"Great," John beamed without stopping. "Couldn't be better."

8

Shirley had been given the week off from the grocery store. Again, she didn't ask for it, but her boss told her to take some time at home before the trial. It was this that reminded her the trial was starting the next day. She was grateful for the days off, but she had no plans of stepping foot in the courthouse. Her husband and the fraternity of snarling Kershaws would keep the bailiff plenty busy without her. Donald asked if he could keep going to school as if nothing was happening, and she thought that sounded like a terrific idea.

She was awake early that morning and got ready as if she was going to work. Except she put on her favorite linen dress and stuffed her blush and mascara in her purse before sidling down the stairs and getting in the truck. Dwayne didn't need to know she wouldn't be at work. If he wasn't concerned with his job, she would turn her attention elsewhere too. And on that clear fall morning, as it had been for days, her attention was on the open road.

9

The new shirt and slacks were folded and stacked on the metal table in his cell. Next to it was a notepad that he'd been doodling and journaling in until his pen ran out of ink. The guard laughed when he asked if he could have another. He stared at the clothes, imagining walking out into a crisp, blue-skied day into freedom.

The apprehension he had been feeling about his future faded when he met his new lawyer and saw him in the courtroom. As timid and careless as his court-appointed attorney had been, Mr. Frazier was charismatic and confident. That sureness seeped into Gabriel as they sat side by side. He was yearning for the trial to be over so he could unfasten the choking top button of his new shirt and walk from the courthouse between Martín and his mother.

10

In the early evening, as the blue skies began to fade into a painting by another god, Alma pulled into the jail parking lot. She scanned the lot for John's truck but didn't see him. She vaguely remembered, in the lonely darkness outside of Uvalde the night before, she'd told John she was visiting Gabriel and asked if he'd join her. Alma crossed the macadam still in her hospital uniform. She was reaching for the door when she heard the familiar hum of John's truck. She heard the door creak open and slam closed, then his boots against the blacktop.

"Hey Alma," he called. "Glad I didn't miss you!"

"Hi John, how are you?"

He reached for the door handle and opened it for her. "I'm good, Alma. Really good."

Gabriel shared some of his optimism with them, telling them Mr. Frazier said the whole thing should be over in a week or two and then he'd be home. Alma feigned excitement, pretending it was that easy. Exoneration from the county court was not freedom from the vitriol that had begun to simmer in town. It was not an end to the letters or the threats. It was very likely just the opposite.

Walking from the jail, Alma looped a hand through John's arm. "Can I sit in your truck for a minute?" she asked.

John opened the passenger door for her and climbed in next to her.

"I don't know what to say about last night."

"We don't need to say anything," John said.

"I know, but I want to. I think maybe we shouldn't be doing that during the trial."

"Because of what the lawyer said?"

"No," Alma said. "It's because I think we're nervous about the trial. Or desperate for something. I don't really know."

"That's not how I feel."

"I don't think that's how I feel either. But I think we should be sure. Don't you?"

John nodded. "I understand. I'm sorry if I did something wrong."

"You didn't. Really. I just think we should keep our hands to ourselves, I guess. Until the trial's over."

"Okay."

"I don't want things between us to get mixed up with whatever's about to happen."

"It seems pretty mixed up already."

"Yeah," Alma sighed. "Yeah, it does."

John watched Alma drive from the lot, then turned east. If he wasn't going to spend his night with Alma, in the cool midnight breezes of the Frio River, he'd spend it getting drunk in Hondo. Maybe he'd still be riding a buzz tomorrow in court. He wasn't hurt. He wasn't even entirely surprised. But he'd fought against his desires for months. They had sprouted slowly over weeks, then multiplied like a weed overnight. His longings consumed him, and without Alma's touch, he was afraid it might devour him.

Slick-smelling alcohol and cigarette smoke took his mind from Alma when he threw open the door to the Deep Elem Bar. The bar was more crowded that time of the evening, but the stool from his last visit was open. The bartender greeted him and brought a glass of George Dickel. He was working on his first when Les sat next to him.

"Hey stranger," he said.

"Hey, Les. Thought I might not see you tonight."

Les shrugged. "Where else would I be?"

The men drank and talked, finding they had just enough in common to keep their conversation sputtering along. Near the end of John's fourth whiskey, the door opened and a draft ran the length of the bar.

"I gotta piss," Les said, standing from the barstool. "And she's looking for a seat, so I'll let her have you."

The woman in the doorway looked like a dream. Maybe it was the whiskey, maybe the spurned lust boiling in him. It could've been any combination of things, but when she sat next to John, he felt electric once again.

"What are you having?" he asked. "First one's on me."

"Lone Star," she said. "Thanks, cowboy."

"From around here?"

"No," she said. "Just passing through."

"Me too. I'm from down the road a bit."

"I'm from down the road too."

"What are you doing in Hondo? In *God's Country?*" he crossed himself.

The woman laughed. John could feel her shoulders relax as she settled into the stool. "I guess I just went for a drive and ended up here. Looked like a nice place."

"It's funny how Texans think dive bars and honky tonks are nice places, isn't it?"

"Well," she took a long swig of beer. "Aren't they?"

John looked at her. She was absolutely striking. Her roughened edges only made her more beautiful. "Does your husband know you're here?"

"Is that really your best line?"

"No, but I'm not going to waste my best line if you've got a husband."

"I'm divorced," she said vaguely. "Or something like it."

"Cheers to that," he tipped his glass toward her.

"Do I get to hear that line now?"

"Oh, Jesus. I guess so. I was going to say 'You're hotter than a tin roof in July.'"

The woman smirked. "Does that usually work?"

"Not a single time."

"Well, I'll let you buy me another beer."

"Was it that pickup line?"

She laughed then. "Not in the slightest. But your boots are clean and you smell nice, so I'll stay."

John smiled proudly. "Name's John. It's nice to meet you."

"Nice to meet you too," she drained the rest of her beer. "I'm Shirley."

TIES THAT BIND

When it feels like nothing's real
and no one's standing on your side,
you can find me in the Indian Nation skies.

John Moreland

1

"THIS, LADIES AND GENTLEMEN, is a simple story of revenge. Robert Kershaw, God rest his soul, was killed. Did he once play a harmless prank on the accused? He surely did. And who among us hasn't played a harmless prank? I know I've been on both ends a time or two! But did I feel the need to murder them? Did any of you? Surely not, or we wouldn't be together here today. So why did Gabriel Jiménez feel the need to kill young Bobby *with his own knife*? Those are the questions that I, along with my partner, will answer for you.

"The defense will spend days telling you folks how Bobby's murder was self-defense. They'll beg you to believe that the young man accused of murder, sitting over there, was so afraid — afraid *for his life* — that he felt it necessary to stab Bobby Kershaw in the stomach while he was trying to play at an arcade.

"In the coming days, you will hear from several students who witnessed that innocuous prank days before the murder. You'll hear from witnesses of the first time the accused attempted to attack Robert. Then, most importantly, you'll hear the sworn testimony of young men that witnessed that heinous attack on Bobby's life, along with the law enforcement officers and paramedics that were among the first on the scene. Included in that group of witnesses is none other than Robert's younger brother, Donald, who was an unwilling witness to his brother's fatal assault.

"In the end, it's simple. Did Bobby — does *anyone* — deserve to be attacked and left to die? I promise young Bobby is dead. And we will hear from the paramedics that valiantly attempted to save him, and the coroner that pronounced him dead. I believe this was surely vengeance. That's not something we can check the pulse of. I believe all of this started as an act of revenge. But was it murder? That is clear to me, but the ultimate decision will be yours."

The strain of the prosecutor's chair when he sat echoed through the room like an explosion. One of the men on the jury was staring at the carpet in front of them. Three stared at Gabriel. The woman at the end of the jury box sniffled quietly and wiped the corner of her eye discreetly. Another woman kept her eyes on Alma, who was sitting somberly in the front row.

Ray Frazier rose into the silence. "Ladies and gentlemen of the jury," he bellowed into it. "This was an attack. I'm not here to dispute that. And it was, as Mr. Wolfe said, a heinous attack. We'll have witnesses and doctors to attest to that as well. But, contrary to what Mr. Wolfe will lead you to believe, Robert Kershaw was not the victim of that attack. Of course, no one can argue that Robert Kershaw is dead, and the tragedy of his passing is one felt by everyone in this courtroom — including me. We won't even force you to pretend that that young man, Gabriel Jiménez, didn't put the knife in Bobby's abdomen. But we will show you, proven through testimony and evidence, that Gabriel acted in self-defense.

"Now, if I were to ask you to save either your life or the life of the juror seated next to you, I am sure all of you would pick yourself. And why shouldn't you? It's nothing to be ashamed of! Save for my wife and our beautiful daughter, I would save my life over any other if need be. Now imagine: your only sibling — your best friend — is being ruthlessly attacked by a boy, years older and a foot taller. Your brother is begging for mercy from vicious punches and kicks. Imagine a knife is pulled from that older boy's boot and held in front of your brother's face. Then that boy — a head taller and almost a hundred pounds heavier — comes toward you, promising to kill you. Imagine that, ladies and gentlemen. Put yourself in that situation, and tell me you wouldn't use a knife if one was in your hand. To protect yourself. To protect your brother.

"That is not a decision I wish any of you ever have to make. But Gabriel did. And he chose to protect himself and his brother, as I think all of you would have as well. This was not murder. Of that, we will soon agree."

Once again, the room fell silent. The same juror wiped her eyes. Some of the other jurors watched Martín as he threaded his arm through his mother's. They were only minutes into the trial and already they were overwhelmed with the weight of the decision in front of them.

The lawyers made it sound so easy. It's this way or that way with no space in between. No room for happenstance or ambiguity. There was more space than they'd realized between this side or that. Kershaw or the others.

2

The first witness was sworn in after Ray Frazier's opening statement. The jurors rubbed their necks and did their best to focus. The witness was a student at Uvalde Regional High School. A short and slight girl with long, perfectly straight brown hair. "Rebecca Bennett," she said when the prosecutor asked her to tell the jury her name.

"And where were you on the afternoon of September 6th?"

"At school. It was the first day of school."

"You were having lunch at the same time as Gabriel and Bobby?"

"Yes sir," she said.

"And can you tell me, in your own words, what you saw?"

"I saw Bobby walk across the cafeteria toward—" she pointed a nervous finger toward Gabriel, "—him. He was sitting alone. Then Bobby grabbed his shoulder and patted his back, I guess. It looked like he might've ruffled his hair or gave him a noogie?"

"A noogie?" the prosecutor raised an eyebrow.

"Yes sir, like this," she made a gentle fist and rubbed it into an imaginary head of hair in front of her. Just as they'd rehearsed. The jury laughed lightly, as the prosecutor hoped.

"And then what happened?"

"Then Bobby walked back to his table."

"Did you witness any other interactions between Bobby and the accused that day?"

"No, sir."

"What about any other day?"

"No, sir."

"Thank you for your honesty, Rebecca. No further questions."

Mr. Frazier stood and smiled at Rebecca. "Do you remember what you had for lunch that day, Miss Bennett?"

She thought. "No, sir. I don't," she said.

"I believe the school lunch menu said they were serving chili on September 6th. Does that sound correct?"

"Could be," she shrugged. "I don't remember."

"Well," Mr. Frazier sighed. "Gabriel remembers what was for lunch that day. And it was chili. Because Bobby Kershaw shoved Gabriel's face into it, didn't he?"

"No."

"Are you sure that's not what you saw?"

"Objection!" called the prosecutor. "Asked and answered!"

"Of course," Mr. Frazier nodded. "Do you remember a student by the name of Brian Leger tripping during lunch that day and dropping his lunch tray?"

"Objection, Your Honor," the prosecutor stood again. "Relevance?"

"Please get to the point quickly," the judge said flatly.

"Miss Bennett?" Mr. Frazier prompted.

"No, sir. I don't remember that."

"But it could have happened?"

"I guess."

"No further questions, Your Honor."

3

John Ellis sat in the second last row of benches. He watched the back of Alma's head as often as he watched the proceedings. He held a notepad on his lap, which he used to take notes on ideas he had during the trial like he was on the legal team. He was scribbling a few notes when the next witness was led to the bench. When he looked up, his mouth hung open and the paper fell from his hand and fanned out against the floor.

"Could you please state your name for the jury?"

"Dr. William Hendrick. I'm the principal at Uvalde Regional High School."

John grabbed at the notepad on the floor, his eyes stinging. His face and neck went hot. He instinctively began gnawing the inside of his lip.

"How long have you been the principal there?"

John was so dismayed he barely heard the testimony. His ears were filled with waves of static, like water was sloshing around inside them.

"When was the first time you met Gabriel Jiménez?"

"To be honest," Dr. Hendrick said, "I still haven't officially met him."

"Gabriel never came to you in regards to his interaction with Bobby in the cafeteria?"

"He did not."

"Is it out of the ordinary to not formally meet new students?"

"I rarely meet all of the new students during the first week of school. I get to know all of the students throughout the school year, but Gabriel was only there four or so days so I never had the chance."

"Did you hear the testimony of Miss Rebecca Bennett?"

"I did."

"Would the incident she described usually cause a student to seek a conversation with the principal?"

"No. That would be out of the ordinary."

"And neither Gabriel nor Bobby nor any other students in the cafeteria at that time, came to speak with you about the incident on September 6th?"

"Correct."

"Did *anybody* speak with you about the incident at lunch on September 6th?"

"None of the students that were present. I had a faculty member come to me and mention he thought he had heard something, but I assured him I hadn't heard anything from the students or other faculty."

"What did that faculty member say?"

"That he was concerned with a student."

"Which student was that?"

Dr. Hendrick looked directly at John Ellis. His eyes glared as he answered. "He didn't say. I suspect it was nothing more than hearsay."

4

The rest of the day was filled with similar testimony. *Yes, I was at lunch that day. No, I didn't see anything.* A line of students came in and out of the courtroom one at a time, as if it was some sort of field trip. John feverishly took notes. Some he thought might be useful, but others were to keep his mind from the anger he struggled to keep contained. Bullet point 13 of his notes: *Fuck Dr. Hen-Prick.*

When the judge announced the end of the day, John remained seated until Alma and Martín smiled at him from the end of his bench. Gabriel's attorney stood near them. "Mr. Frazier," John shuffled down the bench. "I was the person that went to Dr. Hendrick."

"I know," Mr. Frazier said flatly.

"I should testify then. Tell the jury about Gabriel's bruises. Tell them that I knew something happened."

Mr. Frazier pinched his lips. "I'm not sure that's the best idea, but I'll keep it in mind. There are still a lot of witnesses for the prosecution. It's very early," he said as a close to the conversation and took a step toward the door.

John grabbed his arm. "I saw the bruises," he said. "Why wouldn't you want me to say that?"

"Alma and Martín, we'll meet both of you in the hallway in just a moment," he said with a feigned smile. When John and the attorney were alone in the courtroom, he took a step closer. "I don't think it's a good idea for you to testify. I don't even think it's a good idea for you to be here at all, and if I had the power to, I'd make you stay home."

"Why are you so against me trying to help?"

"I'm against your relationship with Alma. And the way that's going to look to the jury. It's another landmine I've got to tiptoe around. So if you want my opinion, if you really want to help Alma, stay away until this is over. Alma dating Gabriel's teacher — the same one that stuck his nose in this from the start — doesn't look good. If a jury smells shit, they don't check their own boots. They assume the defendant tracked it in."

"You want me to stay away?"

"Yes, Mr. Ellis. It's my job to get Gabriel acquitted, and I know that's what you and Ms. Jiménez want as well. So, my advice hasn't changed."

John found Alma and Martín in the courthouse foyer. They walked silently to his truck and drove across town in silence. When they pulled in front of the house, Alma sent Martín inside and stayed in the truck.

"Are you upset?" she asked.

"No— well, yeah, of course— but not at you."

"You're upset about today?"

"Of course I am!" he scoffed.

"It's only the first day. What's got you so upset?"

"Because they were lying!"

"You think they were all lying?" Alma asked.

"Some of them probably didn't see anything. But some of them were lying. They had to be. Unless Martín and Gabriel are."

"They wouldn't lie to me."

John sighed. "This whole town is so afraid of the goddamn Kershaws they won't even say a dead one was an asshole."

"Maybe not everyone in this town hates the Kershaws like you do."

"If they don't, they should," John said. "Best to avoid those motherfuckers." After a minute, he apologized. "I'm sorry, Alma. I'm just worked up about what my principal said."

Alma squeezed John's hand and walked across the front yard.

John pulled away so fast his tires chirped into the evening. It wasn't Alma he was getting away from. It was the whole town. He forced the pedal into the rubber floorboard and didn't let up until he was just outside of Hondo. Out of reverence for the place, for *God's Country*, he slowed and worked to calm himself.

At the Deep Elem Bar, she was already sitting at the bar. He sat next to her with forced confidence. "Shirley," he said.

"Thought you weren't going to show," she said without turning.

"Who could leave a woman like you high and dry?"

"Different day but still that same big talk," she smiled.

"Let's drink," he said. "Then we can dance." He promised her the other night he would dance with her. He was too far in the bottle that night to do more than stagger to his truck and fall asleep on the bench seat. But when he woke with a gleaming headache, he remembered enough of the charming woman he'd met the night before; remembered their date for the next night; remembered some of their conversation. He remembered Shirley.

5

John and Shirley two-stepped for a few songs. John was finally feeling comfortable and hitting a stride when the band kicked into "I Don't Claim To Be An Angel." John felt the sweat coating her back under her dress. With each turn, he pulled her closer. John's boots stubbed her toes, still they danced closer than the other couples. *You'll hear talk around town of the things I used to do,* the band played. *I don't claim to be an angel.*

"I could use another beer," John said when the song ended. They stood at the bar when the band started playing "Love in the First Degree." If they thought anything of it, they didn't say. There was no recognition between them, no discussion of their unknown connection.

"Not that I don't remember anything from last night," John said. "But where did you say you were from?"

Shirley swigged her beer. "Utopia."

"Utopia? That's not too far up the road. Not much of a town though. No wonder you came down here for a honky tonk."

"Not much of a Utopia." She watched him, waiting to see if he caught the joke. The joke Dwayne hadn't understood years ago.

John laughed. "But *this.* This is damn near a utopia."

Shirley smiled and leaned on the barstool so her shoulder rubbed against his.

"Even been to Paris?"

"No," Shirley smiled. "Not even the one in Texas."

"That's the one I meant. It's as close to Paris as Utopia is to a utopia."

"There's a Paradise, Texas too."

John laughed. "And I bet it's anything but. Did you know there's a town called Ding Dong, Texas? I bet that's an aptly named place."

"You're lying!" Shirley's smiling face shone in the neon lights.

"I couldn't make something like that up!"

"What about you? Where are you from? Out past Ding Dong?" Shirley asked, swirling her half-empty beer.

John tapped the bartop. "Valentine," he said. He promised to never go back to the place the last time he drove from it, but maybe he'd never go back to Uvalde either. The barstool he sat on at the Deep Elem Bar, next to that beautiful stranger, was as close to home as any town he'd ever been.

"I think I've been through it. Maybe on my way to El Paso."

"Yeah, going through it at eighty miles an hour is the best way to see it. Guess neither of us are from God's Country."

"What do you do?" Shirley asked.

"I'm a teacher. But being a teacher isn't what it used to be. Maybe I'll quit and write a book or work as a welder or something."

"Can you weld?"

John shrugged. "As good as I can write." He downed his beer and ordered another. "What about you? Do you work or do you just sit around Utopia looking like a million bucks?"

"I work. And I look like a million bucks," she winked. "I work at a grocery store. Worked there since I was a teenager. The boss is good to me."

"I wish I knew what a good boss looked like. Only ever worked for pricks," he sighed. "It's hard to believe there's a store in Utopia though. Can't imagine there's enough business for it."

"Just canned and dry goods mostly," Shirley lied. She wrapped her fingers around the beer bottle so they wouldn't shake.

"What happened to your husband?" John asked. "Is he gonna bust through that door looking for a fight?"

Shirley rolled her eyes. She was thankful she could be honest again. "I don't think he would notice you if I brought you home and took you to bed right in front of him."

"He's a drunk?"

"Yeah. And an asshole."

"Most of them are."

"What about you? You wouldn't be the first cowboy to give me a line about being divorced."

"Oh, I'm as divorced as they come. My wife ran off on me a while ago."

The band counted into "San Antonio Rose," and Shirley stood and pulled John's shirt sleeve until they were both on the dance floor, boots sliding on the wood, closer than before. John felt her under his hands, the muscles in her back tensing in time with the fiddle. He leaned in and could smell her perfume. It had the alcohol tinge of cheap, five and dime perfume, but it drew him in all the same.

There was something he recognized in her. He could feel it in the sureness of her legs and the gentle grip around John's hand. He recognized in her that same threadbare mercy, the ragged virtue, that stayed with him like a hair on his tongue. He could hardly avoid attempting righteousness. He'd worn his tires bald on the high road. And in her way, Shirley was the same. Some do what they can to do right, still the things they touch crumble in their caring grasps.

Alma was made of the same cloth, but she was far from John's thoughts then. That desire still burned in him somewhere, but with enough Lone Star beer and her perfume clouding his head, Shirley was just enough.

"This feels just fine," John whispered to her.

Shirley put a cool hand on the back of his neck. "How could it be wrong?"

6

Uvalde called itself the City of Trees. Hondo claimed to be God's Country. But those forsaken miles between were neither timberland nor heaven. The highway slashed through it, providing passage to the mirages at either end like a River Styx. Shirley, in the yellow truck, sped west on it. She'd left Hondo before John but pulled off the highway in Sabinal. If he was following her tail lights by chance, it would look like she was going north to Utopia. She didn't know where John lived. He said he was from Valentine, but she knew he hadn't driven six hours into Hondo to meet her. But it didn't matter then. He was a handsome stranger with a clean Stetson that listened to her and watched her expectantly like every movement was worth seeing.

The dread of Uvalde filled the air like humidity as she neared. A javelina and two of its reds skittered across the road at the furthest reach of her headlights. She thought about those snarling, screaming things. Somewhere between a pig and a rodent, with a glut of hostility and yellow razors for teeth. She was sure they smelled too. Javelina and her husband weren't too dissimilar, the more she thought of it.

Shirley pulled the truck next to the trailer and went inside. Dwayne was sitting on the battered plaid sofa in front of the television. An orange and white Whataburger bag was on the floor by his feet, along with a collection of crumpled wrappers.

"Where you been?" he barked over the television.

Shirley wiped at her lips. She'd put lipstick on that morning, then left some on John Ellis. "Worked late," she said. "Then I went for a drive. Nice night out tonight."

"Where you drive to?"

"Just around. Out as far as the state park then turned back."

"Past midnight."

Shirley checked the wall clock. It was almost one. "Like I said. Beautiful night."

"What time'd the store close?"

"Same time it has for twenty years."

"Don't get smart with me, bitch! I would think your boss might give you off to go to court today. Seeing as your son's killer is on trial."

Shirley shrugged. "Guess not. Been busy with Thanksgiving's coming quick."

"Sit here," Dwayne patted the scratchy couch cushion next to him.

Shirley sat next to him, her bottom on the edge of the cushion. "What are you watching?"

"Was watching an old Western, but that was hours ago. You don't wanna give me a kiss?"

Shirley stared at the commercial on TV.

"I know you ain't been driving," he said.

"I don't know what you're talking about, Dwayne. I'm not getting into nothing with you tonight. I have another early morning tomorrow." She put her hands on the cushion to stand up, but Dwayne grabbed her wrist.

"Sit on down," he hissed. "Tell me where you been."

"I told you."

"I've drove that truck near into the ground and never gotten out of it smelling like smoke and booze. Know that store of yours don't sell it either."

"For God's sake! I'm not putting up with this. If anyone in this house's been drinking, it's been you."

Dwayne smiled with his yellowed teeth. "Course I've been drinking. But I can still smell it on you. Coming in smelling like a goddamned barroom."

"I'm going to bed," she said and snatched her wrist free. "And don't follow me to the bedroom either."

"Don't worry," Dwayne sneered. "I won't. I can't hardly stand the smell of that cologne you brought in."

Shirley disappeared down the narrow hallway and locked the bedroom door behind her. Her heart pounded into her neck. She peeled off her dress, balled it, and held it to her face. It did smell like cigarettes and liquor. And it smelled like John. She came up for air then dove back in. She was used to a man that smelled of lubricant grease and stale tobacco and sour sweat; earthen on bitter on acetic. But John, it seemed, was a different breed altogether.

Shirley was like a beaten dog; even the smallest amounts of kindness — like putting a rock down rather than chuck it at her — were blessings enough. The way John spoke rather than snarled, clasped her rather than grappled, put a beholden heat in her.

When she buried her nose in the fabric, she could still feel the pads of his fingers on her back. She pulled off her underwear and lay in bed, then reached down and breathed him in again.

7

The next morning, John was parked at the school by the time the janitor unlocked the front doors. He was unshowered. His hair pushed back in a slick, his mustache in need of a trim, the back of his shirt lined with wrinkles. He went inside and stood by the door to Dr. Hendrick's office.

"He's usually not in until the first period bell," the secretary said when she came in and sat behind the front desk.

"I'll wait," John replied gruffly. His mind was busy preparing what he wanted to say. He'd practiced during the drive from Hondo the night before, while he fell asleep, and on the drive that morning.

After almost two hours standing guard by the door, Dr. Hendrick meandered into sight. He smiled and said hello to the secretary and a parent at the front desk. When he saw John, his eyes held him then flicked away. He lost his composure, but only for a short moment. "Surprised you're here and not in court today," Dr. Hendrick said.

Everything John had planned to say was set aflame and burnt like the words were gasoline-soaked rags. "You motherfucker!" he growled. "Trying to make *me* look like the asshole?"

Dr. Hendrick looked toward the parent, who pretended not to hear. "In my office," he said under his breath and unlocked the door. He let John in and slammed it behind them. "What in the everloving fuck are you doing?"

"What am I doing? What are *you* doing?" John pushed a chair out of the way and stood in front of the principal's desk. "Testifying in court? Sticking your nose in something you know nothing about?"

"Sticking my nose in something! That's fucking rich, John! If that isn't the pot calling the kettle a swinging dick! When the county prosecutor asks me to go to court and tell him I didn't hear anything about those two kids, then that's what I'm going to do."

"You did hear something about those kids! I told you something was going on a week before they started pulling knives out! This blood is on your hands. I hope you know that."

Dr. Hendrick laughed. "And what's on your hands, John? That kid's mom? You don't look like you've showered in days so I bet you've got her all over you."

"She has nothing to do with this. You can never just keep your nose out of everyone else's business."

"I hate to tell you, but I'm the principal here so everyone's business is my business. That's how this works."

"Everyone's business except the only kid in this whole goddamn school that actually needed help. You remember what you said that day, Bill? You said 'You know how they are.'"

Dr. Hendrick looked straight ahead. Past the cloud of animus between them, and through John. John stood with his hands on his hips, waiting for another reason to swear at him.

"Listen," Dr. Hendrick said. "I've been the principal at this school for twenty-some-odd years. You haven't liked me since the day you were hired, and I've never been all too keen on you either. But the students seemed to like you, so I kept you around. Now though, I'm out of excuses to be kind to you. If you were working an oil field and called your boss a motherfucker, you'd get stuffed down a mineshaft. You understand me?"

"Not at all," John said flatly. "But it sounds like a threat."

"Let me make it simple then. Thanksgiving break starts in about a week. I want your classroom cleared by the time you leave that day. We'll have a replacement for you by the time classes start again. Until then... thin ice."

John's eyes flared. "You're fucking kidding me," is all he could think to say.

"Kidding you? You've barely been here for the past month, then you show up looking like that, smelling like whiskey, and call me a motherfucker in front of a parent? No, John, I'm not kidding. The only reason I'm not firing you today is because the union would have a fit."

John clenched his hands together. "Don't worry about the union," he said and went to the office door. He opened it slightly then turned back toward Dr. Hendrick. They stared across the room for a moment.

"What, John?"

"Fuck you," John said and left the office, walking out of the school for the last time. There was nothing in his classroom he couldn't do without.

8

Alma woke from a nightmare hours before John, across town, stormed from the school. In the dream, she was sleepwalking with her eyes wide open. The house was exactly as she'd left it when she went to bed. A half-empty glass of water on her nightstand, the digital alarm clock glowing red into the room, a pile of unfolded laundry by the foot of her bed. Her body carried her through the house and into every doorway. She would stand for a long moment, then continue and open the next door, standing in it for another minute. First, the bathroom. Then Gabriel's room, still untouched since the night he went to the football game with Martín. After that, the linen closet with neat stacks of towels. Then the utility closet that smelled like ammonia. Martín's room was next. When the door opened, the bed was empty and perfectly made.

On it went until Alma stood barefoot in the kitchen. The back door swung open and the nighttime breeze blew through her nightgown. On the far side of their short backyard was a carpet of brush and an ancient knotted oak that stood over it. A branch grew horizontal to the ground, stretching ten feet from the trunk in a perfect line before continuing its gnarled path. There on that strange platform branch, cast dimly in the moonlight, were bodies. The ropes around their necks, around the tree, creaked when they swung. Their toes drooped lazily, having given up on finding purchase in the thorny undergrowth. They hung in perfect order, each with a length of rope cut to size so their feet were at the same level.

Alma's legs took her forward, closer to the tree. Somewhere in her throat, a dry scream fought against sleep. Through the sagebrush and bracken, she could feel each pinprick of the thorns embedding into the soles of her feet. The bodies twisted and swayed in the wind.

She was close enough to smell the dried urine that ran down their legs when her eyes moved to look at their faces. Her vision moved on its own, and another cry was smothered in her throat. The body hanging in the middle was Martín. To his right, Gabriel. And the left, Alma.

When she woke with tears running into her pillow, she ripped the sheets from her legs and ran her fingers over the bottoms of both feet. She put a hand on her throat. Just a dream.

Alma pulled sweatpants on and went down the hall in the predawn. A light beamed through the slit under Martín's door. She opened it and saw him sitting crosslegged on the edge of his bed.

"What are you doing up?" she asked him. "Trouble sleeping?"

Martín rubbed his face. "Were you having a bad dream? I thought I heard you."

She crossed the room and sat next to him. "I was," she said. "About you and Gabriel."

"Me? Why me?"

"Well, you're still my boy, aren't you?"

Martín straightened his legs and kicked his heel against the metal bed frame. "Yeah, but I'm fine."

Alma let the conversation breathe. The way mothers learn to do when raising boys. Letting them feel like the conversation is at their tempo, the information and emotions leaking out on their time. "Are you fine?"

"Yes, Mom. I'm fine." They sat for a minute. Alma tried to concentrate on the sound of his heel against the metal. Otherwise, she would hear the dry squeak of the nooses. Martín let out a long breath. "This is all just weird."

"Weird is right."

"Sometimes—" Martín stopped and swallowed hard. "Sometimes I feel like I started it."

"Oh, Martín, you didn't start anything. Neither of you did."

"Do you know about the milk?"

Alma nodded. "The lawyer told me."

"That's what he was so mad about. That kid. That's why he beat me up."

"That boy was mad at everything. Some people are just like that."

"But I made it worse."

"I don't know, Martín. What made him so mad when he put Gabe's face in a bowl of chili?"

Martín thought for a while. "It could've ended there if I didn't make things worse."

"Do you believe that? That it would've ended there?"

"Sometimes," Martín said and wiped a tear away.

She let the tears fall and kept her hand in a careful rhythm on his back, afraid a change would cause him to clamp his emotions back into the crate he seemed to store them in. And when she could feel his shoulders tighten and pull back, she knew he was better. He wasn't fixed in any way, but he was better.

"Do you want me to go to court today?" he asked.

"That's up to you. You don't have to, but you know you can if you want." She watched him weigh his options then said, "I have an idea. It's still early. Let's make something for breakfast."

Alma put on a pot of coffee and started pulling groceries from the fridge. A stick of butter, a package of bacon, a tight sleeve of Jimmy Dean sausage. Martín padded in and sat at the table. "Can you make French toast?" he asked.

"Of course I can," Alma went back to the fridge for eggs. She opened the crate and saw a single egg cradled inside. She plastered a smile on her face and went to the coat rack to get a sweater. "I'm going to run to the store to get eggs. Want to come along?"

"Oh," Martín turned. "It's fine. Don't go to the store just to make

French toast."

Alma pulled the cardigan around her. "I am absolutely starving for French toast since you said it. You coming?"

"Can I stay in the car?" he asked. When Alma nodded, Martín went to his room and grabbed a pair of sneakers, then went outside in his pajamas.

The grocery store was just opening when they pulled into the lot. Alma was thankful their car was one of only a handful. "Want anything else?" she asked, then went inside. Martín rolled his window down and counted the dents in the door of the yellow pickup truck a few parking spots away.

Alma went to the dairy cooler and grabbed a dozen eggs. But the secret to her French toast was vanilla, sugar, and nutmeg in the egg wash. Afraid she would check the pantry and find that tiny McCormick bottle empty, she went looking for some.

A thin woman about her age came from one of the aisles and almost knocked the eggs from Alma's hands. The woman was cinching a green apron around her waist. Her eyes were red and puffed, her fingers trembling a bit while she worked the knot.

"Sorry. Do you work here?" Alma asked.

The woman nodded.

"Baking aisle is this way, right?"

"Aisle 6," the woman said shortly as she walked away and worked a name tag through the fabric on her apron.

9

Alma made an entire loaf of Wonder Bread into French toast. Both of their plates were piled high with it, even after they finished eating. The entire house smelled like coffee and grease. Martín and Alma sat for a while after they were both full, pushing chunks of food through lakes of syrup and taking cautious bites of cold egg.

"Mom?"

"Still hungry?" Alma teased.

"I'm okay with you and John."

"What do you mean?"

"I mean, like, I know he's not coming over to watch TV with me."

"Oh," Alma tilted her head. "Well, he's just a friend. He's been a big help with everything going on."

"Yeah, I know that. But I'm not blind. Well," he squinted his good eye, "Only half blind."

"Martín, it's—"

"It's fine, Mom," Martín stopped her. "He's always been nice to us. I like him. Gabriel does too."

"He has been good to us. Maybe I'll ask him to come for dinner when the trial is over."

"Okay." Then after a minute, Martín asked, "What is it going to be like? After the court stuff is over?"

Alma studied him. Her son, who had seen so much, who had been moved around like a foster. Who had been cut by hurt so deep and so often it took years for scabs to form and when they did, they grew into scars as thick as iron.

"I don't know," she said. "I'd never lie to you. I hope things quiet down, but I don't know."

"Yeah. Quiet would be nice," Martín said.

"Quiet would be nice."

10

Jack MacAnally was the prosecution's second witness that afternoon. He wore one of his father's polyester shirts. The sleeves were rolled three times and buttoned around the excess fabric. Nearly a foot of shirt was tucked into his jeans. They were his best jeans, but both knees were faded and caked with dirt so heavily that two days of his mother's scrubbing still couldn't pull all of it from the denim. He was shown into a room and left by himself with directions not to touch anything. Within a half-hour, he'd downed the pitcher of water on the table. An hour after that, his bladder felt ready to burst. He left the room and wandered the halls for a while before finding a bathroom down a random corridor. His mind had been so focused on not pissing down the front of his newly washed jeans that he couldn't remember how to get back to the room he'd been in. Jack spent the next half-hour cracking doors open and peering inside. Some rooms were empty but stacked with papers, some had books covering every inch of the walls, and some had men in suits and ties that hollered at him to get lost as soon as he poked his head through the door. When he finally found the room he'd been in, a bailiff was waiting inside.

"Where the hell have you been?" he grabbed Jack's arm.

"I had to piss," Jack shrugged loose.

"I told you not to leave the room."

Jack shrugged again. "Next time I'll piss on the carpet then."

The bailiff led him to the courtroom where he was introduced and sworn in.

"Good morning, Mr. MacAnally," the prosecutor said. After the volley of banal questions, he asked, "Could you please tell us about your relationship with Robert Kershaw?"

"We were friends. Met in first grade and we've been friends since."

"Were you with Robert on the night of September 7th?"

"Yeah. We were walking around town."

"Walking around Uvalde?"

"Yeah."

"What kinds of things were you doing around Uvalde?"

"Not much. Mostly walking. Maybe get something to eat if we got the money. Find some other friends."

"And is that what you were doing on September 7th?"

"Probably," Jack said. The group that was with Bobby that night had called around after he was killed and agreed no one would mention what else they'd been up to that night: throwing rocks at passing cars from the embankment near Nueces Street, and stuffing their pockets with stolen candy bars from the H-E-B.

"What were you doing when you first saw the Jiménez brothers?"

"Just standing."

"Where were you standing?"

"Down the street from the H-E-B. I didn't see them right away. Not until they were coming toward us. They were on a bike."

"Did you or anyone else recognize them?"

"I never saw them before. Bobby said something like he might've known them."

"What did Bobby say?"

"I— don't remember," Jack lied.

"What happened then?"

"Then they rode toward us all and the one pedaling reared back and threw something at us."

"What did he throw?"

"I couldn't tell at first. He threw it so high. But then I saw it was a jug of milk."

"A gallon of milk?"

"I don't know. A jug."

"Right," the prosecutor smoothed his tie.

"And what happened then?"

"That thing exploded when it hit the ground. Right in front of Bobby. Covered his jeans and boots pretty good."

"Did Bobby or anyone else do anything after that?"

"Bobby didn't. Think he was pretty well surprised. Just kind of watched them ride away for a second."

"Is that all that happened that night?"

"No. They said something then."

"Who?"

"They did," Jack jutted his chin toward Gabriel. "Shouted at us. Well, at Bobby I guess."

"What did they shout?"

"One of them shouted something in Spanish."

"Do you remember what was said?"

"Yeah."

"Would you mind telling us? In English, please."

"Objection!" Mr. Frazier stood. "Speculation. Are we really going to take the translation of a high school student as expert evidence?"

The judge regarded him vaguely. "No, Mr. Frazier. But he was a witness to this event and the jury has a right to hear his testimony on that event. Overruled." Then, turning back to Jack, he said, "Answer the question, son."

"He called Bobby a '*de puta.*' Or something like that."

"And what did you take that to mean? In English, please."

" — I don't want to say," Jack gnawed the inside of his cheek.

"Son," the judge looked down at him. "Answer the question."

"He called him a fat motherfucker," he looked at his boots. "As far as I know."

Something between a gasp and a yip escaped from one of the jurors, like the man next to her had accidentally stepped on her toes.

"Did you feel threatened at that time?"

Jack shrugged. "They didn't want to be our friends, I could tell that."

"Did you see which of the brothers threw the milk?"

Jack looked at Gabriel. "He did."

"And do you know which of the brothers yelled at Bobby?"

"He did," he said again. He wasn't lying. Not really. In his mind, he was sure. And if he was questioned further — really grilled on how he knew — maybe, at some point, he'd admit it was because to him Mexicans were all the same.

11

Donald skipped his last period class and snuck out of the school through a side door, disappearing into the streets of Uvalde. He walked a few blocks until he was in front of the courthouse. He checked the tall cast iron clock standing on the sidewalk and then went inside, staying near the walls of the hallways. When he found the courtroom, he went around the corner and leaned his back against the cold stone wall. He hid there until people began trickling out. From around the corner, he watched his father exit and head toward the front doors. When he was sure any Kershaws had left, he crossed the hall and went into the courtroom. He spotted the prosecutor and walked to him with his head down.

"Mr. Wolfe?" he said sheepishly.

"What is it, son?"

"I'm Donald Kershaw."

"I know that. What can I do for you?"

"I— well— I was hoping I could talk to you."

"I don't have much time right now, Donald. What is this about?"

"I just wanted to talk about my... I forget what it's called. When I go up there and talk."

"Your testimony. What about it? Does your father know you're here?"

"Yeah. Sure."

"Tell me what this is about."

"I don't really know what to say."

The prosecutor sighed and shoved the rest of his papers into his briefcase. "Follow me," he said and was already walking away.

Donald followed him to a conference room. The lights were off but soft, late afternoon sunlight leaked through the windows. The prosecutor sat at the end of the table and rubbed his eyes. "What's the problem?" he sighed. "We talked about this already."

"I know. But I don't think what everybody's saying happened is right. It feels like lying."

"Happened when?"

"At the arcade."

The prosecutor leaned back and crossed his arms. "What are you talking about? What's the issue? We talked about what you saw — *what everyone saw* — what the police report says. What exactly is the problem?"

Donald struggled to put his finger on the problem. He sifted through his doubt and anxieties about standing in front of that room, with the judge looming over him, with that Mexican boy staring at him, and telling everyone the same thing the prosecutor told him to say. He compared that written story of that night with the movie reel playing in his mind, of what he'd actually seen. Somewhere along the line, the truth became skewed.

"I don't know if I want to say what everyone else is going to say. I don't know if I believe it."

"Well, you believed it enough to tell the police. And it didn't seem to be an issue when we discussed your testimony the other night."

"I know."

"Listen," the prosecutor said. "You're nervous. I get it. I've seen it a thousand times before. My advice is this: go home, don't think about it so much, and when it's time to get on the stand and tell your story.

Tell it like we practiced."

"Okay."

"Does that sound like something you can handle? I need to be able to count on you, Donald. Your testimony is important."

"Okay."

"Good. I'm glad we could work this out. Without your testimony, we might not be able to keep that kid in jail." Then he stood and left the room without a word.

Donald leaned against the long table for a while, wondering what they'd worked out. His confusion remained. He'd known the weight his words would have with the jury, but the prosecutor put a face to it when he said they could keep the Mexican kid in jail. He thought about that; the kid that sat in the courtroom every day in the same shirt and slacks, going to jail until he was a wilted man. It made him want to vomit. He could feel bile in the back of his throat. But thinking about what would happen to him if he told the truth, about what his father might do to him, made him shudder. Whichever story he told, there would be retribution.

12

The evenings were beginning to grow cooler in the Hill Country. The jail had been suffocating with unbearable humidity when Gabriel was first closed into his cell. But as his months there collected, the sweltering hours without air conditioning turned to nights without heat that were as cool and damp as a root cellar. Everything in the cell was metal, and a chill ran through him any time he touched it.

He'd given up on the small desk — not much more than a metal shelf bolted onto the wall — because every pen stroke or movement of his arm placed his skin on a new frigid section of metal. The biting cold toilet seat was a necessary evil.

Gabriel sat hunched on his bed, a thin blanket wrapped around him like a funeral shroud. A guard came to his cell and clanged his baton against a bar. The guards felt it necessary to do that whenever they stood in front of the cells as if Gabriel was too witless to exit if they'd simply unlock and open it.

"Let's go kid," the guard barked. "Shower time. Leave the blanket."

Gabriel dropped the blanket and felt a chill run through him. The prison jumpsuit was so large on him it felt like the air blew directly over his naked body. He was cuffed and led down the corridor toward the showers. Five concrete stairs connected the small cell block with the inmate showers. It seemed a clever trick to keep the prisoners from attempting to flood the main building, but it was only the work of a shoddy government contractor. Gabriel wore his rubber sandals, as thin and slick on the floors as pieces of cardboard. He'd slipped up the stairs after showering every day for his first couple of weeks. Even with dry feet, he was careful not to lose what little traction the sandals had on the painted floor.

"Move," the guard nudged him from behind. "Quit walking like a pussy."

Gabriel, by instinct, started to turn. Not to fight or even to respond. But in that helpless way, to maybe convince himself he'd heard wrong.

"Don't even think about it," the guard snapped. "You turn around and I'll cave your fucking skull in."

Gabriel stepped forward, careful even in his cautious footsteps to not cross the guard further. He didn't recognize the guard, but he wouldn't know most of them by sight. He'd grown accustomed to dropping his gaze when they neared; staring at the cracked floors when they spoke to him or shackled him. They weren't his friends. Most of them made that clear. To look them in the eye, to study their faces as if they were feeling each other out, was pointless. Perhaps even dangerous. There was nothing to feel out, no social formalities or cues to watch for. The dynamic between Gabriel and whichever uniformed man stood in front of him was clear.

He was thinking back on the pile of vaguely cruel indecencies he'd experienced at the jail. He wondered if it really was the first time a guard had called him a pussy. Sure, they'd called him other names because he was Mexican and was going to court every day fighting against charges of a white boy's murder. But something about the guard's willingness to say it in the brazen openness of the cell block shocked him as much as the cold air against his skin.

At the top of the stairs, Gabriel took a practiced step down, his toes clenched against the bottoms of the sandals so they wouldn't fly across the showers. That momentary pause was enough. His head was down and he was leaning forward, toward the next step, when the guard shoved him. With a hand on each of Gabriel's shoulder blades, the guard sent him soaring headfirst down the stairs.

He landed on his right shoulder at the bottom of the stairs. The right side of his face hit the concrete next. His momentum carried him forward a few feet, his nose and cheek scraping against the floor. Like a thumb on a sheet of sandpaper, he felt the skin on his cheek rip loose in a thousand tiny cuts. When he reached his right arm out to push himself from the ground, he felt a flash of pain down his neck through his arm. He put his other hand up to the shoulder and felt a bulge where his collarbone had snapped in two.

The guard put a gruff hand under his armpit and dragged him to his feet. "Hell of a fall you took there," he said. "Must've slipped on these steps. Not the first guy to take a tumble like that."

Gabriel tried to move his right arm from the guard's grip and winced from the bolt of pain. "I didn't—" he started to say, but the guard gave him a nudge toward the showers.

"Wash yourself off. And hurry. If you get blood on that shirt, we gotta throw it out."

He stood under the fetid water and washed his face with one hand. The water on his open cuts felt like acid. The water ran through them like gutters, then spread across his chest and legs before spiraling around the drain in a crimson whirlpool.

Later, while Gabriel was being seen by a doctor that had been called in, Jess Travis sat at a desk and filled in a small stack of paperwork. He wrote the report to reflect the fact the boy slipped on the top step and fell straight to the bottom. Jess, of course, immediately offered help in the manner he'd been trained. He signed the papers and forged a signature for Gabriel Jiménez, then filed it where it would stay until it was moved to a storage box and taken to some dank and forgotten room.

Either the warden didn't know or didn't care that Jess was a Kershaw. Even if he had the inclination to figure it out, he'd find a muddled and convoluted lineage that caused even Jess to wonder if he really was kin. Not that it mattered much. The Kershaws were a fraternal organization more than a family; difficult to gain entry, but once inside membership was lifelong. Jess's father proudly claimed himself a Kershaw uncle. But so far on the fringe of the family was Jess that it took him months to realize the young Mexican boy in the county jail was the one accused of killing Bobby. He'd never met Bobby and only knew of him after he was killed.

When he made the connection, he kept his eyes peeled for a solitary moment with the kid or a time when the other guards had their backs turned. But his patience ran out quickly, and the first night he was tasked with escorting the kid to the showers, he decided it was high time. After calling the kid a pussy, he looked to the other guards to gauge their reactions. None of them had glanced up from their magazines.

The fall was harder than he'd expected. The kid must have only weighed a hundred pounds, so Jess's shove sent him flying across the showers. For a fleeting moment, he felt a twinge of pity when the kid looked up and half his face was bloodied. Then, again, when he watched him showering one-armed and realized his collarbone was broken. But it passed as quickly as the scent of mint leaves on a summer breeze. He hadn't gotten to wear the badge and carry a baton from doling pity. He'd grown coarsened by being named Jess. Then he refined his snide and ruffian demeanor over years, like a blade on a whetstone, as a member of the Kershaw family.

13

The sun rose in a fury on Saturday morning. It cleared the low clouds that had been fogging the hills and dried the grasses so they could rustle in the eastward breeze. The entire town of Uvalde rose to feel washed in clarity. The people were so thankful for the dry heat and the day off that there was hardly a word of gossip about the trial or that Mexican boy. It seemed to some the skies hadn't been so clear, the air so bright smelling, since the night the boy was locked away.

John Ellis was up at sunrise, sitting on his front porch in boxer shorts and a Texas A&M sweatshirt. One hand held a coffee mug on top of his leg, and the other pinched a cigarette. Even with winds as clear as Texas had ever made, John felt a cough nagging the back of his throat. Down deep, somewhere even a minute of hacking couldn't assuage.

Though he'd refused, the doctor in Uvalde had scheduled an appointment for him to see a specialist in San Antonio months ago. John ignored the phone call reminders and decided to not show up to his appointment. But, at the Uvalde doctor's insistence, the specialist's secretary continued scribbling his name in the schedule every month. Last night, another phone call appeared like a poltergeist. *This is Marilynn from San Antonio ENT. I'm calling to remind you of your appointment scheduled for tomorrow at 11 o'clock in the morning. Thank you.*

Maybe if the air wasn't so clear, if Merle didn't seem so content lazing on the porch all day, if he'd woken up with his throat feeling better, he would have canceled it again. In a last-ditch, he dialed Alma but there was no answer. So John showered and dressed, and drove to San Antonio.

The doctor was a man about his age. When he asked what John did for a living, he said he was a teacher before he remembered. John was sent from one room to another, each with beeping and whizzing machines, smelling their tinges of bleach. By the time he was left in a room and promised the doctor would be right with him, his throat felt like he might never speak normally again.

When the doctor came in, he sat on a rolling stool with his knees almost nudging John's. He pulled some pamphlets from a rack on the wall and handed them to John like a sidewalk preacher. He told him the best way forward would be check-ups regularly, and to see a doctor with any major changes. A slap on the knee and a pat on the back, and the doctor left John alone in the room. His stomach moaned but his throat was too sore to eat.

Near the outskirts of San Antonio, John pulled to the curb and found a pay phone. It rang five times, and John was ready to put it back in the cradle when she picked up.

"It's John," he said.

"Hi, John. I tried calling you earlier."

"You did?"

"Yeah, it's a beautiful day today. Figured me and Martín could use some fresh air. Want to join us for a walk?"

"I would, but I'm calling from San Antonio. But if the weather's good again tomorrow, I'll be around."

"What are you doing in San Antonio?" Alma asked.

"Just had an appointment. Doctor's appointment for that cough. Canceled it for three months until I figured it was a nice enough day for the drive."

"Hope it wasn't serious."

"You know how it is," John said. "Lots of poking and prodding. Leave feeling like you were on sale at a cattle auction. But give me a call tomorrow morning. I'll be around. And tell Martín I said hello."

"I will. Bye, John."

John hung up and walked down the street to a diner. They had a sign outside promising chicken corn soup, and that seemed about as much as he could handle.

14

There was close to a case of spent beer bottles between them. They'd been sitting for hours, enjoying the last, unexpected aftershock of warmer weather. They each held a sweat-beaded bottle and had a pair at the leg of their lawn chairs. One for cigarette ash and the other for tobacco spit. Dwayne popped the lid from another, digging around his bottom lip for the soggy clump of Skoal. He threw it in the direction of their neighbor's yard, the clod disintegrating into diseased shrapnel.

"You seen my truck around town?" Dwayne asked the other man.

"Your truck?"

"That's what I said."

"Naw, haven't seen it. And that son of a bitch is hard to miss."

"Old lady's been taking it out a lot."

"You let her drive your truck?"

Dwayne scowled. "It ain't about letting her. That bitch's sneakier than hell. By the time I'm up, she's gone with the truck."

"All that just to drive to work?"

"Claimed her foot hurt."

Both men laughed. "Like we ain't coming home every day hurting head to goddamn heel," the other man said.

"I know it."

They let their cigarettes burn to the filters. Their bottles left damp rings on the legs of their faded jeans.

"But," Dwayne said. "She ain't just going to work."

"Where's she going?"

"Claims she's just been driving," Dwayne spat into the yard. "Came home the other night smelling like a barroom."

"You don't say."

"Pulled in well after midnight too. Said she'd been going for a drive. Ain't that some bullshit?"

"Maybe she's going to court," the man suggested.

"I've been there. Haven't seen her."

"Well, where do you think she's getting to then?"

"No idea. Smells like Stetson cologne when she comes home sometimes."

"That cologne smells pretty good though, don't it?"

"Shut the fuck up."

"Just saying," the man swigged his beer. "You should follow her one time. Then you'll know."

"With what car?"

The man lit another cigarette. "I'll do it," he said then, exhaling blue smoke. "Ain't got anything else going on. Don't mind driving either."

"What're you gonna do?"

The man worked it over in his mind, constructing his halfwit, drunken-minded plan. "I'll park down the street before sun up and watch for that yellow truck. Can't miss the fucking thing, even before sunlight. Then just follow her," he shrugged.

Dwayne swirled beer around the bottom of the bottle. "Alright," he said. "Monday morning?"

"Sure." Then, after another cigarette, the man asked, "What're you

THE DEVIL IN THESE HILLS

gonna do to the guy?"

"What guy?"

"The other guy. One she's meeting up with."

"Who said she's meeting up with another guy?"

"Come on. You think she's two-stepping with a lady that wears Stetson cologne?"

Dwayne scoffed. "Never know anymore. Kids with blue hair and pierced dicks and shit now."

"No shit," his friend shook his head. "So, you gonna slash his tires or what?"

"Will you shut your goddamn mouth?"

"Just saying. I feel bad for the cowboy that got wrangled up with Dwayne Kershaw's old lady."

"There ain't another guy. Shut up about that."

"But — just saying — what if there is?"

Dwayne threw an empty bottle into a stone mound across the yard, where it shattered in a wet crunch. "I'll fucking kill him."

15

Shirley had off on Sunday. The truck was already gone when she woke up and peeked through the blinds. She fixed herself breakfast and ate the eggs and toast standing in front of the sink, looking out over the backyard. A pile of beer bottles and cigarette butts littered the yard, only one of the chairs was still upright. The sky was clear again, but the day seemed clouded with dread. Without the truck, she was sentenced to the trailer. Since she'd met John, the walls of her home, of her life, seemed to be creeping in. Even the coffee was more bitter than usual, the toast noticeably drier.

"Morning Mom," Donald padded into the kitchen.

"Hi, Donnie. Want some breakfast?"

"Sure."

Shirley cracked two eggs in the cast iron, flipped them when the edges of the whites turned brown, and slid them onto a plate. "You want toast too?" she asked.

"Just bread," Donald said.

She put two slices of Wonder bread on his plate. The eggs and bread disappeared quickly, leaving only a faint yellow swirl of yolk. Shirley sipped her coffee from a mug that said *World's Best Mom* in faded letters. A gift from her boys on a Mother's Day years ago, though she knew it was Donald who chose and paid for it. Bobby probably didn't even sign the card himself.

Donald watched her cradling the mug. He was glad she was home that morning. Something about it seemed right. But he was sorry he'd have to bring up the trial and risk ruining it. "I talked to Mr. Wolfe the other day," he said.

"Mr. Wolfe?"

"The lawyer. From Bobby's trial."

"Sure. Of course," Shirley's grip on the mug tightened. "I didn't know you were going to court on Friday."

"I didn't. Well, I didn't go to the trial. I went to talk to him after. After school."

Shirley nodded. She attempted to toe the line between maternal listening and disinterest. Try as she might, and feeling the shame it brought, she couldn't seem to care about the trial. Whether that Mexican boy went to prison or not had little effect on her life. She'd heard people say *It would at least be some consolation, but nothing can bring Bobby back.* And she was thankful for that. She had loved her oldest son by instinct, and at the time it seemed enough. But with him gone, her life suddenly seemed breezier. Her favorite child had been spared, and Bobby was finally forced to pay cash on the bets he'd waged since he could talk.

"I'm worried about getting up there and talking," Donald said then.

"Why? Just answer the lawyer's questions."

Donald scraped his fork through the pattern of egg yolk. "That's what I'm worried about though."

Shirley sipped her coffee. "Don't be."

"Mom," Donald said, pleading for her to emerge from the haze she carried around herself, which buffered her from the rest of the town. "Please."

She put her mug on the table and sat forward. The edges of Donald's eyes were squinted, a sign she knew meant tears were approaching. "Why are you worried?" she asked.

"Mr. Wolfe said my story could put that boy in jail for a long time. Is that true?"

"I guess so. But it wouldn't be the only reason. You're not the only person testifying."

"What if I lie?"

"Don't do that. Why would you lie?"

Donald shrugged. "Would I get in trouble?"

"Yes, you would get in trouble. Why would you want to lie?"

"And what about if I lied before?"

"When?"

"When the policeman asked what happened that night."

"You lied to the police?"

Donald shrugged.

"What did you lie about? Why would you lie?"

Donald stared at his plate. "Everyone else was. Bobby's friends all did. They said the Mexican kids started it."

"I figured those boys didn't start it. No surprise Bobby did, I guess."

"I heard what they were saying and just told the policeman the same thing. Now I'm worried I'll be in trouble. I asked Mr. Wolfe what to do but I don't know."

"What did he say?"

"He told me to tell the story like I told the cop."

Shirley picked at a fingernail.

"What should I do, Mom?"

"I think you should tell the truth. Whatever that means to you. You should try to do the right thing."

"Even though I already did the wrong thing?"

"It's either one thing wrong or two."

"I guess."

"I know what you must be feeling. You've got Kershaw blood and I know that means you want to protect each other. I get that. I'd protect you over anything too. But maybe that other boy is just as much a brother as Bobby or anyone else."

Donald sighed. "I guess." He dropped his plate in the sink and went back to his bedroom where he was left to once again wonder how an answer could be no answer at all.

16

John was hacking over the side of his bed, trying to down a glass of water, when the phone rang. The clanging made his brain feel leaden. He coughed as hard as he could and swallowed down the rest of the water before picking up.

"John, it's Alma."

"What's wrong?" He knew from her voice's cadence. From the lack of melody in it.

"I just got a call from the jail. Gabriel was hurt last night. Apparently, he fell down some stairs and got a little banged up."

"How bad?"

"Not too bad, they said. But I'm going over to see him if you want to come along."

"Yeah," John looked around the bedroom, scanning for a clean shirt. "Let me get dressed and I'll pick you up." He hung up and wrestled into an outfit, threw some ALPO in Merle's bowl, and pulled on his hat. He arrived at Alma's house fifteen minutes after she'd called.

"Thanks for coming," she said, climbing into the truck. "You look nice."

"No I don't," John laughed. "I haven't showered and I've been keeping Hungry Man in business lately."

"I'll cook you something today. For lunch, and you can take the leftovers home."

"You don't have to do that. You're not my mother."

Alma reached across the truck and squeezed the back of his arm. "Good thing too."

John held his breath for a moment, then said, "What do you think happened with Gabriel?"

"They just said he fell and had to see a doctor but he's okay."

"Do you think he actually fell?" John asked.

Alma rolled her window up as they pulled into the lot. "If he didn't, he'll tell us."

After the gauntlet of paperwork and metal detectors and pat-downs, Alma and John were finally seated in the visiting area. Gabriel was led in, and when Alma saw him round the corner, her eyes spilled over with tears. She fought to keep them from rolling down her cheeks. Gabriel's right arm was in a sling, and half his face was bandaged with gauze. She'd seen patients at the hospital that had been shot, stabbed, run over — even one that was dead for a minute — that looked better than Gabriel did then. Even under the layers of gauze, his face was swollen, the skin a vicious red. Alma was reminded of the morning she was shown to Martín's hospital room, where he was even more heavily bandaged and swollen. *How much more could she take?* she wondered though she knew she would, without a thought, shoulder the burdens of her sons. Her chest constricted until it felt like whatever was inside was about to shatter.

"Gabriel, *mi hijo*. What happened?" Alma wiped her eyes. "Are you okay? Did they give you Tylenol? Something to take the edge off? Is your arm broken?"

"No," Gabriel said. "Not my arm. It feels broken here," he pointed to his collarbone. "They gave me something last night. Maybe to help me sleep but I still couldn't. It was too cold and I couldn't get the blanket around me with one arm."

"How does your face feel? Did you break anything there?" John asked.

"I don't think so. It was bleeding last night, but it feels better with all this over it."

Alma clasped her hands. "Tell me what happened."

Gabriel adjusted the strap of his sling. "It's fine," he said. "It was nothing." Then, for the first time he could remember, he lied to his mother. "I tripped down the stairs."

Somber nods went around the table then, and the silence slowly turned to other topics. The trial, and the beautiful weather after those cold and damp nights. Gabriel asked what they had planned. Alma usually lied and said she had nothing planned, that he wasn't missing anything while he was in his cell. But John answered and told him he and Alma and Martín would make some lunch and maybe go for a walk. Alma watched for Gabriel to slump of his shoulders or for a tick of a frown, but he smiled and asked John if his cooking was getting any better.

When their visit was almost over, and the guard would soon be plucking Gabriel from the table, he put a hand to the weeping gauze over his face. "Do you think God tests us?" he asked. "Gives us just as much as we can bear just to watch what we do?"

"I don't know," Alma said. "It feels like it sometimes."

"What do you think, Mr. Ellis?"

John sighed. "I don't think about God much, to be honest. Is that how you feel?"

"I didn't use to think about it much either, but I've got time now to think about a lot of things. The way I think it works is God uses us like pack mules. Have you ever seen one loaded halfway? They're always carrying as much weight as they can. That's what I think God does. Puts exactly enough on our backs so we can trudge on. So much weight that even a pound more would break our backs."

John and Alma were silent. John turned the idea over in his mind. "Then why do some people carry so much more than others?" he asked.

"Mules can carry more than horses," Gabriel shrugged. "It doesn't have to make sense, and it doesn't have to be fair. Some people can just carry more weight, I guess."

Alma wiped tears away and asked, "How close is your back to breaking?"

The guard came then, clasping a hand around Gabriel's good arm. Gabriel stood but his eyes stayed on his mother. "Closer every day," he said. "But I'll drop these packs soon."

17

Alma cooked chicken with rice and beans for lunch. Martín's jaw was starting to feel better, and he'd graduated from eating only potatoes to heaping plates of rice and beans. John watched him scoop mounds of it onto his plate and joked, "I hope no one lights a match in this house tonight or the whole neighborhood might go up." John and Martín ate second and third helpings, then Alma packed the rest for John. Martín went to watch television, and John and Alma sat at the table, his stuffed stomach aching, and the coffee pot gurgling.

"Gabriel's going to be okay," John said. "I broke my collarbone when I was in middle school. Heals pretty fast."

"I know. But what about everything else? Maybe the rest of it won't heal so quickly. Or not at all."

John sat back.

"I'm afraid I lost the son I knew as soon as they took him to jail," Alma went on. "How could I expect him to ever come home and just be a boy again? He's supposed to finish high school and maybe go to college after all this?"

"He'll get the help he needs," John said. "Someone he can talk to. Tutors. I can try to help too."

"I'm glad you'll be at the school too. If he goes back."

John pursed his lips. "I forgot to tell you," he lied. "I quit."

"Quit what?"

"My job. At the school."

"John! Why would you quit?"

"Well, I had a— disagreement with my boss."

"Because of what he said in court?"

"We started there."

Alma poured their coffees. "What are you going to do now?"

"Maybe I'll be a country singer. Or move to Alaska."

"Is that so?" Alma laughed. "I remember you being embarrassed when I heard you humming."

"Yeah, I guess that's out then."

They sipped the scalding coffee, trying to pace the conversation and the tension between them. John hadn't thought of Shirley since the day before when Alma invited him for lunch. Whatever space she'd been filling was occupied once again by Alma, at least on that blue-skied Sunday.

"What about your back?" John asked after a while. "How close is yours to breaking?"

Alma swirled her coffee. "I don't know. I think mothers can handle things like this better than they realize. Not that it doesn't hurt. But it's hard not to be thinking ahead. That's what we're used to."

"How could you be used to something like this?"

"We're not used to it, but I don't think it surprises mothers when something terrible happens. Not really. When you have a child, you realize in that split-second that the rest of your life is going to be spent worrying about them. Every single second that worry will be on your mind. Thinking about all the things that could go wrong every day. Stressing whether today or tomorrow or the next day will be the day because some instinct tells you it's coming. Or at least to be ready when it does. But you go to bed and laugh at yourself and feel foolish because you'd thought something could've ever happened to your perfect children. Then one day, you don't feel foolish anymore because you were right. You knew since the day your belly starting growing that it would happen eventually. You prayed and begged to be wrong. And thank the Lord, most mothers are. But it's something we all carry, I think. Something we all share. It's a weight on our backs, and the worst part is the only way that weight goes away is because something terrible finally happens. It's a second of lightness at the same moment your child becomes a tragedy."

18

On Monday morning, Donald was the first one awake in the Kershaw house. He showered and put on the same ill-fitting suit he wore to Bobby's funeral. He was sitting at the table, nibbling a piece of dry toast, when Shirley came into the kitchen. She sat across from him.

"You look nice," she said. "Nervous?"

Donald nodded and put the toast down, the chunk he'd been chewing stuck in his throat. "Maybe you could come with," he said.

"To court? I'm sorry, Donnie. I don't think I could handle that."

"Could you at least drop me off then?"

"Of course." Then after a minute, she asked, "What are you going to say today?"

Donald pinched pieces of dried crust between his fingers. He watched it clump together, then fall apart. "What I told the cop. That those Mexicans started it. I don't want to get in trouble saying something different than everyone else."

"I see."

"Are you mad at me?"

"No, Donnie. As long as you're okay with it."

"Okay," Donald said. "We should get going."

Shirley pulled a sweater on and they went outside to the truck. The morning was cutting and dewy, but the yellow sunrise glowed an assurance the day would be warmer and kinder. They drove into town and Shirley parked a block from the courthouse.

"Are you sure you won't come in?" Donald asked.

"I'm sorry," was all she could say. She watched Donald walk away. His slacks were getting shorter every day. She shifted the truck into drive but kept her foot on the brake, watching the town move; people walking toward the courthouse, standing in sun-soaked patches of the city square, ebbing and flowing in and out of the diner. She rolled the window down and wished she smoked. The morning warmed and stilled while she watched. When the sidewalks seemed calmer, she went across the street to the diner. She ordered a turkey and mayo sandwich wrapped in butcher paper, and ate it sitting on the curb in the shade of the truck. Then, before she could talk herself out of it, she stood and walked from the safety of the yellow pickup toward the courthouse.

19

"Officer Simmons," the prosecutor said. "Could you please tell us what is included in this police report?" He handed the officer a stack of papers.

Officer Simmons flipped through it. "This is the police report I wrote regarding the events on the evening of September 9th."

"Could you please read your report?"

"I met with multiple witnesses the night of September 9, 1983, at approximately 22:00. Witnesses agree on the following events: The victim arrived at Pocket Change Arcade at 882 South Main Street at approximately 20:00 hours. Soon after, an altercation took place between the victim and both Martín Jiménez and Gabriel Jiménez. Witnesses report punches and kicks were first initiated by both of the Jiménez's. At some point, while the victim and Martín Jiménez were on the floor, Gabriel Jiménez reached into the victim's waistline and removed his knife. When the victim stood and attempted to walk away, Gabriel Jiménez stabbed the victim in the abdomen."

"Thank you, Officer. Can you tell us who you are referring to as 'the victim' in your report?"

"Robert Kershaw."

After Officer Simmons finished his testimony, the prosecutor brought several other witnesses to the stand. They all confirmed, in varying degrees of detail, what the police report stated. The prosecutor carefully crafted the order of the witnesses. He knew the jury would be freshest for Officer Simmons and his clear, concise testimony. They could read the report themselves and see a clear picture of the events. The prosecutor was also holding an ace that he was placing on the table as his last witness. The boy had been getting increasingly anxious about his testimony, but that would play even better in front of the jury.

Donald was sworn in and took his seat on the witness stand. The padded leather seat was warm from the line of Bobby's friends that had sat in it already that morning.

"Good morning, Donald. Could you please tell us your relationship with Robert Kershaw?" the prosecutor started.

"Bobby is my brother," Donald said quietly. "*Was* my brother."

Donald answered the preliminary questions, trying hard not to look anyone in the eye. He could feel the jury's questioning gazes, and he figured the Mexican boy's eyes probably held something like pleading. But as he became more comfortable with the cadence of the ask and answer, his eyes scanned the gallery.

In the third row behind the prosecutor, he saw his father. He wore a flannel shirt buttoned tightly to the collar. Donald had rarely seen him without a cap, so he stared at his thinning, slicked back hair. Dwayne's eyes were locked on his youngest son, seething but smug. They were Kershaws and they fell in line.

"And you were with your brother on the night of September 9th?"

"Yes, sir."

"Could you please tell us, in your own words, what happened that night?"

"Me and Bobby and some of his friends were at the football game, but Bobby said he wanted to leave."

"And then what happened?" the prosecutor prodded.

Donald looked around the gallery again, trying not to look at any face for too long or too deeply. There were a few people standing against the back wall of the courtroom; stragglers that hadn't been early enough to find seats on the long wooden benches. Or people just passing through while they were near the courthouse, so they could tell their friends they'd been there whenever someone brought it up.

Among them, Donald found a familiar face. Shirley had the collar of her sweater pulled around her neck, and her face was down but her eyes held Donald's. She smiled thinly when Donald found her.

"Donald," the prosecutor interrupted. "Could you tell us what happened after that?"

He put his hands together and squeezed them until the pain sent flashes of light through his view of the courtroom. His father stared at him through narrowed eyes. But his mother watched him with the same gentle and proud gaze that had watched him his entire life.

"Then," Donald mumbled. "Then… um… he… Bobby said that he—" then he coughed and brought a shaking glass of water to his lips.

"Would you like to take a break, Donald?" the prosecutor asked.

Donald shook his head. His mind was made up. He was going to tell the jury the truth. Not his or their stories, but the truth. He closed his eyes and said, "Bobby saw the brothers and said he wanted to follow them, so we left the stadium and went a couple places until we found them at the arcade. Then Bobby went to them and started punching the older one."

A few of the jurors furrowed their brows. One of them looked toward the prosecutor as if he was asking if Mr. Wolfe wanted him to escort the boy from the courtroom.

"Those other boys didn't start anything. Bobby did. He had the bigger one on the ground and was beating him, then he took out his knife and waved it in his face. I don't know how, but it ended up getting knocked to the ground."

"Your honor," the prosecutor cut in. "I would like to request a recess."

The judge watched the boy on the witness stand, his shoulders heavy with shame but words still on his tongue. "Do you need a break, son?" he asked.

"No sir."

"Okay. Then finish telling your story."

Donald sipped the last of the water and went on. "The skinny brother — that one — picked up the knife and told Bobby to quit it. But he didn't. He kept beating the bigger one and then stood up like he was going to start on him," he nodded toward Gabriel. "Bobby said he was gonna kill both of them."

The prosecutor slumped and returned to his table, where he shuffled through papers that were rendered meaningless.

"Son," the judge said, "why is your story so different from the rest of your friends'?"

"Because I was scared. I told the police what I heard everyone else saying. But they only talked to Bobby's friends. Everyone else scattered before the police came."

"Do you know it's a crime to lie to a law officer like you did that night?"

"Yes, sir."

"And you could get in some serious trouble? Go to jail, even."

"Yes, sir."

"Are you telling the truth today?"

"Yes, sir." Then Donald looked at the scrawny Mexican boy whose hands had grasped Bobby's knife. "I'm sorry," he said. To the boy, and to everybody.

A wave of commotion rippled through the courtroom; through the prosecution, through Alma and Martín in the front row, through the jury, and through the Kershaws that stippled the gallery. But Donald looked over all of them and looked to the woman standing against the back wall.

I'm proud of you, she mouthed.

20

A few rows in front of Shirley, sitting in the middle of the gallery, somewhere between her and Alma, was John Ellis. She hadn't picked the back of his head from the other men in the crowd. They maintained their thin veil of anonymity for at least a few hours longer. But a head she had recognized was Dwayne's. His oily hair with a ring pinched around his head from a ball cap. She could tell he was simmering by the way his shoulders rose and how his chin twitched to one side.

She watched Donald climb from the witness stand and disappear into the backstages of the courtroom. When Donald was gone, the judge called for a recess but Shirley had already slipped through the door and was back in the truck, rolling away from town, by the time Dwayne or John had left their seats.

Outside, Dwayne's friend sat behind the wheel of his black GMC pickup. He'd been spinning the radio dial, trying to find something to keep him awake, when he saw Shirley climb into Dwayne's truck. As promised, he was parked down the street from the Kershaw house by sunrise and followed Shirley when she drove Donald to the courthouse. He parked a half block away and watched her with disappearing excitement. The only thrill he'd had so far was when she went to grab an early lunch across the street. He walked behind her, then ducked into a shadow until she emerged with a sandwich. Disappointed it was lunch rather than a smoking gun, he struggled to keep his eyes open enough to watch the yellow truck.

When she pulled from the curb and turned east, he was behind her. He rolled the window down and lit a cigarette. While Shirley weaved through the small grid of downtown streets, he kept close behind. But when they reached the highway, and the world and road flattened and emptied, he could see her up ahead from a half-mile away. By the time Shirley crossed into Hondo, he thought she might have seen him and was stringing him along; taking him an hour into the nothing of Texas to teach him a lesson. But Dwayne's friend followed her to the Deep Elem Bar, parked across the street, and watched her walk through the doors like a regular.

21

After an abbreviated afternoon in court, John met Alma in the foyer of the courthouse. "Want to have dinner tonight?" he asked. "I can bring over some take-out."

"I would but Mr. Frazier wants to meet with me. He said Gabriel's defense is going to have to change after that Kershaw boy's testimony."

John smiled. "That's got to be good news. I'm pretty sure that kid was the first person to tell the truth this whole time."

"We'll see," Alma shrugged. "I don't want to get my hopes up just yet."

"Okay. I'll see you tomorrow?"

"Why don't you come over later? I should be home by eight."

John nodded and tried to seem indifferent. "Yeah," he said. "Maybe I'll stop by."

With the rest of the evening ahead of him, John unbuttoned the top of his shirt and turned onto the highway. It'd been a few days, but he could still taste George Dickel whiskey from the Deep Elem.

He walked in with a cigarette hanging from his lips and found a stool near the door. Les, the bartender that called him an old pal, poured him a whiskey and brought him a beer on the house. John stubbed out the cigarette and, after the first swig of beer, the scratch in his throat became a tickle and he roared in a coughing fit for a minute. Les brought him a glass of tepid, iron-tasting water that he chugged. "Your girl's down there," Les said then. "If you're trying to avoid her, that coughing ain't helping."

John looked down the bar and saw Shirley, her hair in a ponytail, little make up, and a sweater wrapped around her. He grabbed his drinks and went to sit next to her. "Didn't think I'd see you today," he said.

Shirley smiled when he joined her. "You say that like it's a bad thing."

"Not at all." He rifled through his pockets for quarters and turned to the jukebox. "Anything you want to hear?"

"Play some Merle Haggard."

John beamed. He dropped four quarters in the jukebox and lined up two by Merle and two by George Jones. When Merle started singing, John said, "I've got a dog named Merle, you know? He's a mutt, but I found him along the highway when I was listening to Haggard."

"That so?" Shirley said. "Along the highway?"

John nodded proudly and told her the story of the drive through Texas and how he'd come home with the smiling pup. Shirley was listening to John close enough that she didn't hear George Jones singing. *Borrowed angel, belongs to someone else.*

After another round, John stood and said he was going to get some fresh air and a smoke. "Fresh air and cigarettes don't go together," Shirley smirked. But she followed him outside, where they stood on the sidewalk and enjoyed the last glowing orange embers of sunset over the Hill Country. Shirley took a drag from John's cigarette but wrinkled her nose when the smoke hit her lungs. John laughed and coughed and smoked. Shirley hooked her arm into the crook of John's and they watched cars whiz by until the cigarette was burnt to a column of ash.

Across the street, under the disguise of the sunset, Dwayne's friend sat in his black GMC and watched John and Shirley. By the time they were laughing arm-in-arm, he was shaking his head with a crooked scowl. "That son of a bitch whore," he muttered when they went back into the bar.

John left the Deep Elem after another beer and climbed into his truck. His tires crunched under the gravel and macadam of Hondo's streets. The black GMC followed behind him like a shadow.

He expected John to pull off in Sabinal, to take the exit and wind through that town until he pulled into a random driveway. By the time they reached Knippa and its half dozen streets, he was surprised trailing John had brought him so close to home. But when they passed by and John turned off Route 90 in Uvalde, the man muttered "*You've gotta be fucking kidding me*" over and over like a mantra.

He stalked John's truck through town; past city hall and the courthouse, by the abandoned opera house, and beyond downtown. He pulled past John when he parked along the curb. When the black GMC stopped around the corner, he recognized where he was. He'd driven with Dwayne to that part of town, to that street, to that house, to hand deliver their threatening notes to the mailbox John was parked next to.

22

After being led through hidden hallways of the courthouse, Donald only realized he was outside when he felt a breeze tickling the back of his neck. He looked around and saw the town was mostly empty. When he got his bearings, he walked the sidewalk around the back of the courthouse. He searched for his mother and the yellow truck but it was already gone. Donald wondered then if he'd actually seen her.

Not knowing what else to do, he started walking home. With each step, the picture of his situation cleared. Each time his shoes hit the pavement, he felt another dollop of his father's rage. He could hear the entire Kershaw family tree gnarling together to snare him in its branches and bury him within its roots. Halfway there, he knew he couldn't go home. At least not until his mother was home. Donald stopped at a random street corner and sat. He leaned his back against the stop sign and felt the seams of his pants straining.

He made sure the street was empty before he cried. For the first time since he died, Donald missed his brother. Not because he wanted him back, but because dealing with him alive was somehow easier than the past months. The bullying and ribbing he endured seemed tolerable. Wistful, even.

Or maybe Bobby dying forced him to grow up. To realize there was no love in his parent's marriage; there was no love in his father at all. The only love that existed in their home was between Donald and his mother. Perhaps Bobby's death didn't change a thing. It only stripped away the peat growing over the sharp, cracked rocks of his family. Without that false covering, the true width of each fissure could finally be seen.

Donald wiped his face with the sleeve of his jacket. He had a friend that lived a few streets away. It was still early in the day but his friend would be home from school soon. Until then, he would go there and sit on the porch steps and cry.

23

Dwayne got a ride home from court late in the afternoon. He was silent the whole way. When he arrived at the trailor, he flung the screen door nearly off its hinges. He bellowed for Donald and went into each room like a burglar, upending belongings and furniture. Dwayne even went to Bobby's room and trashed it. At some point, he stopped looking for Donald and focused only on ravaging his sons' rooms. In the kitchen, he kicked a chair until it splintered into arbitrary pieces. He reached inside the fridge, grabbed a beer bottle, and threw it across the kitchen into the wall. It exploded and sent sopping foam dripping down the wallpaper.

He sat for hours, drinking the fridge clean of beers, then reaching deep into cabinets for dusty bottles of grain alcohol. His anger boiled. The burn in his throat from each slug of liquor reminded him of his outrage. The broken chair and soggy splotch of wall were emblems of his ire. He held it tightly, careful to not let any of it loose until Donald was home.

Later, his friend came into the kitchen. Dwayne hadn't heard the door. His ears droned with alcohol and choler.

"Jesus, Dwayne," the friend surveyed the trailer. "How'd you hear already?"

"What?" Dwayne slurred. "Hear what?"

"About Shirley. I came right over to tell you."

"Tell me what?"

"Oh, Dwayne, buddy," the friend shook his head. "You're not gonna believe this." He'd smoked three cigarettes in quick succession parked near the Jiménez house before driving to tell Dwayne. "Shirley was all the way out in Hondo today."

"Hondo?" Dwayne spat. "The fuck's she doing there?"

"She was at a bar. Was there for a while. But she came out and had a smoke with some guy."

Dwayne brought the glass bottle to his lips and growled at it all.

"But—" his friend went on, "You ain't going to fucking believe this. Guess who it was?"

"You gonna fucking tell me?" Dwayne exploded.

"Some guy from Uvalde. I followed him all the way back here. Guess where he is right now? At that fucking Mexican's house."

"Don't fuck with me."

"Dwayne, I ain't fucking with you. Not even a little. This guy's been with that spick and now he's sniffing around at your old lady."

"Who is it?" Dwayne fumed. "Who is he?"

The friend shrugged. "Pretty tall guy with a mustache and a Stetson. Doesn't narrow it down much."

"Was he wearing some queer pearl snap unbuttoned down past his tits? Driving a Chevy?"

"How the hell'd you know that?"

"I know him," Dwayne staggered to his feet. "He's that goddamn teacher that's been in court every fucking day." He shrugged into a denim jacket and grabbed the liquor bottle by the handle. "Let's go," he said. "I know where he lives."

LEAST OF THESE BROTHERS

Mama's been crying in the kitchen,
Daddy's done left in the truck.
He's headed down to the ABC Store
to get a little more fucked up.

Waylon Payne

1

IT WAS ALMOST MIDNIGHT, and the last fumes of Monday night were rippling over the Texas hills. Donald walked home with his feet dragging along the sidewalks. When he rounded his street corner, he took a sweeping path that allowed him to check the house and driveway. The yellow truck wasn't parked outside, but there were lights on in the kitchen. He stood and stared at the windows, waiting for shadows. After a while, the night chilled him through his suit and he climbed the steps to the front door. He willed the door to open gently and breathlessly craned to look into the house. He could smell cigarettes and liquor, but the house was quiet.

In the kitchen, he found the debris of his father's rage. Donald got the broom from the pantry and swept the bottle shards into a corner. Then he collected the matchwood pieces of the chair and set them aside in a crooked pile. He screwed the caps onto the heavy glass liquor bottles his father had left behind and hid them in the cabinet under the sink. There was a leftover piece of meatloaf in the fridge that he ate cold. It tasted old, with a hint of freon staleness like it'd been sitting in the casserole dish for weeks. But he shoveled it and went back for the crumbs of beef in the bottom of the dish.

Donald was heading to his room to change out of his cheap suit when he heard tires on the gravel outside. The truck door slammed and Donald stood in the hallway waiting for his mother. But he heard heavy boot steps and rowdy laughing. Donald was going to slink into his bedroom and hide, where he would pray his father was too drunk to find him. He was a step away from the door when Dwayne and his friend barreled inside.

Blood filled the deep wrinkles on their hands and splatters ran down the front of Dwayne's jeans. Donald was so shocked by their savage appearance that he froze. Dwayne flipped on the hall light, leaving a faint red streak along the plastic switch cover. He laughed when he saw Donald. "There he is! The other son of a bitch that's due for a beating!"

2

The ribbon of highway between Hondo and Uvalde was empty, save for the yellow truck. Shirley passed the miles thinking of the handsome cowboy that made her feel buzzed. And her son who dauntlessly stared down the Kershaw clan and cut their roots away with honesty. All was well over those miles through the ragged caliche.

Anything outside of her reality was a paradise. Maybe she would empty the bank account she'd had since she was eighteen, bundle the cash together, and drive the rusted truck until the engine gave out. She could leave Dwayne behind. Take Donald along and start over somewhere past the horizon. Maybe John would follow them. She could make him a home and be a wife. Maybe she'd pour kerosene through the aisles of the grocery store, touch flame to that godforsaken green apron and drop it, lighting up the whole thing. If she was lucky it might burn the whole town to cinders.

But as she neared the glowing light that hung over Uvalde, her delusions fell away. Like every night she'd driven as far as she could stand, she returned to Uvalde and her abhorrent husband. Anywhere else was utopia, but home was the barbed hook pierced through her cheek.

There was a black GMC parked in front of the house. The truck was a sure sign Dwayne would be snot-slinging drunk. She hoped to slip through the front door and to the bedroom, where she could bury her head in a pillow to drown out the men's rowdiness. She was already cringing, anticipating the hollering that would be thrown her way. Instead, mixed with the choir of drunken friends was a pleading whimper.

Shirley shouldered the door open and ran to the kitchen. Dwayne and his friend were standing over Donald, hissing and bent so their liquor-soaked breath was hot on Donald's face. Shirley threw her purse onto the floor. The chiming of spare change and Altoids tins got the attention of the men. They turned away from Donald, and Shirley saw him. Donald was slumped in a chair, one of his eyes already swollen shut with an earthen purple bruise. His lip and nose dripped a steady stream of blood onto his white shirt.

"Who did this?" Shirley screamed.

Dwayne laughed. "Who the hell do you think?"

"Who did this to him?" she repeated. Then, when the pieces connected, she muttered her denial. "No, no, no, no…"

"Just teaching him a lesson," Dwayne said with a wry smile. "Since it seems like he forgot what it means to be a Kershaw." Dwayne turned from his wife and smacked Donald across the face as quick as a whip.

Donald muttered something but had no fight left.

"Touch him again and I'll kill you," Shirley said. It was the same promise her brother had given their father when she was a girl. The one that ended with a pistol blast in their backyard, and their father's unceremonious burial.

"He's my son. I'll teach him a lesson however the hell I want."

"He's my son too."

"Yeah," Dwayne scoffed. "Showed that today. All I'm doing is beating that Walker blood out of him. Like I should've done to you a long time ago."

"Don't you put a hand on him again."

Dwayne shook his head and put his filthy hand in Donald's hair, then told his friend to give him a swing. His friend punched Donald in the stomach and doubled him over.

Shirley pushed Dwayne from behind and sent him sprawling onto the faded linoleum floor. "Fuck you," she fumed. Dwayne clambered to his feet and was in front of her in two strides. He wrapped his bloody hands around her neck and lifted her against the wall. He squeezed his chest into her and put his mouth to her face.

"You're due for a beating too," he hissed. "I know you were out in Hondo tonight. And I bet you don't even know who you were fucking around with."

Shirley looked somewhere beyond him.

"Or did you know you and that spick are fucking the same guy?"

Shirley gasped on instinct. She deflated as soon as it slipped from her mouth.

Dwayne squeezed her throat tighter. "I knew you been messing around on me," he snarled. "You've as good as got spick in you now. I'll be damned if I'm ever touching you again, you goddamned whore."

Shirley glared at him and, with every scrap of force she could collect, spit in his face.

Dwayne released his grip on her neck and she fell to her knees. His hands were across her face before she could draw a breath. Again and again, he brought his hands and fists to her with all the hatred he'd been harboring since the day they'd wed. Shirley felt blood dripping from her face and into her hair. She'd driven home smelling like Stetson cologne, but all she knew then, with her husband's hands thrashing against her, was blood and bile.

3

John drove across town with another helping of leftovers on the passenger seat. He rolled his window down and lit a cigarette. He could still feel Alma's hands on his. If the night had been warmer he might have asked to take her for a drive.

John pulled into his driveway and saw light shining through the house. The front door was hanging open. He was suspicious, but he'd often let the door cracked open so Merle could come and go as he pleased. John noticed wet footsteps on the porch, so he went back to the truck. He reached under the seat and grabbed his revolver.

He stuck his head inside and saw the light over the kitchen table was on, casting long shadows down the hallway. Speckling the floor were more footprints. Two sets, going from the kitchen and out of the front door. He turned back to the porch and surveyed the yard. He sat on a lawn chair and smoked another cigarette while watching the street. It was completely still and absolutely quiet. There wasn't enough breeze to rustle the trees.

John stubbed the cigarette and went inside. He crouched in front of a footprint and realized it was dark, sticky blood. He followed them to the kitchen and, when he turned the corner, heard a shriek throughout the house. It was only when he was on his knees — his head pinched between his fists so tightly he saw stars — that he realized the wailing noise was his. If he pushed against his eyes, maybe he could erase what he'd seen. If he screamed loud enough, it might open a chasm in the bloody kitchen floor and cause another truth to rise up. But as much as he willed it, nothing stopped the patter of blood dripping from the edge of the table. In the spotlight of the bulb above the table was Merle. He lay on the table, cut the length of his underside like a field dressed buck.

4

John slept with his head on the kitchen table, his arms making a wall around him. A partition that protected him just enough to sleep in long moments where he woke slightly sweated and dry-eyed, not sure if he'd slept for a second or an hour. He had drunk the rest of an open bottle of Jim Beam, then opened another and drank most of that too. It went down hard. He forced each swig down his throat, trying to ignore his companion laid in front of him. Merle's body disgusted part of him. The sight and smell of the viscera and blood curdled his stomach. But he couldn't think to be anywhere else. That sickening scent of death was the last warm grey coals of his dog's existence, and he couldn't bear to leave it.

During some shapeless time of the morning, John called the police. He dialed the operator and asked for the department's direct line. It wasn't an emergency, he told the woman. He was patched through to a cop who took John's information and listened to his description of the footprints in the hallway, of his slain dog on the table.

"Were there signs of a break-in?" the officer asked.

"No. I usually keep my door unlocked," John said. He wondered if his tongue sounded as heavy as it felt.

"You're sure you don't want us to send a vet?"

John winced. "No use. I'm sure of it."

"We'll be there in about an hour to take an official statement and collect any evidence."

"Okay." Then he added, "Will you want to take photos of my dog? The way he is now?"

"Yessir, that would all be evidence."

John ran a hand through Merle's patchwork fur. "I moved him already," he lied. "Buried him first thing. I'm sure you can understand."

The officer was silent for a moment. John could hear a piece of hard candy clacking against his teeth. "Of course," the cop said. "Just try not to disturb those footprints."

"Sure," John said and hung up. He bent over his dog and wrapped both arms around his neck. His sleeves sopped up blood and ruined the fabric of his favorite shirt. Before the police came, he went to the backyard and dug a grave in the hardscrabble dirt. Merle had a secondhand couch cushion that he used as a bed, a bedsheet that was ripped and stained, and a bleach white ham bone that'd been a table scrap from years before that he carried with him. John collected those possessions, then laid them at the edge of the grave before putting Merle inside.

He was shoveling dirt over him when the cops arrived. The uniformed pair stood and watched John work in the cold morning light, sweat collecting in his beard and blood-stained sleeves. He let them watch and allowed them to wonder. Anything, so long as nobody saw his dog the way he had died.

5

After the cops were gone, their reports written and signed, John sat on the sofa and stared at the black television screen. He'd thought about getting up and flicking on whichever channel he'd left it dialed to, but he would watch it as closely as the blank screen so he didn't bother. He called the Jiménez house four times but there was no answer. He fought against feelings of frustration toward Alma for being at work. John picked up the phone late in the afternoon to call again but put it down when he checked the time. Martín was back in school a few days each week, and he would be getting home. John didn't want to hear anybody's voice but Alma's.

The police had sent a woman to help clean the blood from the kitchen. John offered a hand with mopping up the blood from the Formica tabletop, but after a few swipes, he tasted metal under his tongue and ran to the porch to vomit. When he came back, the woman was on her knees scrubbing the area rug under the table. The brush bristles created a pink, blood-tinged foam, like saliva dropped from a shot and panicking doe. John put a hand on her shoulder and shook his head. He pulled the table and chairs against the wall and rolled the carpet. "Don't think that was coming out anyway," John said. The woman smiled soberly and left.

John's stomach was churning on itself but eating seemed like sac-rilege. So he sat and watched the silent TV, which reflected the beginnings of a sunset streaming through the front windows.

He heard the knocking the second time. "Come in," he called from the sofa. The visitor knocked again. John got up with a groan. His head was heavy from a hangover and his limbs were still shaky. He turned the knob and, for only a moment, thought it might be last night's visitors back to finish the job. When he saw who was standing on his porch, he could have confused the shock with a shotgun blast.

"What— what are you doing here?" he stammered. "How did you know where I live?" Then, when the cataract of disbelief evaporated and his vision cleared, he saw the bruises on her face. "What the hell happened?"

"Do you know who I am?" she asked.

"Of course I do," John said. "Shirley. Shirley from Hondo. What are you doing here?"

"No," Shirley said. "Do you know who I am?"

"Shirley," John rubbed his face. "What are you talking about? What's going on?"

"I'm Shirley Kershaw."

Cold ran down the back of John's neck. "You're a Kershaw? I thought you were from Utopia?"

"I'm married to a Kershaw. Bobby was my son."

John leaned hard against the door jamb. He closed his eyes and put the heel of his hands into them. He pushed until he hoped he was blind. "What are you talking about?"

"Did you know who I was?" she demanded.

"What? No, of course I didn't. You said you were from Utopia."

"And you said you were from Valentine."

"Fucking Christ," John rasped. "How did you know I live here?"

"My husband saw us in Hondo. Or someone did. They recognized us, I guess."

"And that's where those bruises come from?"

Shirley stared at the pattern on his shirt. "Has he been here?"

"No," John said. "Why? Is he coming?"

Shirley shrugged. "He said he already taught you a lesson but he's a big talker. That's why I came over. To see if you were okay, I guess."

"Wait," John muttered. "Jesus." He bit his bottom lip until he saw stars. "Someone killed my dog last night."

"Was he old?" Shirley's eyes searched for a safe place to land. "Maybe it wasn't Dwayne."

John stared at her. "He was gutted."

On a different day, Shirley may have reacted differently. Maybe with disbelief. But after seeing Dwayne beat their son bloody, it simply clicked into place in her mind, the way things do when they just make sense.

"What do we do now?" Shirley asked then.

"What do we do? We act like this never happened. Like I didn't two-step with Bobby fucking Kershaw's mother."

"We didn't know, John. *I* didn't know."

"Well, now we do."

"We could still go to Hondo," she said. Shirley wasn't sure why she said it. Something about his bitter sweat and sweet cologne, the splatters of blood on his patterned shirt.

John laughed, and she could feel her chest crumple on itself. For just a moment she felt sadness but it quickly turned to anger. Anger was easier for her to hold. Melancholy required some amount of self-awareness, and it too easily slipped between her fingers when she meant to throw it at someone else. But anger was solid and sharp; it was a sword and shield; protecting her while jabbing others with the sentiments she'd buried.

"I think you're a good woman, Shirley. But I never even would have talked to you if I knew. It's just a big fucking mess now."

Shirley turned to leave. The fantasies of starting again with John, of breaking free from her cursed life, dripped from her limbs like bathwater. She realized every time she had thought her life would be changed by meeting John, it was cheap solace. Once again, she'd bet it all and assumed salvation for a man she hardly knew.

"Shirley," John dropped his eyes. "I'm sorry about Bobby. My brother died when he was Bobby's age. I know how hard it is."

She forced a tight smile. "I'm sorry about your dog," she said and turned away. She'd walked across Uvalde to see John and was almost home again when she realized the words she'd planned to say were still in her throat.

You're the closest I've been to utopia, she wanted him to know.

6

John was heating a frozen dinner when Alma called. "I thought you might call," she said. He could hear it pass over her smile.

"Sorry," John said groggily. "I tried earlier but I didn't want to bother at supper time."

"Oh, that's enough of that," Alma said, but John wasn't listening. He thought he'd heard the jingling of Merle's collar in the bedroom.

He watched the hallway for the dog to appear before he remembered he was gone.

"I've just been busy."

"Good," Alma said. "Busy is good sometimes."

"Yeah."

"Well listen, I wanted to call because both of the boys are testifying tomorrow and I was wondering if you'd be there."

"Oh," John sighed. "I don't know."

"I know they'd appreciate you being there. I would too."

John rubbed his cheeks and felt a random shiver run through himself. "Merle died," he said.

"What? John, I'm so sorry. What happened? Do you want me to come over?"

"No," John said. "No, I'm alright. It's okay."

"Okay. If you need anything, call. And don't worry about tomorrow. I'm sorry I asked. I didn't know."

"It's fine, Alma. Really. It's alright."

"The day after tomorrow is Thanksgiving," Alma said. "Do you have plans?"

John hadn't had Thanksgiving plans, besides Coors, a Hungry Man, and a football game, since his mother died.

Alma broke through the silence. "We usually have an early dinner. I might visit Gabe in the morning if they let me. Turkey's on the table at two, and I want you to be there."

"Okay."

"You'll come? Don't bring anything. We'll have more enough."

"I should bring something."

"Just come over. Thursday at two."

"Yeah," John said. "Yeah. I'll be there."

7

The day before Thanksgiving, the town weaved through frantic grocery store aisles and butchers. Women took down and wiped the china and cutlery they reserved for occasions. Almost every kitchen had pies set out to cool. The streets of Uvalde smelled that day of the sticky, fruity syrup that bubbled on the rims of each pie.

Martín and Alma drove through town early. If he smelled the sickly sweetness, it would have turned his nervous stomach. He'd lain in bed the night before and stared at the ceiling with suspicious eyes. He turned on the bedside lamp and held a book in front of his good eye but the words swirled into a hole of anxiety. The night eventually faded into a vaporous predawn morning. His nerves made the day feel like it couldn't be grasped, like everything was a half-step out of reach.

By the time he was seated in the witness stand, Martín was exhausted. His limbs were heavy against the thick wooden chair arms, and his head was unsteadily balanced atop shoulders. Gabriel's attorney asked him a litany of questions before asking about Bobby.

"Had you met Robert Kershaw before the evening of September 7th?"

"No."

"Did you throw a gallon of milk in the direction of Robert Kershaw and his friends?"

"Yes." He struggled to speak more than a few words at a time, so he wanted to keep his answers brief.

"And did you know, at the time, that it was Robert Kershaw?"

"Yes."

"How did you know it was Robert Kershaw?"

"Gabriel told me. He… said it was the kid that beat him up at school." Martín's tongue was beginning to struggle against him.

"Were you trying to threaten Robert and his friends by throwing the milk?"

Martín thought about that. The question wasn't one he could answer with a single syllable. He had never considered what compelled him to hurl the milk jug at Bobby. It would be impossible to trace Bobby's death back to a true cause. Why stop at the milk and not go back to the first time Bobby's sneered? Or the first time he called a Mexican a wetback with his own voice?

"Not really," he said. "I think I did it to… make Gabriel feel better."

"And did it make Gabriel feel better?"

"No," Martín looked at his brother. "He wanted the milk for… cereal and was mad I wasted… it."

"Can you tell us your account of the night of September 9th?"

"Me and Gabriel went to the football game that night, but we left… early to go to the arcade. We… went straight there and then played… the Star Wars game for a while. Then we were playing Donkey… Kong when I got pushed from behind and hit… my head on the machine. I started… getting punched in the head and… my face. I ended up on the ground and I… was getting kicked. Bobby got on… top of me and started punching me again."

"And who was doing all of this to you?"

"Bobby Kershaw."

"What else happened after those events?"

"Then he reached into… the back of his jeans and… took out a knife. He held it in front of my face and said…" Martín stuttered. "He said that he wanted… to kill me."

"Do you remember anything happening after that?"

"No. I think I was knocked out."

When the prosecutor had his chance to cross-examine Martín, he handed him a folder and smiled. "Mr. Jiménez, this is your medical record from Uvalde Memorial Hospital in the days after September 9th, is that correct?"

Martín flipped through the folder and shrugged. "Sure."

"And in your medical record, the doctors diagnosed you with — among other things — a moderate brain injury. Some symptoms of that include speech problems, severe headaches, and memory loss. Have you experienced any of those symptoms?"

"Yes."

"Do you remember being taken to the hospital in the ambulance?"

"No."

"Do you remember being taken for your surgery?"

"No."

"Do you remember what the weather was like on September 9th? The night you allege Robert Kershaw attacked you?"

"No."

"Do you remember what you or your brother or Robert were wearing that night?"

"No."

"But you remember — in detail — what happened starting the exact moment Robert Kershaw entered the arcade?"

Martín could feel the electricity in the courtroom. He sensed the pressure of the anxious ears around him. He recognized something was happening, the way the ocean shifts suddenly before a tidal wave, and hoped his answer wouldn't be the rumble that caused the water to swallow his brother. "Yes," he said. "I couldn't forget that."

8

For the first weeks of the trial, Gabriel was brought into the courtroom with his wrists cinched in handcuffs. But, with his right arm wrapped in a sling, the metal cuffs were clasped around his ankles. A long chain hung between his legs and jangled against the carpeted floor with each step. The jury looked him over and looked amongst each other, as if to say they would discuss it later. When Gabriel was taken to the witness stand, he jiggled his leg and tapped his toe in nervousness, and the courtroom was filled with noises like sleigh bells until the judge scolded him to stop.

In the days before, Alma had interrogated Mr. Frazier to make sure Gabriel testifying was in his best interest. "He's shy," she warned. "He's going to be so nervous." But the attorney promised the jury would be willing to forgive nerves and timidity with the story he would tell. "Why is it about how it's going to *play for the jury?*" she asked. "What about whether it's going to put him through everything that happened again?"

"I understand that. But I think the real tragedy would be Gabriel spending the rest of his natural life in prison, and I think you'd agree."

While Gabriel was sitting in the withness stand with cold cuffs pinched around his ankles, he and Mr. Frazier were in a battle for his life.

"Was there anything that happened between Robert Kershaw and yourself that led to his attack on you at lunch on the first day of school?" the attorney asked

"No," Gabriel answered. "I had never seen him before."

"Can you describe what happened during that attack?"

"I was sitting by myself at lunch. It was my first day at the school. I was about to eat my chili when I heard someone come up behind me. He grabbed my head and my hair before I turned around and he started swearing at me and shoved my face into the bowl."

"What kind of things did he say to you?"

"He— um— called me a spick and told me to go back to where I came from."

"And then he forced your face into the chili?"

"Yeah," Gabriel's voice fell away like a radio from a car passing by. "It was so hot and it got in my eyes and it really burned. It was running down my neck and splashing onto my shirt. I remember feeling the bowl against my face and I thought my face was going to break."

"Thank you, Gabriel. Let's skip ahead to the night of September 9th at the arcade."

Gabriel painstakingly recounted the story of that night, much as Martín had just told it. His eyes were stinging and he focused on keeping tears in rather than what he was saying. When he caught a glimpse of his mother wiping her own eyes, his mind sharpened and he felt more comfortable under the weight of his testimony. *You did nothing wrong*, he repeated to himself. The same as he had for months.

"And how did you end up holding that knife?" his attorney asked.

"Bobby was holding it in front of Martín's face and he knocked it out of Bobby's hand when he started threatening Martín."

"What was he threatening?"

"He was saying he was going to kill Martín."

"And the knife landed in front of you?"

"Pretty close to my feet," Gabriel said. "I just reached down and grabbed it. Then I told Bobby to get off him."

"To get off of Martín?"

"Yeah. I said it two or three times. And when he got up he started coming toward me."

"What happened then?"

"He said he would be glad to kill both of us. He kept walking toward me. Probably four or five steps. Then when he raised his fist at me, I— uh— I shoved the knife at him, and I guess he was— I guess that's when it went— went into him."

Gabriel let tears run down his neck. He barely felt them well in his eyes or drop over his lids and run down his cheeks. He didn't notice his mother watching him wide-eyed with a tissue held under her nose. He didn't notice John Ellis standing against the back wall looking tired and disheveled. And only his attorney saw one of the jurors — an older man — wipe his eyes. Methodically and awkwardly, like he'd hardly wiped tears away before.

"Did you feel threatened when Robert Kershaw was stepping toward you?"

"Yes."

"What were you afraid of at that moment?"

"I was afraid of him. I knew he wanted to kill Martín and I knew he was going to kill me for stopping him."

"Do you think you did the right thing by protecting yourself?"

Gabriel gulped the silent air. He pinched his eyes shut and felt a rush of tears run down his face and soak into his collar. "I think I saved me and Martín's life. But I don't know if I did the right thing. Bobby's dead and I obviously wish he wasn't. I wish the whole thing had never happened. It was either him or me and my brother, and I don't think having to make that choice is right. There was no right thing."

"Thank you, Gabriel. I'm sure Mr. Wolfe would like to ask you some questions now. We could take a break if you'd like."

"I'm okay," Gabriel shook his head.

The prosecutor stood and smiled at Gabriel. "Thank you for sharing your testimony with us, Gabriel. I'm sure it took a lot of bravery to do so. Now, I just have a few questions for you."

"Okay."

"That day at lunch, when you allege Robert Kershaw attacked you, you also mentioned you didn't have time to turn around. So how can you be sure it was Robert that attacked you?"

Gabriel's eyes dried and he stared at the prosecutor. "I saw him walking away," he said.

"Is it possible he could have just been walking past, and you were actually attacked by someone else?"

"I know it was him."

"You're sure? Even though you couldn't turn around to look at who it was?"

Gabriel picked his fingernails on each other. "I think so," he said finally.

"You mentioned getting chili down the front of the shirt you wore that day, but it was never brought up as evidence. What happened to that shirt?"

Gabriel looked at his brother. Martín's eyes closed and his head hung. "Me and my brother tried to wash it," Gabriel said. "We washed it and tried bleaching it. We were afraid our mom would be mad it got ruined. She'd just bought it for me."

"And then it disappeared?" the prosecutor smirked.

"I hid it from my mom for a day or two then I threw it away. Probably on Thursday."

"I see," the prosecutor sighed. "Lastly, is it possible Bobby also felt threatened by you and your brother? After throwing milk at him and pointing his own knife at him?"

"I— I don't know. I don't think he was afraid of anyone. He's just— he was just mean."

"Well whatever he was, *was* is the right way to say it now, isn't it?" the prosecutor looked at each of the jurors and sat, dismissing Gabriel and his chiming shackles.

By noon, both attorneys had recapped their case with great detail and drama, and the judge directed the jury on their next tasks. They filed into a room next to the courtroom where they would decide whether Gabriel Jiménez would see another Texas sunrise outside of his prison cell.

9

John worked in his kitchen on Thanksgiving morning. He stood in the glare of the dingy yellow light over the stove and worked an opener around the rim of a handful of cans. Alma told him not to make anything, but his mother had taught him better than to arrive at a holiday meal empty-handed. When he arrived home from court the day before, he'd gone into a closet and rifled through his mother's old paperwork. Eventually, he found her small wooden box of stained and wrinkled recipe cards. He fingered through them until he found a recipe he could handle: green bean casserole.

He went to the grocery store late Wednesday afternoon. By then it was mostly empty. The employees looked at him with exhausted commiseration as he milled through the aisles. The shelves were mostly bare, save for some bruised produce and dented cans. The day before Thanksgiving had the same effect on the shelves as an apocalyptic panic. A bag of frozen green beans, a tin can of heavily preserved beans, and a can of off-brand cream of mushroom soup was as much as he could scrounge from the store. The cashier followed him to the door and latched the lock behind him. He planned to make the casserole when he got home but driving from the store in the early evening hours, his eyelids grew heavy. He put the grocery bag on the counter with a clatter and sat on the sofa, where he slept until morning.

With the casserole in the oven, he showered and picked out a shirt that didn't need ironing. He shaved his scruffy necks and put on Stetson cologne. A coughing fit enveloped him when he opened the oven door to check the bubbling dish. By the time it passed, his face was red and speckled with sweat, his throat battered. He spent the next few hours staring at the cooling casserole and sitting in ways that wouldn't wrinkle his shirt. Finally, around noon, he went out into the warm and docile day and drove to the Jiménez house with a careful hand on the translucent pink Pyrex dish on the seat beside him.

Alma was bent in two with her face in the oven when John came in. She wore a white and navy striped dress and had curled her hair. She was barefoot while she cooked, but a pair of pumps sat next to the table. John thought he'd drop the casserole when he saw her.

"Alma," he gaped. "It's really good to see you. Really good."

"Hi, John! Happy Thanksgiving!" she greeted him with a hug and a kiss on the cheek. She took the dish from him and set it among the other offerings. "I told you not to bring anything," she said. "But I'm glad you did. This is one of my favorites."

John looked over the table. Already, there were steaming dishes of potatoes, corn, stuffing, asparagus, and another green bean casserole that looked much more appealing than the one he'd made. "I had to fight for the stuff to make it," he laughed. "Went last night right before they closed. So if yours is better, let's just say that's why."

"Okay," Alma smiled. "That's what we'll say."

"Did you visit Gabriel this morning?"

Alma nodded. "He seemed in good spirits. He's glad the trial's over."

"This waiting on the jury is nerve-racking though."

"That's if you've got any nerves left," Alma huffed. "Hopefully they don't have too much to think about."

"Yeah," John said. "How's his face? Look any better?"

"Those scrapes are a sight but he says he feels okay."

"Yeah, his collarbone will heal before he realizes it. But those scrapes on his face must be a killer." John felt the word spring off his tongue and float between his lips. He would have sucked all the air from the room if he could bring the word back to his lungs.

Alma's hands around a wooden spoon stilled, but she forced a smile and said, "What about you? Are you feeling okay? I was so sorry to hear about your dog."

"It was nice to be busy this morning. If you can call that cooking," he jutted his chin toward the casserole. "I'm alright though."

"I didn't realize he was sick."

"Oh— well— he wasn't. It was pretty… sudden."

A timer shaped like a bright red tomato rang and Alma bent to take the turkey from the oven. It steamed and sizzled, and wafted a smell of rosemary and fat through the kitchen. Alma turned back to him, flushed but smiling, and John thought all of it looked delicious.

After they'd eaten, with half-empty Pyrex and Corningware surrounding them, John and Alma sat back in their chairs with cups of coffee. "That was amazing," John said. "I always eat well when I'm here, but you really outdid yourself today."

"I figured a big meal wouldn't hurt you," Alma teased. "You could put some fat on those bones. Seems like you lost half of yourself since the first time you came here. You could get rich selling your diet trick to women."

"Budweiser and Marlboro," John scoffed. "The secret to having the body of a god."

Alma smirked and her lips split like she was about to say something, but she bit her tongue. They sipped their coffees in silence. When John got up to pour another cup and coughed over the sink, she put her mug on the table and leaned forward, ready for when he sat across from her.

"What happened to Merle?" she asked then. "Did he run out in the road? Did you have to put him down or something?"

John stammered. "It was just— he was getting old. You know."

"You're a bad liar, John. You've only lied to me a couple times but you haven't fooled me yet."

John swirled his coffee.

"If you don't want to tell me, that's fine. But I won't stand for being lied to."

"He was killed," John blurted. "I went home from here the other night and he was on the kitchen table cut from his chin to his tail."

Alma gaped. "How could that've happened?"

241

"It was Bobby Kershaw's dad."

"Oh John, I don't think so. You've always been paranoid about people in this town since the trial, but no one would kill your dog over it."

"It's not just that," he paused. "I'd been going out to Hondo some nights. Remember that bar we passed when I took you to meet with the attorney the first time? I went back there a few times and— and there was a woman there that, I guess, took a liking to me. We had some drinks a couple nights and danced a little, but nothing else. I'm not lying, Alma. Nothing else."

"I know you're not lying. When you lie, you pinch your lips together until they almost disappear."

John, by instinct, puckered his lips slightly and licked them. "And by some sick joke, that woman was Bobby Kershaw's mother. I'm not kidding. And apparently, her husband found out and he showed up at my house while I was here and killed my dog." He squeezed the mug handle until he thought it might shatter. "Probably came looking to kill me but settled for the dog."

Alma was quiet for a while. She breathed deeply and studied the table. She was careful to put all parts of the enigma together before she spoke. "It's almost funny," she said finally. "All this wide open space, and a handful of us have gotten so tangled up together."

John coughed in the middle of swigging his coffee and almost spit it across the kitchen. Alma took her fingers and pinched a clump of cold bread stuffing and put it in her mouth. "When you called from San Antonio, I'm pretty sure you were lying too."

"When?"

"You lips just did it again. When you called from San Antonio after a doctor's appointment."

John sighed.

"You said everything was fine. Is everything not fine?"

John wanted to shrivel into the folds of his chair cushion. "We don't have to do this today," he said.

"Whatever there is to say, I'd like to hear it." Alma parted the dishes and reached across the table for John's hand.

"It's not good," John said. "He said it's— he said that it's cancer. That it's been cancer for a while, I guess. The coughing and the weight. I guess it makes sense, and I guess I probably knew it for a while anyway. That's probably why I kept skipping the appointments. But I didn't think it'd be so bad."

"Cancer?" Alma moaned. "Where?"

"My throat. And my lungs. Probably other places too but they stopped looking."

"I'm sure there's some kind of treatment for you, isn't there? Did the doctor talk to you about that? Maybe we should get a second opinion?" Her nature as a mother dictated the response; the desperate helpfulness, the frantic and aching planning.

John shook his head. "He said it wouldn't help. It's too far along and it won't help."

"So he just gave up on you? John, there's always something you can do."

John grasped Alma's hand in both of his. "Nobody's giving up," he said soberly. "The doctor told me to go on with the time I've got, and that's what I mean to do. That's what I'm doing right now."

Alma wiped tears away. Her breathing broke apart into the choppy waters that precede stormy sobs. "How much?" she cried. "How long?"

"A year. Maybe a little more, but probably less."

10

Through each neighborhood and down each street, families congregated together and chanted their thankfulness. They shoveled lunch and dinner and pies into their mouths and ripped open beer cans in front of football games before giving in to greedy midday naps.

At the Kershaw house, Donald rummaged through the fridge and the pantry to find lunch. He found a box of dehydrated potatoes that became a bowl of suspiciously smooth mashed potatoes in a minute. He spooned it to his mouth slowly, careful of his split and scabbed lips. Donald thought one of his front teeth was cracked from the other night. He'd examined it in the bathroom mirror but he couldn't see anything wrong, so he was left to habitually work his tongue over it.

He didn't remember much from that night. He could remember sitting in the courtroom with everybody facing him. He remembered his mother standing with her back to the wall. But after climbing from the witness stand, the day became foggy. Based on the bruises, split skin, and dried blood over his face and neck, he knew his father hadn't taken his testimony well. It wasn't the first time his father had risen a hand, and it wasn't the only time it had come crashing down on him.

Since then, his father had been gone more than he'd been home. His yellow truck must have been parked elsewhere in town. Probably between a friend's house and the package store for another case of beer. His mother was home, in a sense. Donald had found her lying in bed for most of the day, or sitting hunched on the sofa and watching television mindlessly. She'd hardly said a word to him since his testimony. She'd hardly said a word at all. Donald wanted to reach out, to push the hair from her face and meet her in the ether of their shared pain. But he couldn't think of the first words so he said nothing.

Donald thought when he'd wake up Thanksgiving morning, the kitchen might be filled with smells of sage and starches and pie filling. But when he padded through the house, he saw the kitchen as it had been; dishes piled in the sink, a pan with congealed grease growing fetid on the stovetop, empty liquor bottles collected on the countertops. Maybe, he told himself, his mother had just forgotten it was Thanksgiving.

Sometime after supper, his father came home. Donald went to the kitchen and stood around the corner and out of sight. He heard his mother climb from the bed and close herself into the bathroom. She turned the lock and started running bathwater. When Dwayne came in, he was mumbling to himself. He staggered to the sofa and collapsed there, face down with a leg hanging off. From the kitchen, Donald could smell the yeasty scent of beer coming from him. He watched from around the corner for a while, making sure his father was passed out.

Donald went to his room, opened his nightstand drawer, and pulled out a folded sheet of paper. It was from the same notepad his father had used to write his caustic letters to the Jiménez family. Donald smoothed the paper and brought it to his parent's bedroom, where he laid it on the bed, on his mother's side. It had only taken a minute to write it. He'd known what he had to say for a while.

Mom,

You were the only one that ever showed me some-thing like kindness. I don't think I would have known what that felt like without you. I was born into a bit-ter world with a mean brother and a hateful father. You told me so many times to do the right thing but I'm not sure right and wrong mean anything to any-one else. If God wanted me to be kind and tell the truth, I don't think he would have made it so hard to do. I know it's not true for everyone, but for me, in this life, kindness has become too heavy to carry. I don't know if either of us were ever really meant to be happy. I guess it was just never in our cards. So instead of growing mean like my last name wants me to, I think I'd rather start over somewhere else.

Donnie

He tiptoed down the hall and went outside. The keys were still swing-ing in the truck's ignition when he climbed inside. Donald's face no longer pained him. The tightness in his chest had unfurled. He was ready to start again.

He turned the key and twisted the radio dial until a station came in without static. *Out into the morning light where the sky is all ablaze, this looks like the first of better days.* Donald tapped to the rhythm on the steering wheel with his thumb. When the song was over, and a commercial for a sale at the H-E-B came on, he reached under the seat. His fingers gripped the cool metal. He brought up the revolver and laid it on his leg. *Looks like the first of better days.* He gripped the gun and pulled the hammer, and winced only when the barrel rested against his cracked tooth.

11

Shirley had always known she was cursed.

But in the kindest mercy her life had shown her, she wasn't the one to find Donald. Of course, she had reason to avoid the truck, to stop herself from peeking through the blinds, after she'd heard the gunshot rumble through the neighborhood. She was sitting in tepid bathwater when she heard it crack. When she stepped from the tub an hour later, she saw the note displayed on her side of the bed. She folded it and put it in the nightstand drawer without reading it. She prayed the bullet had found Dwayne's insides, but when his drunken snores continued to fill the house she could have known. She could have guessed what the note said also. She knew what happened, if only her mind had let her.

It was Dwayne that found their son. He was showered and dressed early and bore no scars of the drunken night before, in that uncanny way alcoholics manage. Shirley lay awake on the bed while he dressed but she was easy enough to ignore. Especially since she'd stopped talking. The morning was humid and the truck's windshield held a thin veil of dew, so it wasn't until Dwayne opened the truck door that he found him. Without knowing what to do, he closed the door and walked away. He walked all the way downtown and went into the diner. It was the only place open. He sat at the counter, and when the waitress asked if he wanted coffee, he told her. "Donald shot himself," he said placidly. The waitress called the police who took him back home. There, they removed Donald from the truck, placed the gun in an official-looking bag, and took photographs of the cab. They were careful to document each of the innumerable specks of blood, the collections of other matter.

Shirley watched from the front door. In some miasmic and half-blind way, she saw them carry Donald's body like a sack of hog feed. She watched Dwayne stand around and answer their questions and hand over his identification like he had no hand in driving their son to do what he'd done.

She was incensed at the sight of her husband. But more than anything, she was furious with Donald. She fumed that he'd done something to leave behind what he saw as an unwelcome world. Hadn't her life been more miserable? Haven't her years shown her how vile the world can really be? Donald knew nothing about a hateful world, she thought. Most of all, she hated Donald for doing what she could never summon the courage to do.

12

John had fallen asleep on Alma's sofa. The television was babbling softly when he woke up. He and Alma had talked for hours last night until he said he was exhausted. "We can talk about it until I'm out of time, but it won't change a thing," he said finally. "I'd rather we not talk about it anymore." Then he stretched out on the couch to watch the Detroit Lions game and fell asleep watching the sky blue jerseys crisscrossing the astroturf.

The house was quiet that morning. He dumped the dregs of coffee from the day before and brewed another pot. Opening the fridge, he was awestruck by the amount of groceries inside. He was heaping ingredients into his arms to make an omelet when he heard a chair pull from the table.

"Morning John. Are you making me breakfast?"

"Sure," he checked the groceries piled on his arm. "As long as you want a bacon, cheese, tomato, green pepper, and hot sauce omelet."

Alma laughed. "Why don't you make one of those for Martín. That'd give me heartburn until next Thanksgiving."

Alma watched him work over the stove. He was distracted and continually overwhelmed. But eventually, he rolled a hunk of egg and produce from the pan that, in some ways, resembled an omelet.

"How did you sleep?" John asked when he began making another.

"I didn't, really. This waiting makes me too nervous. I hate waiting."

John turned, his eyebrows high. "Is that why you made me drive you out to the state park the first night I came for dinner? Because you hate waiting?"

Alma raised her coffee mug to her lips to hide a smile. "I was the one that said no more until after the trial, wasn't I?"

"Mmmm," John nodded triumphantly. "I guess I know why you're so anxious then."

13

By the afternoon, John, Alma, and Martín were crammed together on the sofa to watch television. They watched vaguely, each lost in their own minds.

Alma was worried if the jury didn't come to a decision in the next few hours, the judge would allow them to disperse for the weekend and the prickling anxiety lapping against her would carry through to Monday. John was thinking of Merle. A dog on the show Martín was watching had the same bouncing trot Merle had. And Martín was wondering how long it would be until they moved again. No matter what the jury decided, Uvalde had shown them they were no longer welcome. If they ever were. Staying in the town would drown them in the slow-rising tides of resentment — either theirs or the town's.

As one episode turned to another, then a different show began, they continued to swirl in their thoughts, wading into waters that grew deeper by the hour. The brisk afternoon began burning into early evening. Martín was sleeping fitfully, and John had plucked a novel from a bookshelf and was flipping through it. Alma was about to make dinner when the phone rang. The call lasted less than a minute.

"That was Mr. Frazier," she said. "The jury's ready. They're reading the verdict at 5:00."

Alma disappeared into her bedroom to change while John paced around the house. Martín had slept through the phone ringing so John let him sleep. In the kitchen, John picked through a small bowl of candy and mints. He unwrapped a caramel and slipped it in his mouth but the syrupy sweetness coating his tongue turned his stomach. He was leaning over the sink to spit the candy out and calm the waves of nausea when Alma came behind him. "Martín is changing his shirt then we can head over," she said.

The curbs surrounding the courthouse were clogged with parked cars. They had to park a few blocks away and walk. The fresh air suited John's lungs and Alma's nervous stomach. Inside, people milled around the hallways in anxious conversations. John grabbed Alma's

THE DEVIL IN THESE HILLS

hand, Alma grabbed Martín's, and they fought toward the courtroom door.

"Gallery's full," the bailiff said when they reached the door.

Alma stepped forward. "This is my son's verdict."

The bailiff looked them over before opening the door. The only empty seats remaining in the entire gallery were behind the defendant's table, the judge's plush chair, and the rows of juror's seats. The three of them crowded into the wooden bench and waited, with shaking hands, for Gabriel's fate.

Gabriel was led in, his face swollen and scabbed, and his arm still tied in a sling. Even through the angry inflammation covering half of his face, they could see how much weight he'd lost, how sunken and despondent his eyes had become. His attorney turned to them. "I was telling Gabriel this earlier," he said. "People always say if the jury doesn't look at us, it means they voted guilty. But I don't buy that. We'll know when they read it and not a second sooner."

John and Alma exchanged glances. They'd never heard that before but now they watched each juror's eyes as they walked in. Only one of them so much as glanced at Gabriel.

The judge thanked the jurors for their time and civility. He asked for the sealed verdict and commanded Gabriel to stand. "I will accept no outbursts while or after the verdict is read. Bailiffs are standing by and any outbursts will be met with charges for contempt of my court. This is your warning." He gave Gabriel a long stare before unfolding the sheet and reading over it.

"We the jury," he read, "unanimously find the defendant, Gabriel Jiménez, not guilty of murder in the first degree."

John felt as if he was floating from the bench. Alma crumpled into him, keeping him grounded, and sobbed into the fabric of his shirt.

Martín nodded slowly. Gabriel waited patiently for the bailiff to remove the shackles around his ankles. In minutes, he was between Alma and Martín. Where he belonged.

RETRIBUTION

Javelina, knocking at my door.
Javelina, coming back for more.

Red Shahan

1

DRIVING TO THE COURTHOUSE, the three of them had fit comfortably across the bench seat of John's pickup truck. But on the drive home, they were crammed into the truck cab. It was a small inconvenience that, John thought, showed how deeply their hopelessness had seeped. They'd made no preparations for Gabriel's homecoming, perhaps to avoid a jinx or swells of optimism that would only make the following days more difficult. None of them fully expected Gabriel to be allowed to walk from the courthouse, but they'd kept their doubts mostly silent and took each other's quiet as optimism. But as he climbed into the truck and sat hunched on Alma's lap, there was hardly a thing on the earth that seemed more natural.

"We haven't done this in a long time," Alma said with a wide smile.

The bumps bothered Gabriel's collarbone but he didn't complain. He didn't feel he had the right. He held onto the jittering anxiety and his wary passivity in silence. Why had he thought those feelings would just disappear after the verdict? It would be years until they began to fade from him in the slightest.

"What would you like for dinner?" John asked him. "Anything you want."

Gabriel shrugged. He hadn't made a decision for himself in months. His meals were slopped onto trays and given to him. His hours were scheduled by someone in the statehouse. Showers and clothing were charity rather than basics. "I don't know," he said. "I haven't really thought about it."

"Well, what have you been hungry for?" John asked.

In truth, he hadn't been hungry for months either. The things he craved — transparency, normalcy, the halcyon years of his hard up but happy childhood which seemed to drip away like blood on the tip of that knife — filled him much like rat poison, growing solid and leaden in his stomach. The absence was not an empty space but, rather, a festering burden.

Finally, he said, "I could eat a Whataburger."

"Now that's a choice!" John laughed and drove them away from the courthouse.

John and Alma sat at a booth along the window while the sun began to set and the boys shoveled french fries and burgers. Alma watched her sons with an untiring smile. John went back to the counter after they'd collected a pile of spent wrappers in front of them and ordered another burger. He handed it to Gabriel. "This'll go well with the beer we'll have tonight," he said.

"John!" Alma scolded. "He's not drinking beer tonight."

"If tonight isn't occasion enough to have some beer then what is? Just one for the Jiménez boys. It won't do any harm." He turned to the brothers. "Will it?"

"I think it's a good idea," Martín shrugged. "Mom could have one too."

John laughed. "Now *that* is a hell of an idea! Let's get outta here before your mom can say she's too tired to join us."

Back in the truck, Alma leaned toward John and said, "Joke's on you. I don't have any beer at home."

"Not a problem. I've got some at mine. I'll pick it up on the way." He tapped his boot to the radio. "Hope Budweiser's okay with you guys. Not sure what you usually drink," he smirked.

Turning onto John's street, he saw a car parked by his driveway. He eyed it as they neared and parked behind it, his headlights lighting the interior and casting a shadow around the man that sat behind the wheel.

"Stay here," John said and climbed from the truck. He walked between their bumpers and went to the curb. Standing next to the car he saw — with only some relief — it was a patrol car. The officer was already climbing out. He was older than John, with scraggly and unruly eyebrows under his cowboy hat.

"You live here?" he asked.

"I do," John said.

"Are the Jiménez's with you?"

John stared. "Why?"

"We went to the Jiménez house but nobody was home. Someone suggested checking here."

"Why are you looking for them?"

"There's a—" the cop hesitated, "*group* downtown. Near the courthouse right now, but we wanted to be cautious and let them know."

John rubbed his chin. "I take it they're not happy about the verdict?"

The officer nodded.

"And now there's a mob in town?"

"I wouldn't say it's a mob. But we wanted to make sure the family was aware so they could be safe."

"Okay," John sighed. "What should they do? Is it safe to stay here? At my place?"

"Only took me a couple minutes to find you here," the cop said. "Off the record, my advice would be to get them out of town for a day or two."

John nodded.

"Might not be a bad idea for you to stay with them too."

He nodded again. "Will you have someone parked outside their house?"

"The Jiménez house? I don't think so. We don't have the manpower, but I'll keep an eye out."

"Okay, thanks. I appreciate that."

The officer nodded and climbed back inside the patrol car. He drove toward downtown, where a faction of men were riling each other like howling dogs.

John got into the truck and saw Martín had cracked open the passenger window. The brothers were staring at the dashboard. Alma looked at John with silent unease.

"I guess you guys heard that?"

"Enough of it," Martín said.

John drove west. There was hardly a word spoken until they entered Eagle Pass. Gabriel was balanced half on his mother's lap. His shoulder was smarting. To fit inside the truck cab he'd been ducking his head for over an hour and his neck was getting stiff. But finally, a blaring sign for the Royal Ridge Motel came into view.

John paid for two rooms but Alma insisted they stay together. The room was cool and quiet. The air conditioner in the window buzzed like a neon light. Martín flicked on the television but stretched out in bed when every channel was covered with static. The air conditioner, the static, the steady thrum of traffic outside all lulled them into an easier sleep than they'd felt in months. John was the last one awake and he thought then that, all things told, the day could have gone worse.

2

Under dim halogen streetlights, a crowd pulsed in Uvalde's town square. Kershaws stippled the congregation like chickweed — invasive and paltry, but too pervasive to ignore. As some among the mob shouted for the boy — that liberated killer — to be sent back to Mexico, Gabriel slept less than a mile from the Rio Grande and the illusory partition it represented.

3

With light beginning to stream through the motel room drapes, John took the phone and stretched the cord into the bathroom, and closed the door behind him. He turned on the shower, sat on the toilet, and dialed the Uvalde sheriff's department.

"This is John Ellis," he said. "I'm staying out of town with the Jiménez family, and I wanted to see what things are like there."

"As in Gabriel Jiménez?" the woman asked.

"Yeah. Just wondering if we should stay here another day or if Uvalde's quieter today."

"Well," the officer thought. "It's still early, but I'd imagine that crowd is still by the courthouse. I can't guarantee it would be safe for you yet. But maybe check back tomorrow."

"Okay."

"Also," the officer hesitated. "I'm telling you this in confidence. But Dwayne Kershaw's youngest boy killed himself the other day. Thanksgiving day."

John sat on the edge of the toilet seat and set his jaw. "Bobby Kershaw's brother?"

"That's the one."

"Jesus Christ," John muttered.

"Just figured you all should know."

"Yeah," he sighed. "Thanks. If anything changes, give me a call. I'm at the Royal Ridge in Eagle Pass. Room 117."

"You got it."

John hung up and set the phone on the bathroom floor. He stripped and climbed into the shower. He cranked the handle until the water scalded. *Bobby's brother. Shirley's son,* he thought. *What a fucking mess.*

4

Dwayne and Shirley were at the funeral home making arrangements when the verdict was read. Dwayne moseyed through a room filled with coffins. He ran his dirty hands over their high-gloss crowns and squeezed the padded interiors as if he was picking discount furniture. Finally, he turned to the funeral director and said, "The green one. That was his favorite color."

Blue, Shirley would have said if her grief had allowed. *His favorite color was blue.* But she hadn't spoken a word since Dwayne laid a hand on her and her silence only grew heavier, more haunting, after

Donald shot himself. She'd wondered for years how her mother could withdraw so deeply within herself when tragedy struck her family, but she understood then — when she felt loathing in her husband's hands, and when he so easily turned that hatred onto his own son — how easy it is to disappear. To find a rare place of refuge only within her delusions, which were insignificant by any measure yet unable to be spoken.

Driving from the funeral home, they saw a small gathering in front of the courthouse. Dwayne parked and disappeared into the crowd. "What's going on?" he asked someone. "The hell's everybody standing around for?"

"The fucking spick," a man grunted. "He got away with it. Can you believe that shit?"

Dwayne searched the growing swarm for a familiar face until he found the friend that had tailed Shirley to Hondo. "Dwayne!" the friend called. "Been looking for you! Were you in there?" he nodded toward the courthouse.

Dwayne shook his head. "But I heard."

"Ain't no fucking thing as justice anymore."

"Donald shot himself," Dwayne said simply. "Took my pistol and put it between his teeth."

"The fuck are you talking about, Dwayne?" Then realizing it wasn't a joke, he lowered his head gravely and loosened the corners of his mouth. "When?" he asked softly.

"Thanksgiving. After I came back from your place, I guess."

"Goddamn," he sighed.

They stood in silence, feet apart, not knowing what else to do. In a different life, they may have clapped each other on the back, or put an arm around another, or even embraced. Instead, they did what they've always done. What was easiest. They turned their indignations in a different direction. Like rising bile, it was easier for them to vomit their ire onto someone else rather than taste it on their own tongues.

So they whipped the crowd from an unfastened faction of dissenting voices to a mob of frothing agitators. Anyone who was there only to hear the verdict, or to gossip about its meaning, quietly backed away from the crowd as afternoon turned to evening.

They swelled and began to boil over in the grassy square at the center of Uvalde, under the long shadow of the courthouse. They grouped and fueled each other's vitriol. Behind them was the dilapidated Uvalde Opera House, and at its corner, mismatched and stuck to the building like a leech, was the former office of John Nance Garner.

Stories were often passed through town that he haunted the office. Perhaps his ghost was watching as the horde swelled and began moving toward the courthouse. It would have offered an unobstructed view of the men grabbing branches and rocks, and throwing them at courthouse windows; of the red-faced men screaming for justice; of others promising it by their own means.

5

"Were you calling one of those hotline girls in there?" Alma asked with half a smile when John came out of the bathroom. A towel was wrapped around his waist and the phone hung lazily from one hand.

He forced a smile. Gabriel and Martín were sitting up in bed with groggy eyes. "You guys hungry?" he asked.

Gabriel shrugged. "Those burgers didn't sit too great with me last night."

Martín waved a hand in front of his nose. "That's for damn sure!"

"Martín!" Alma scolded.

"Guess it's a good thing we didn't drink that case of beer then."

"Yeah, good thing," Alma said. "I could use a coffee."

"I'll find some coffee then," John nodded. He went back to the bathroom and dressed in yesterday's clothes. "I'll be back in a few minutes. Lock the door behind me," he said and walked into the motel parking lot. He went to the front desk and asked the woman where he could find coffee and donuts.

She lifted a fat finger to John's left. "Two blocks that way."

John balanced a dozen donuts and two paper cups of scalding coffee on the walk back to the motel. He knocked on room 117's door with the toe of his boot and heard a breath catch inside. "It's John!" he called through the door and heard the lock unlatch. "Sorry," he said, setting the coffees on the nightstand. "My hands were full. Didn't mean to scare you guys."

"The police called. From Uvalde," Alma said quietly. "They were looking for you."

"What did they say?"

"Said the group from last night is a few Kershaws and a couple of their buddies sitting around the park now."

"That's good news, I guess. Do you want to head back home then?"

Alma looked to the boys, deferring the decision to Gabriel.

Gabriel chewed the inside of his lip. "I don't know," he said. "I didn't really think I'd be able to choose where I could go, you know?"

"Gabe," Alma reached for his hand.

"You really didn't think you'd get out?" Martín asked.

Gabriel shrugged. "I wasn't counting on having any good luck after all the bad."

"Maybe things are looking up then," John offered.

"I don't know. But I don't think I want to go back there."

"To Uvalde?"

Gabriel nodded. "It never felt much like home. I can't imagine it will now... After everything."

Alma squeezed Gabriel's hand but dropped her gaze. "My job is in Uvalde. And we have a lease on the house. I wish it was as easy as just not going back."

"Then it is," Gabriel looked at her. "Then it *is* that easy. We moved how many other times? I'd rather be the new kid at another school than the kid that killed someone."

The traffic outside continued flying past. "I think he's right," Martín said finally. "We don't want to be in Uvalde anymore and nobody wants us there either."

Alma sighed. "I don't know how I could make that work. I'm sorry boys."

"Can we talk for a second?" John cut in. "Outside?"

Sitting in John's truck, parked outside of their room, John said, "We can figure this out."

"I don't know," Alma said. "I don't know if things will just work out for us. Not to mention I feel like we'd be running away. Like it's teaching my boys that they can just drive away from their problems. I don't want them to think it's okay to give up."

"Give up? This whole thing is happening because those two wouldn't give up! It's not running away either. That town's done nothing but cut you and then pick at the scabs they made. My advice would be to get the hell out of Uvalde and make sure Martín and

Gabriel know it's not with your tail between your legs."

"I know. But what about the house? We still have half of the lease left. Where would we go?"

John tapped the steering wheel. "We can call the landlord. Tell him that as long as you're living there, the Kershaws will want to burn it down, so it's better to just let you leave."

"Really?"

"Sure," John shrugged. "Why not? Where do you think you want to go? Back to Fort Worth?"

"I don't think so. Might as well go somewhere nobody's heard of us."

John thought about places he'd driven through, the moss green highway signs with town names he'd never heard before. The highways that snaked through jagged bluffs and undulating hillsides, heavenly mountains and lifeless plains that connected one rodeo town to another. "I stayed in a really nice town a year or two ago when I was driving with my brother for the rodeo. Small city called Fort Collins. Pretty far north from here in Colorado."

"What's it like there? I've never been to Colorado."

"It's beautiful. Honestly. Under the Rocky Mountains. Even has a good college in town. The people were some of the nicest I'd met that summer."

"Okay," Alma said before she could convince herself otherwise. "Fort Collins then. Easy as that, I guess."

"If you and the boys are okay here for another day or two, I can get your stuff boxed up and we can hit the road."

"That soon?"

"If you're not turning back then you might as well move on."

"You're right. It'll be better for everyone that way. Let's go tell the boys."

John was reaching for the door handle when Alma put a hand on his elbow.

"John," she said shyly. "What about us?"

The truck door hung open and filled the cab with humid morning air. The wind was heavy. A storm was rolling in.

"I don't know." It took him a minute before he worked up the gall but eventually, he said, "I think you've been through enough. You don't need to be around me at the end."

Alma shook her head. "I want you around. I want to be with you. Until... then."

"No, Alma. I'm not doing that. I don't need you to see me like that. You sure don't need to see it. I don't want you taking care of me if I can't do it myself. You deserve better than that. You deserved better than all this shit too, but you've got a choice in this. I'll be okay. I'm glad I had the chance to help you and the boys while I could. But you don't owe me a thing."

Heavy tears streamed down Alma's cheeks. She wiped them impatiently, but their paths filled in with every blink. "I'm not leaving you," she said. "So if you're staying in Uvalde then we are too."

"You're being selfish now."

"Me?" Alma cried. "Don't tell me I'm the selfish one! You're telling me to drive off and leave you alone to die! All because you don't want someone to help you? Is that really what you want your life to come down to? Give your pride a break! If it's the last thing you do, let someone help you."

John stared through the windshield, watching the motel room curtains ripple. "The doctor told me how it's going to be. At the end. He said 'Until you get to heaven, it's going to feel like hell.'" He held in a cough. "I don't want us to have a year or two together if half of it's going to be like that."

"Well," Alma sniffed until she found her resolve. "We could either have those days together, or we won't and wish we did. And I want them to be with you. Even the hard ones."

John hesitated. "Let me think about it. I'll pack up your place and I'll think about it."

Alma leaned across the bench seat and kissed John's stubbly cheek. "You know I love you, John Ellis," she held a hand to his chest. "Just don't tell your pride."

6

By the next afternoon, most of them had grown tired of their own anger. The courthouse offered them no response. It seemed to them justice was deaf and ill-intentioned as well as blind. It was a beautiful Saturday, and as much as those men despised their brown-skinned neighbors, lawns needed cutting, dogs were in need letting out, and the Texas Longhorns would be on ABC protecting their undefeated season in a few hours. So the mob fizzled as steadily as it had grown.

Dwayne, his friend, and a few of their neighbors were sitting under a patch of trees, their backs leaning heavily on the trunks. Someone had brought them a case of beer earlier and it disappeared as quickly as the morning's dew.

"We could burn those wetbacks' house down," one of them offered half-heartedly.

"Yeah!" another chimed in. "Teach those fuckers a lesson."

"Since those goddamn jurors won't!" someone agreed. But none of them attempted to so much as stand.

Eventually, Dwayne got up and brushed the front of his jeans. "I gotta get home," he said. "Donald's funeral is Monday if you feel like it."

The men dropped their eyes dutifully. It was as much as they could manage in the way of sympathy. Dwayne walked to where he'd parked the truck the day before. It was still there but Shirley was gone. She must have slipped from the seat and walked home. He was almost surprised she hadn't stayed in the truck waiting for Dwayne to tell her what to do.

After Dwayne was gone, the rest of the men dispersed within an hour. The day was already getting warmer, and tomorrow was Sunday. They silently reasoned they couldn't have continued their seething riot through the Sabbath. But more likely, it was that their anger seemed less powerful when it didn't anger others. They were candles burning on a gasoline-soaked floor, but their heat had burnt the wick to ash without lighting another flame. They'd attempted through the night to pass their anger like a virus, but they'd only managed to sweat out their own fevers.

7

Donald's gleaming coffin was on display in the United Methodist Church on Monday morning. The mortician tried, but in the end, the casket was closed. Inside, Donald wore the same suit he had worn to Bobby's funeral. The opalescent green coffin shimmered against the mahogany altar as the line of mourners filed through. The lines were massive compared to Bobby's calling hours. Word of what happened had traveled through the streets of Uvalde like a piece of litter. A mother had lost both of her sons in the same year.

Shirley stood next to Dwayne and accepted the condolences offered to her. She took their words and hugs, their solemn faces and grasping hands, and folded them up, placing them back inside the envelope, and putting them in a drawer like a stack of greeting cards. Without the heart to throw them away but unsure what else to do, they would sit forgotten until they vanished.

She had thought about running off before the funeral. For close to twenty years, she'd thought about it. Each time Dwayne's hands found her in ways she dreaded, in ways that left marks, she thought about it. But she would find a reason to stay until the next morning — the laundry needed hanging, Donnie needed a ride to school, the strawberries on the counter would get soft if she didn't use them soon. And by the next morning, leaving seemed too arduous to stand. She convinced herself that staying wasn't apathy. That it wasn't enabling the cruelties of her life. Excuses were made, but only when warranted. If leaving was simple, so righteous, why would it feel so perilous?

Staying was her choice. It was *a* choice. She was sure of it. It may be the only decision she'd made for herself, but she wasn't being kept captive. She'd driven to Hondo and danced with John, but chose to return home. She could have run away then. But she came home each night because she had no reason to leave. Or that's what she thought. And thinking otherwise would have fractured her like kindling under a boot.

Where would she go anyway? She'd dreamt for years about that oasis up the road. *That fucking Utopia.* She could vanish from Dwayne's

271

life and spend her silent days there. The unwonted surroundings, the liberation, could give voice to her suffering. She'd gone as far as driving through the place to get a taste of it. And it turned out Utopia tasted as corrosive as poison. Or maybe it was bitter like medicine.

She almost left after Bobby was killed. She thought about running off with that cowboy from Hondo. Dwayne slapped the indifference from her for a while. And without Donald, she hardly had cause to live, no less stay. But her boss was expecting her back at the grocery store next week, and she'd hate to lose that job after all the years she'd worked there.

Driving that hideous yellow truck around the Texas Hill Country was as close as she'd edge toward leaving. The highway didn't end where she'd turned the truck around those nights. She could have followed it for miles, for days, if she wanted. The razor's edge of the highway dropping away from the horizon was like the edge of the limestone bluff she dreamt of climbing. Either turn around and return to the life that was cursed from the start, or fall off the horizon into the baptismal waters of beginning.

Shirley hated her husband, but she needed him. Not for anything he did, or the solace he had once provided. She needed Dwayne because she hated him. He was prey for the shotgun blasts of her hapless life. She could blame him for her sons' deaths and wash her hands clean of the guilt owed to her. Liability is sticky and leaves a residue on every hand it touches. But hate is easier to carry; it smooths everything over like a mold. Shirley hated her husband more than she'd ever loved anything, and that was what made her stay. Because in despising him, she could ignore the ways she hated herself.

8

A loaded U-Haul cut across Uvalde late Monday morning. John Ellis's truck was in tow. A duffel bag stuffed with some of his clothes and toiletries was thrown on top of the Jiménez's boxed belongings. He was glad to drive from the town, even though he'd be back in a few weeks to pack the rest of his things and stomp a FOR SALE sign into his front yard.

Martín sat next to him on the U-Haul's bench seat, bumping through the streets for the last time. He was happy to help, to keep his hands busy and his mind clear. He could feel the town working itself from him in rivulets of sweat. Uvalde was quiet and if he were unloading the truck and it was his first time there, he might have thought it was a kind and pleasant place.

Bells chimed above the Methodist church. John counted five tolls and checked the dashboard clock. It wasn't 11:00 yet, and he knew what the bells were signaling. Donald Kershaw's funeral had just begun.

"Do they always ring like that on a Monday?" Martín asked from the passenger seat.

"No," John said. "Not always."

Donald's suicide weighed heavy on John, but it was only one of the many jagged thoughts in his head. As they always did, they would rub against each other and their edges would wear smooth. He would not tell Alma or the boys about Donald's suicide. If they eventually found out, so be it. But he refused to have their memory of it be in his voice.

Gabriel was already having nightmares without that knowledge. On his first night out of jail, he was calmed by exhaustion. But after a day of rest, his mind began scrambling to make sense of it all. He'd wake up with his dark hair stamped to his sweaty forehead and his eyes searching the room. Alma would give him questioning looks while Martín was distracted by the TV, but Gabriel didn't want to talk about it. He said his collarbone was hurting, but they knew his pain was elsewhere.

Gabriel and Martín's playfulness had fallen out of them like pocket change, but their fraternal bond was still abiding. The night before, Gabriel was having another nightmare. John was snoring and their mother was still, so Martín reached his hand out from under the covers and held his brother's shaking arm. He felt guilt over Bobby's death and Gabriel's months in jail, but he was determined to bury the blame in coaxing Gabriel back to himself.

At the outskirts of Uvalde, John rolled the window down. He and Martín took deep breaths of the fall air. For years, John had sworn this town still smelled sweet, a relic of the *guajillo* manufacturing Uvalde was built around. But driving from it that day, he thought the smell wasn't the treacly scent of honey after all. The way it caught the wind and filtered through the mosaic limestone, John thought it was the cloying sweetness of rot.

9

Jess Travis stood in the receiving line, tapping his pant pocket where seventeen cents jingled inside. The old woman in front of him

turned to give him a disapproving look, but he'd been too busy checking his watch to notice. The queue was longer than he'd expected. It
stretched down the side of the chapel, through the bleach-smelling
hallway, and into the lobby. The sun was brilliant in the narthex and
the windows made it sweltering. Jess felt sweat dripping down his
back below his polyester uniform.

He was off that morning but he'd dressed in his prison guard
uniform. His gold nameplate was pinned proudly above his breast
pocket. He wanted Dwayne Kershaw to remember him from Bobby's
funeral. Maybe Dwayne had even heard what he did to that Mexican
kid when he had the chance. *Good thing too,* he might say. *Now that
the little fucker's back on the streets.*

When the line finally dwindled and the metallic casket was in view,
he wiped droplets of sweat from his forehead, smoothed the part of
his hair, and checked his gold nameplate.

He lowered his eyes and shook Shirley's hand gently, offering
hushed sympathy. Jess was surprised by how weary Dwayne looked.
Jess shook his hand and grabbed his shoulder. "Hell of a thing," he
shook his head. "Can hardly make sense of it."

Dwayne nodded.

"You'd think those spicks would've at least had the decency to stay
the night."

Dwayne dropped Jess's hand. "They're gone already?"

Jess nodded and pulled on Dwayne's shoulder. "It's alright though,"
he said in Dwayne's ear. "I heard where they went."

"Where?"

Jess eyed the woman behind him. "Eagle Pass. Hopefully they're
hopping the border back to where they belong." He added a sly smile,
but Dwayne was staring into the holy nothingness of the chapel. Just

when he thought it had passed, the fever that burned inside Dwayne
for months came back with a quaking shiver. The court and its jury
may have supplanted justice, but Dwayne saw a chance to serve it
himself. If a stranger — that sweating prison guard — handing him a
gavel of finality while he stood under a crucifix wasn't a sign from the
Lord, then He never existed.

"You staying for the banquet?"

Jess shrugged.

"You should stay. I'll talk to you then."

He was pushing a pile of potato salad around a paper plate when
Dwayne sat in the folding chair next to him. "Who says they're in
Eagle Pass?" he asked.

"They do," Jess said. "They called the station and said so. Even
gave their room number."

"That so?"

"You calling me a liar?"

Dwayne shoved a finger in his mouth and dug around his teeth.
"How far out is Eagle Pass? Bout an hour?"

Jess shrugged. "Never been, but that's what I'd say."

"You got a truck?"

"Parked outside."

"Good. I'm ready to get the fuck outta here anyway. Let's stop at
my place on the way out."

Jess stood and unclipped his keys from his belt loop. "Your trailer
isn't on the way out of town."

Dwayne faced him and clamped a hand on his arm. "Unless you
got two loaded shotguns in your truck, we're stopping at my place."

"Okay," Jess said, beginning to understand the cost of his admission into the Kershaw ranks.

After backtracking through Uvalde, Dwayne and Jess cut through the alien nihility surrounding Highway 481. Jess's truck strained from the dust and speed, but he coaxed it to ninety miles per hour by the time they crossed the Nueces River. They would be at the Royal Ridge Motel in a half-hour.

10

Near the grassy banks of the Rio Grande, Alma and Gabriel sat against their motel headboards watching The Price is Right. The screen was covered in a flurry of static, but the brightly colored set made it easy enough to play along. Alma was anxious for John and Martín to come back in packed the U-Haul. John still hadn't told them whether he would move to Colorado, only that he would drive them and help them get settled. Alma had turned from John for weeks, only to find it was exactly what she craved. John had shown her family more kindness than she thought they deserved, and she couldn't bear to think of him suffering through his last days alone.

"What would you have done if I didn't get out?" Gabriel asked suddenly.

"Out of where?" Alma asked.

"Out of jail. What would you have done?"

"We would have stayed in Uvalde. Of course we would've. Or wherever you were. We wouldn't have just left you behind."

"What if they said it was still dangerous for you to stay?"

"We would have stayed anyway."

"Even if you couldn't visit me?"

"Gabriel," Alma sighed. "It's no sense in talking about this. You're with us and we're all going to move on together."

"Okay," Gabriel said. "Is Mr. Ellis really coming with us?"

"I asked him to, but he wanted to think about it."

"Okay."

"Do you want him to come with us?"

"Yeah, I guess. He's always been nice to me."

"He has."

"Why?" Gabriel asked. "Why was he good to us?"

"I don't exactly know. I think for him it was the right thing to do. I'd like to think there are still people that think that way."

"Maybe I'll ask him then. We'll need a lot to talk about on the drive."

"John is sick," Alma blurted. She didn't know why it came from her mouth, but it felt good to confide in her trusted son. "I'm not sure if he told you or Martín, but I think you should know."

"I kind of figured it. He got really skinny and he's always coughing."

Alma looked over the gaunt body her son had developed in jail.

"How sick is he?"

"Sick," Alma said. "He could use some kindness for himself now."

Gabriel was falling into an afternoon nap when a truck pulled into a parking spot just outside their motel room. Its massive headlights, fogged orange like setting suns, shone into the windows next to the door. The diesel motor fought itself, exerted from the afternoon sun.

"Mom!" he called to his mother in the bathroom. "John and Martín are back!" She'd told him not to open the door, but Gabriel climbed from the bed and began working on the door chain. He reveled in his freedom to unlatch a door and walk freely across the threshold. To unlock a deadbolt at his choosing, to be in sole possession of his key to something more.

Outside, he heard the truck doors creak open, heard the muted steps coming toward the door. The footsteps stopped and Gabriel heard hushed words from the other side. He was just grabbing the doorknob when Alma came out of the bathroom.

"Gabriel!" she shouted across the room. "Don't open the door!"

11

Dwayne and Jess pulled in front of the motel room. "This is it," Jess said, jutting his chin at the rusted room numbers nailed to the door.

"You sure you heard right?" Dwayne asked while ripping open a box of shotgun shells.

"I heard right!"

"Alright," Dwayne said. "Then let's go."

He tried walking quietly, but his Tony Lama boots sizzled on the blacktop with each step like meat dropped into a scorching pan. He'd been rehearsing it in his head while they drove. He wanted them to be stunned to see his shadow in their doorway. Dwayne wanted their last seconds to be moments of shock and panic. They thought they'd gotten away with killing his sons, but justice could be avoided only as well as his shotgun blasts.

A step from the door, he held up a hand to stop Jess. Through the sheer curtains, he'd seen movement in the room.

"The hell are you waiting for?" Jess whispered.

"Shut the fuck up, would you?"

Dwayne listened to the chain clinking against the door and realized he was holding his breath. When the doorknob rattled, as if someone had grasped it from inside, he raised the shotgun and aimed it at the door, just below the brass room numbers. Dwayne pulled the trigger before the door could open.

The middle of the door exploded into splinters. The mangled door swung open and Dwayne heard a scream inside the room. He stepped over the body crumpled in the doorway. Whatever had been opening the door was now unrecognizable. Its features were reduced to a pile of flesh on the carpet and wallpaper. Dwayne fired again before his eyes could adjust to the dingy motel room. The shotgun clicked empty so he reached into his pocket, stuffed the red wax cartridges in place, and fired again. The blasts thundered until the woman's screams were stifled. He continued after the television screen shattered and left a gaping hole. Dwayne continued reloading and pulling the trigger until the entire motel room was bloodied shrapnel.

By the time it ended, Dwayne's ears were ringing like a dial tone. Jess Travis sat dazed behind the wheel of his truck. He hadn't fired a shot. Dwayne climbed into the truck and dropped his shotgun on the floorboard.

"I'm done," he sat back. "Take me home."

12

It was pouring rain when the truck fled from the Royal Ridge Motel. Droplets collected on the windshield and refracted the blue and red lights of the patrol cars speeding south. They didn't look back to see where the police were headed. Their demons were behind them. Left to wither and rot in a cheap Texas motel room. In the end, everything turned out the way it should. Justice came after all, even if it was in a scattered pile of rubble.

The truck barreled past Utopia going eighty. In Eden, they stopped for gas at a Texaco station. He filled the tank and walked to the pay phone.

"Just checking in," he said. "Don't think I told you where I was headed."

"My god," the woman on the other end gasped. "I've been trying to get a hold of you for hours!"

"Sorry. I've been on the road. Headed north. I'm calling from Eden right now."

"We thought you were dead."

"Dead? We're fine. Totally fine. Just leaving it all behind."

There was silence on the line. Then the woman said, "Two people got shot to hell at the Royal Ridge Motel. An older couple. Probably just passing through on a road trip."

His legs weakened and his shoulder leaned hard against the aluminum pay phone.

"They were in room 107. A couple doors down from you." The

woman from the police station went on. "It was Dwayne Kershaw that did it. Him and a buddy heard you all were there and drove down with shotguns."

"Dway... But we... That's..." he stumbled. He struggled to hold the phone in his fingers. His entire body had gone to static.

"I guess you all were out of there by the time they showed up. Couldn't have missed them by more than a couple of minutes. Seems like they had the wrong room number and just blasted their way through the door and whoever had the bad luck of being in that motel room."

He looked over his shoulder, scanning the Texaco lot. "Where is he now?" he asked.

"I got a call from the sheriff not long ago. I'm the only one left at the station. He said they were barely out of Eagle Pass before the cops were on their tail. Wouldn't be surprised if the whole county heard all those shots, from what they're saying. But they were speeding north out of there — probably back to Uvalde — and a tire blew. Their truck went off the road, got caught in a wire cattle fence, and started flipping. Seatbelts would've saved them but they both got thrown out. Killed them both."

"Jesus," was all he could muster.

"Jesus is right. Three Kershaws dead in less than a year. That poor Shirley. Nobody on this Earth deserves a cursed fate like that."

He climbed back into the truck with a fake smile plastered on his face. Just like with Donald's suicide, John would protect them from the news about Dwayne. They'd been punished enough. He refused to tell them they'd been hunted like varmint.

"Everything okay?" Alma asked.

"Of course! Just let them know we're headed north."

Gabriel looked absently out the window. "Getting outta there," he said to himself.

Near Lubbock, Gabriel said, "Why did you decide to help us?"

"Because you needed help," John said.

"Yeah, but—"

"It's that easy," John cut him off. "You needed help, so I did what I could."

"Why were you the only one that helped?"

"Oh, I don't think I was," John said. "I think there were a lot of people that helped in ways you never realized."

"Like what?"

"That, I can't say. But being a good person is quieter than being mean. Just because kindness gets drowned out by screams and shouts doesn't mean it's not there. Kindness is quiet, but it's always there. If you listen closely."

"Yeah."

"My mom used to say the only thing more contagious than hate is kindness."

Gabriel stared through the window and watched the Hill Country flatten. "I'm listening for it," he said gently.

13

John saw the sign for the town of Abernathy and turned off the highway. The streets weren't familiar but he was certain he could find it.

"What are we doing?" Alma asked.

"I want to show you something," John smiled. Under the blinking stoplight, he saw the brick box just off the road. He pulled the U-Haul into the church parking lot and climbed from the truck, beckoning the rest of them to follow.

They stood on the sidewalk and stared through the glass. "What is it?" Martín asked.

"It's Jesus!" John said. "Jesus In A Box! I passed it last summer driving back from visiting my brother and thought it was the weirdest goddamn thing I've ever seen. I had to see it again just to make sure it was real."

"You shouldn't swear while Jesus is staring at you," Alma warned.

"Better than what happened the first time I saw it," John laughed. "I doubt He can hear me through this glass anyway." He tapped the window and turned to the brothers. "What do you think?" he asked.

Martín shrugged. "Weird is right."

A few hours later, after the rumbling of the highway had lulled Martín to sleep, Gabriel turned from the window. "Why was He in there?" he asked.

"Who?"

"That Jesus thing. Why was He in there?"

John shrugged. "Just for tourists or people like us passing through, I guess."

"No, I mean like why would anybody believe Jesus would be in a box in the middle of nowhere?"

"I don't think anybody really believes it." But after a few miles, he said, "I guess it's not too hard to believe though. We're kind of like that. We could be anywhere. Leave everything behind any time we wanted to. Go anywhere we want. But we stay around and stick to the things we know. Some people only know what they were born into and have no idea what they don't know. Even if we hate it, we know it, and I guess hating things is easier than getting to know new ones.

"Did you ever notice how a horse could be hitched to nothing and he'll stay right where he is? As long as it takes until his rider comes back, he'll be standing right there. I think if we were any smarter than that, we'd try to bolt. Even knowing the rope was around our necks. We either choke ourselves or get away. But we're not smarter, and we're definitely not much braver. We're afraid to go a step too far. One step too far from what we know and the rope starts getting tighter around our throats. But maybe we're most afraid the rope will just drag behind us like it was never hitched in the first place. We sit around and wait for someone to pull the reins and tell us it's okay to move on. And before we realize any different, we've wasted a whole pile of time standing around, walking in circles over the same patch of ground."

Martín had woken up and was listening. Alma held Gabriel's hand in her lap.

"Sometimes the rope is a rein. But I guess for other people it might as well be tied in a hangman's knot. Either way, we're getting away from that dead patch of grass at seventy miles an hour."

Epilogue:
Out Among the Stars

How many travelers grow weary
bearing both their burdens and their scars?
Don't you think they'd love to start all over,
and fly like eagles out among the stars?

Adam Mitchell

1

NORTH OF AMARILLO, where streams and dried ghosts of flood plain tributaries crisscrossed, where the Texas landscape began to contort into its arid neighbor New Mexico, green vegetation was reduced to scattered splotches. Low to the ground and sprawling, like it wanted to remain unseen; an ivy with no lattice or terrain to climb. Its false-lush verdancy was stippled by ethereally white flowers shaped like a phonograph horn. As if they were bells of a bugle and their purity would call like Gabriel's blessed horn to ward off demons crossing the frontier into the Hill Country.

"I love those flowers. They're beautiful," Alma said, watching another drove of the plant through the U-Haul window. "I've seen them before but not that many. They're everywhere."

John sat forward and looked across the truck cab, out of the passenger window. "Oh, that? The state park outside Uvalde was covered with them. All over near the Frio."

"What is it?" Gabriel asked.

"Just jimsonweed," John said. "Grows like a weed anywhere it can. Looks nice from here but those leaves will poke you pretty good."

"They're poisonous too, aren't they?" Alma asked. "I heard people used to make tea out of it but it can kill you."

"Wouldn't surprise me."

"My parents called it devil's snare."

"I've heard that. Feels like a snare if your jeans get caught on those thorns."

"Does it grow in Colorado?" Gabriel asked.

"Maybe," John said. "But not like that." He watched Gabriel and Martín's curious eyes studying the horizon, then looked to Alma who was already smiling at him. "No devil in those hills."

2

SHIRLEY WAS SILENT when the officer knocked on the trailer door and told her Dwayne had died in a rollover wreck. Her face was still when he told her about the elderly couple he'd murdered in Eagle Pass. She closed the door behind him and sat with her back to it and let her shaking breaths echo through the empty house, realizing there was no one to ask if she was alright.

The next afternoon, she hung up on the coroner's office when they called and asked what she'd like to do with the body. She didn't want him lying next to her sons but she didn't know where else he could go. She'd let them decide. Let them bury him in the dry, unwelcoming dirt.

Shirley took the yellow truck on a drive north on Route 83 to the state park. She left the keys on the dashboard and walked the bank of the Frio River. Her foot still hurt, even months later, but she trekked to the top of the limestone bluff she'd stared at after Bobby's death. Each stab to her heel was a penance she paid to the demons she carried. She hiked through the underbrush and bracken until the only thing under her aching feet was the last feet of land. Shirley didn't need time to consider what she would do. She'd been thinking about it since she was young. Whether her feet carried her backward — down the steep trail and back to the truck — or forward to the lightness of the fall, she was making a decision, and decisions had plagued her from the moment she was born. Either direction promised a new beginning. The stabbing in her foot would remain, but the rest of her pain would fall away. With that step, she felt the leaden burdens of her life fall away. New skin took the place of the scars she did nothing to earn. She'd always known she was cursed but for the first time, she felt satisfied.

3

FORT COLLINS WELCOMED THEM with a blizzard. Almost a foot of snow fell the day they pulled the U-Haul in front of their new apartment. Gabriel and Martín climbed from the truck and high-stepped through the drifted mounds. They wore sweatshirts and jeans, white cotton tube socks and Converse sneakers. They'd never owned a winter jacket. Gabriel drew a finger over its surface like he was afraid it would poison him.

"It doesn't feel that cold," he said and put his palm down into the snow. "Try it, Martín."

Martín, as if he were checking a hot pan, put the back of his hand on the snow. Then he pinched some between his fingers, pulled some into his palm, and watched it melt. "How do you make a snowball?"

he asked John.

"Just mush it together."

"With my hand?" he asked incredulously.

"What else would you use?"

Alma laughed and hooked her arm in John's. "You've seen snow before, right?"

"Yeah, I've been pretty far north with my brother. Drove through places in Wyoming that had more snow than I ever knew existed. But I've never seen it falling like this. Have you?"

Alma pulled her cardigan around her and crossed her arms. "I honestly don't remember," she said. "I'd like to think I did when I was a kid, but I can't remember it."

"Well," John held his hands out. "Here it is. A blizzard, no less! Pretty crazy, isn't it?"

"Yeah," she watched her sons carefully forming snowballs with their bare hands, then rifling them at each other. "It's been a year for *pretty crazy.*"

B Y THE NEW YEAR, the boys had mostly lost interest in the snow. Even the mountains, in all their resplendence, had become a part of their landscapes. But they were still not accustomed to the air and the clean brightness of it. Each lungful was as clear and refreshing as a dipper of spring water. John treasured it the most. He could breathe easier than he had in a year, and his coughing seemed to be less violent and less often. He would often leave the apartment he shared with Alma and the boys and go for long walks through the town. John got to know Fort Collins on those walks. He memorized the mountain ridges and their white caps, learned neighbors' names, and found shortcuts home when breathing became too difficult.

It was a Tuesday evening. A school bus would be dropping Gabriel and Martín off in front of the apartment complex within the hour. Alma had found a job as a secretary for a podiatrist in Fort Collins and she would be home soon also. John strolled the edges of Colorado State's campus. It was a beautiful place that reminded him of his time in college. He would often sit on a stone bench overlooking a wide walkway lined with ancient trees, and watch the students mill around the grass oval. But that day, he didn't have time to sit and rest.

He walked to a florist, where a woman helped him pick a bouquet of flowers. He flipped through a stack of cards. *I am so happy I found you,* the one he picked said. *HAPPY VALENTINE'S DAY.*

John carried the flowers dutifully and hoped to have them on the table by the time Alma was home. But when he opened the apartment door, they were already waiting for him. Gabriel, Martín, and Alma were standing around the kitchen table, their faces aglow. On the table in front of them was a cake, a line of candles flickering atop it. They beamed as they sang *Happy Birthday*.

"How did you know?" John hugged each of them.

"You told us!" Gabriel grinned. "On the first day of school. You said you were born on Valentine's Day in Valentine. The Cupid Baby!"

"That's right," John laughed. "I did say that."

"How come you never told me you were called The Cupid Baby?" Alma raised an eyebrow.

"Cause I'm the Cupid Man now," he winked. "Now let's eat that cake."

They had pizza delivered and ate the cake down to crumbs. The Winter Olympics in Sarajevo were on television. John and the boys cheered and hollered each time a ski jumper would land, impossibly, on the mountainous slope. When the programming switched to figure skating, John took Alma's hand and led her to their bedroom.

He almost saw another birthday, but that one would be John's last. That night, before Alma fell asleep with her head on his chest, she asked if he had a good day. "Of course," he kissed the top of her head. "What else could I ask for? I got to spend it with my family."

4

ON THE LAST DAY OF SCHOOL, the principal presented Mr. Gabriel Jiménez with an award for being the school's Outstanding Teacher. "The students adore you," she said when she handed him the certificate.

After finishing high school, he'd gone to college at Colorado State. He relished being able to come home after classes and spend the nights with his mother, to eat her dinners and blurt out guesses during Wheel of Fortune. He was offered a position at his former high school two weeks after his college graduation. Alma cried into his shoulder when he told her. "I'm so glad you're staying," she said.

Martín had moved away a couple of years prior. His poor eyesight and his memory problems never improved and proved too troublesome for him during high school. He dropped out halfway through his senior year and got a job on an oil field in Oklahoma. For the first few years he was there, he would come home to visit on holiday weekends. But eventually he stopped coming around. Gabriel called him every Sunday afternoon, but before long his calls went unanswered, and it stayed that way for almost five years. He'd run out of things to say to Martín's answering machine. It never filled so Gabriel knew they were being heard. Reels of his practiced message. *Hey Martín, it's Gabe. Think about you. Give me a call sometime. Hope you're well. Love you.*

Gabriel was in his thirties then, when he sat in his classroom and stared at the *Outstanding Teacher* certificate on his desk. He jumped in his desk chair when the classroom phone rang.

"This is Greg McCarthy from West-Chase Oil," the man said. "Is this Mr. Jiménez?"

"It is. What can I do for you?"

"Your brother is Martín?"

"What happened?" Gabriel faltered.

"Nothing," the man paused. "Well, not nothing. I don't usually do this, but your brother's been working for me for a few years. I was his foreman. He's a good kid, but he fell into some shit and he's not doing well."

"What kind of shit?"

"Heroin. He's been showing up to work more and more fucked up for a month or two now. I gave him as much slack as I could, but it's a liability for me so I had to cut him loose."

"What?" Gabriel rubbed his forehead. "Are you sure?"

"Yessir. Not the first time I've seen it. This work is decent money but it's hell on their bodies. Someone offers them pills one time and that's all it takes. Almost always ends the same after that."

Gabriel stared out his classroom window, where kids were loading onto school buses and beginning their carefree summers.

"I just wanted to let you know."

"Thank you," Gabriel said. "I appreciate you calling."

Gabriel left the school without telling anyone. The certificate was still on his desk. He unlocked the door to Alma's apartment. The same one they'd shared with John. "Mom? You home?" he called down the hallway.

Alma came into the living room and gave Gabriel a long hug. She was just then beginning to look her age, but her kind eyes remained. "Hi Gabe!" she held him. "I have a Yahoo in the fridge for you. Remember when you were a kid and you always wanted a Yahoo on the last day of school?"

"Thanks, Mom. I remember."

"Want to stay for dinner?"

"I'd love to, but I can't." Gabriel walked with her to the kitchen table and sat across from her. "I got a call from Oklahoma today."

"Martín?" Alma glowed. A Christmas card two winters ago was the last she'd heard from him.

"It was his boss. He said Martín's having some trouble."

"What kind of trouble?"

"He didn't say," Gabriel lied. "But I'm going to pack a bag and drive down there tonight. Might stay a little while. Maybe bring him back here if he wants. Just wanted to let you know. Will you be okay if I'm gone for a few weeks?"

"Of course, Gabe. I'll be just fine. Just don't forget to call."

"I won't."

Alma reached across the table and held Gabriel's hand, rubbing the soft space between his thumb and index finger. "You're a good man," she said. "A good, good man."

"He just needs some help," he stood and kissed her cheek. "Love you," Gabriel said before leaving the apartment and locking the door behind him.

He crossed into Oklahoma at some nameless hour of the night. The sky was clear and dark with stars like pinpricks in its fabric. He stopped for the night deep within the plains. Gabriel stood outside the motel room, looking at the stars and listening to the night's boundless silence. He thought, for just a moment, he heard the familiar rustling of kindness. It was quiet. But he knew if he listened closely, he would always hear it.

ACKNOWLEDGEMENTS

THIS BOOK would not have happened without the support of my partner, Heather. She allowed me the time, space, and encouragement to write this story. She also allowed me to pest her with the minutiae of this book. With her gentle nudges in the right direction, this novel took shape. Her fingerprints cover this story. She put up with my attempt at dramatic readings of each chapter as they were written, and was a good sport through all of my questions afterward. You're a great partner, Heddi.

My mom — again — read this story as each chapter became polished, and offered sage advice throughout. At the end of my previous novel, I promised I wouldn't share another story like a path of breadcrumbs, so I have to apologize again. Maybe next time I'll have more patience. (Although I think we both know that won't be the case.)

Abundant thanks to Carol Kressley, who once again read a draft of this novel and found mistakes that had slipped past me several times. Her keen edits are one of my favorite pieces of mail to receive. With that said, if there are any mistakes in these pages, I take full credit.

Amanda Turcotte, one of my greatest friends, was honest and kind in her reading of one of my early drafts. I wish everyone could have a friend like her.

Lastly, thanks to my dad for his advice, and for pushing me to rewrite this story's original ending. A voracious reader of any thriller he can find (that aren't about a divorced woman in London), he was adamant my final chapters could use more heat — and he was right.

ABOUT THE AUTHOR

Born and raised in rural Pennsylvania, JARED REINERT is a doctor and writer. He lives in New England with his partner, Heather, and their dog, Ellie.

CPSIA information can be obtained
at www.ICGtesting.com
Printed in the USA
LVHW040908260422
717174LV00002B/297